SLAVE OF MYSTERY

& OTHER TALES OF SUSPENSE FROM THE PULPS

MORE WILDSIDE CLASSICS

SLAVE OF MYSTERY

& OTHER TALES OF SUSPENSE FROM THE PULPS

JOHNSTON MCCULLEY

WILDSIDE PRESS

SLAVE OF MYSTERY & OTHER TALES
OF SUSPENSE FROM THE PULPS

"The Great Green Ring" originally appeared in *Detective Story Magazine* under the pseudonym "Harrington Strong," January 14, 1919. "The Only Way" originally appeared in *Detective Story Magazine* under the pseudonym "Harrington Strong," April 1, 1919. "Run to Ground" originally appeared in *Detective Story Magazine*, September 3, 1921. "The Obvious Clue" originally appeared in *Detective Story Magazine* under the pseudonym "Harrington Strong," May 28, 1921. "Slave of Mystery" originally appeared in *Detective Story Magazine* under the pseudonym "Harrington Strong," March 25, 1919.

CONTENTS

THE GREAT GREEN RING

CHAPTER I

THE RING AND THE BET

TALL and broad-shouldered, and not unhandsome, Eddie Brunton had the appearance of a prosperous man of thirty. He wore clothes well, could swing a stick in a nonchalant manner, and seemed to demand the right of way over all others, as he paraded the principal streets of the city.

As a matter of fact, Eddie Brunton was almost as prosperous as he appeared, but his prosperity came through nefarious pursuits. If ever there was such a thing as an all-around gentleman crook, Eddie Brunton was one.

George Larimore was of the same ilk; and between the two there existed a peculiar rivalry of long standing, though they were firm friends, aided each other if officers of the law caused them some annoyance at times, and stood shoulder to shoulder now and then in certain adventures outside the law.

On this day, about four o'clock in the afternoon, Eddie Brunton was walking down a street in the retail district, watching the crowds of shoppers, with an eye to the main chance.

He met Larimore in front of a famous department store, and they stood back against one of the show windows to exchange confidences, not having seen each other for several days.

"Business as usual, old top!" Eddie Brunton declared. "Foolish society woman — foolish letters — quite a sum of money in exchange for them — regular old stuff, but profitable!"

"Yeh?" said George Larimore. "I've been having a bit of good luck myself — just finished a little deal."

"I've nothing to do at present, either."

"Looking for new worlds to conquer, eh?" Larimore said. "I am, too. And since it is our particular business to make the women pay, I don't happen to know of a better corner in all the world on which to look for a prospective victim."

The two precious rogues turned away from the window and glanced at the scene before them. Handsomely-gowned women were coming from the great store and getting into their limousines. Silks and satins, furs and jewels were very much in evidence. Aristocratic lap dogs seemed to be everywhere. There was an atmosphere of wealth and social position about that particular corner.

"Take a look!" Eddie Brunton whispered suddenly, touching

Larimore on the arm.

A woman had stepped through the entrance, and the attendant was calling for her car. She was a gorgeous woman of perhaps thirty, was dressed in the mode of the moment, and seemed to radiate wealth and excellent breeding.

"Class!" George Larimore admitted. "Class that shows even in the midst of a classy crowd!"

"I'd say as much!" Eddie Brunton told him. "And I might add the remark that the classier they are the harder they fall!"

"Yeh? I don't know about that. All society women are not fools, my friend," Larimore replied. "Here and there you find one who has a little common sense."

"Oh, I grant you all that!" Eddie Brunton answered. "But it is in society that you find wives who imagine that they are neglected — and a wife who imagines that is usually prepared to be foolish. That has been my experience."

"Well, just cast your optics once more on the subject of the sketch," Larimore told him. "She is proud, haughty, rich, of course — evidently of an excellent social position. Men like us never would get a chance to mix with a woman like that at a public dance pavilion, because she wouldn't be caught in such a place; but, if she did visit it, she wouldn't even speak to us."

"Rot!"

"Yeh? Maybe you are right, but I have my doubts," Larimore went on to say. "Take another look at her face. That woman is very exclusive, my friend — she hates the common mob. She is getting angry now, because her chauffeur isn't here when he is wanted."

At that moment, an expensive limousine was driven up to the curb, and the chauffeur touched his cap. The attendant sprang forward and opened the door. The woman they had been watching stepped up to the chauffeur and handed him a card.

"Drive me to this address at once, Henri," she commanded. "And please try to pay closer attention after this. I dislike very much to be kept waiting."

"Yes, madame!" the chauffeur replied. He accepted the card, looked at it, put it into his pocket and touched the peak of his cap again.

The woman stepped into the limousine, and the attendant closed the door. There was a traffic jam for the moment, and the limousine could not be moved.

Eddie Brunton turned and met George Larimore's eyes.

"Did you see it?" he asked.

"You mean the ring? I did. I saw it as she handed the card to the chauffeur. Freak thing!"

"What was it?"

"Search me!" Larimore declared. "It looked like a mixture of jade and emeralds to me."

"Well, it's nothing in our young lives!"

"Why not?" Larimore asked. "I'll bet you I could get that ring, if it was worth the time and trouble."

"If *you* could, old boy, *I* most certainly could!" Eddie Brunton declared. "And getting a ring is no easy job at that!"

"You could get it, could you? Maybe so!"

"You seem to have some doubts about it," said Brunton. "You think that I couldn't?"

"I'm not saying that you couldn't; nevertheless —"

"Got your doubts about it, eh? Say, old-timer, I'll just make a little bet with you! We don't know this woman or anything about her status in life. We don't know the least thing about her. She may be the queen of Sheba, the daughter of some millionaire, or just a common adventuress. She is probably some society leader. Now, let's both go after that freak ring, and the one who gets it collects five hundred dollars and a good dinner from the other."

Larimore glanced at him, and then looked once more at the woman in the limousine.

"Why, you poor simp, we couldn't get within hailing distance of a woman like that!" he said.

"Maybe you couldn't."

"Say! I can get anyplace you can!" Larimore declared. "Don't forget it for a moment!"

"Well, is it a bet?"

"To get that freak ring she is wearing — that is the job, is it? And the man who gets it collects five hundred dollars and a good dinner from the other?"

"You're on, boy! You've just closed a wager!" Larimore told him; and began chuckling.

"Maybe you know her already," Brunton said, with sudden suspicion, glancing quickly at the other man.

"I give you my word of dishonor, old thing, that I never saw her until she came from the store a few minutes ago!" Larimore declared. "It'll be a fair deal, all right! Going to welch now, or does that bet stand?"

"It stands!" Brunton said.

"If neither of us can do it within a reasonable length of time, we call it off. I can't afford to spend a couple of months, or anything like that, on a deal like this."

"Suits me — neither can I. When we agree to quit, we quit! But I'm going to get that ring!"

"You think you are!" Larimore said.

The traffic jam was broken. The limousine moved away from the curb. The woman inside was adjusting her veil, and they caught sight of the ring once more — a large, green thing of peculiar design, of emeralds and jade.

The hands of Eddie Brunton and George Larimore met for an instant as the two rogues ratified the wager. And then they both hurried toward the curb to get a taxicab — and so entered upon an adventure the like of which they never had anticipated.

CHAPTER II

THE UNEXPECTED HAPPENS

THERE was but one cab within hailing distance at the moment, and Eddie Brunton caught it. Larimore was forced to go half a block to a stand to get another.

Brunton gave the chauffeur his directions and a bill, and the taxi began following the limousine through the heavy traffic, the chauffeur working up until he was directly behind the luxurious car.

Down the broad avenue they went, stopped now and then by some traffic officer, and finally reached a section of the city where the vehicles were not so numerous.

Eddie Brunton leaned back against the cushions and sighed. It had been a fool bet, he told himself; nothing would come of it, and he was merely wasting time and money. For the limousine was going toward that section of the city inhabited by persons of wealth and social standing, and Brunton supposed the woman he was following was merely being driven home after a shopping tour.

And then he remembered that she had handed her chauffeur a card and told him to drive her to the address on it. That was a peculiar thing, Brunton decided. Why had she not merely told the man where to go? And why — now that he came to think of it — had she not had her gloves on at the time, as any well-dressed woman should have?

"Mystery stuff!" Brunton told himself. "Huh! Maybe getting that ring won't be so difficult, after all!"

He looked back and saw another taxicab some blocks behind. He supposed George Larimore was in it.

"Fool bet!" he told himself again. "Probably both be pinched for annoying the woman before we're through with it. Wish I hadn't been so crazy! Might as well go ahead with it now. I don't care to lose that five hundred and have Larimore hand me a laugh besides!"

Suddenly the taxicab pulled in at the curb, Brunton looked ahead and saw that the limousine had stopped before a house in the middle of the block. The woman got out, spoke to the chauffeur and hurried up the steps to the front door. She was admitted immediately.

Eddie Brunton gasped. He knew that house well. It was nothing more or less than a resort where fashionable women gambled. He had been there often himself, looking for prey, playing games of chance, dancing and indulging in small talk with foolish women.

"Great stuff!" he told himself now. "She looked like class, but you can't always tell. If she's one of these gambling women, I'll get that ring, all right. The only thing will be to beat Larimore to it. That boy's clever!"

Brunton paid his chauffeur and walked up the street. Larimore's taxicab was still a couple of blocks away. The limousine left the curb and went on up the avenue. Brunton darted behind the corner of a wall and watched Larimore pursue the empty limousine. He chuckled and went on toward the house.

Swinging his stick in a manner that seemed to say he was thinking of nothing but killing time, he ascended the steps and pulled at the bell. The door was opened half a foot, an attendant grunted his recognition of Eddie Brunton, and immediately he was inside.

He handed over hat and stick and gloves, and wandered into the large reception room, where he was greeted by the proprietor of the place.

"Haven't seen you lately, Brunton," he said.

"Oh, I've been busy," Brunton replied. "A man has to do a bit of work now and then, you know — can't let business go to the dogs. How is everything, Harley?"

"Couldn't be better, my boy."

"Business good, eh? I saw a new face — came in just ahead of me."

"Ah! Splendid woman — Madame Stalman."

"Splendid, huh? And coming here?"

"They all like their bridge, you know — some of them for stiff stakes."

"I liked her looks," Brunton said. "Introduce me?"

"When I get a proper chance. Can't rush things with a woman like Madame Stalman. She's a bit particular about her friends, I fancy."

"Ouch!"

"You had it coming, didn't you? Go through the rooms, and maybe you can manage to meet her yourself."

Harley turned away to receive some message from one of the attendants, and Eddie Brunton went into the first gambling room. Half a score of men and women were playing roulette; others were wooing the goddess of chance at faro; still others were grouped around smaller tables, playing poker. It was a quiet and orderly scene — a typical fashionable gambling house where the chance comer could not enter.

Brunton did not see the woman he sought. She had gone to one of the private gambling rooms, he supposed. He walked around the tables, speaking to an acquaintance here and there, watching the games and acting as if trying to decide which one to chance himself. He was still chuckling because Larimore had chased the empty limousine. So far, he was ahead in the race, he told himself. At least, he knew the woman's name and that she liked to play for high stakes.

But he didn't seem to be making any progress. He walked into the hallway where the private rooms were to be found. Passing an open door, he glanced in.

Madame Stalman was there, sitting at a table beneath a colored light, shuffling a pack of playing cards acting as if she was waiting for somebody.

Eddie Brunton walked to the end of the hall, turned, and went back slowly. Once more he glanced into the room, and this time Madame Stalman looked up, met his glance — and smiled.

The smile was enough for Eddie Brunton. He smiled in return and stepped quickly inside the room.

"Am I intruding?" he asked.

"Well, we'll not call it that this time," said Madame Stalman, smiling at him again.

Eddie Brunton sat down across the table from her. He watched her as she shuffled the cards, saw the great green ring again flashing back the light. There seemed to be something fascinating about the ring. No person would have called it beautiful, but it seemed to Brunton that he scarcely could keep his eyes off it.

"Stupid crowd outside," he said. "I thought I wanted to play a bit this afternoon, but I guess the mood isn't on me yet."

"No?"

"You are not playing yourself."

"Oh, yes, I am!"

"But —"

"I am playing you!" she said.

"I beg your pardon?"

"Why did you follow me here?" she demanded.

"Follow you here?" he gasped.

"Oh, I know you did it! I saw you watching me as I left the store. You ran for the nearest taxi and followed me. After I got inside here, I watched you walk up the street and hurry up the steps. You followed me. There is no doubt about it. And why?"

Eddie Brunton smiled at her again, though he found that this woman was making him feel uncomfortable.

"Let us say that I was fascinated," he said, speaking in a soft voice that he had found effective with other women. "Didn't you ever hear of a man seeing a woman for the first time and immediately wanting to meet her?"

"Certainly! I've heard of such things several times. Do you mean to say it was a case of love at first sight with you?"

"Now you are trying to make fun of me!" Eddie Brunton accused her. "Just let us say that I was pleased with the sight of you and wanted to find out who you were."

"And have you?" she asked.

"Perhaps. But what did you mean by playing me?"

"I was playing you to see what you would say. It is not everyday that a man follows me. I was wondering just what sort of man you are. Is that surprising?"

Brunton did not know exactly what to say. He felt that this Madame Stalman was making a fool of him.

"Suppose you tell me something of yourself," she went on. "I suppose I am a good-looking woman, but not good looking enough to cause a sophisticated man to follow me. I cannot flatter myself that it was my appearance alone. Was it not the ring?"

"The ring!" he gasped.

She clasped her hands beneath the light, and Eddie Brunton looked at the ring again. It was a dragon of jade, between two and three inches long, almost covering her finger. Emeralds were set in it, emeralds that gleamed in the light like live things.

"A peculiar ring!" he said.

"In more ways than one," she replied.

"Yes?"

"You know all about it, I suppose."

"Really, I know nothing at all about it," he declared.

"And you expect me to believe that?"

"Well — pardon me, but it is the truth. I know nothing at all about your ring, madame. I just remarked that it is a peculiar thing. Is there some history connected with it?"

"If you know nothing of it, why are you so eager to get it?" she wanted to know. "Isn't that why you followed me — to try to get the ring?"

"Why, I —"

"You know very well that it is!" she interrupted him. "Sit very still, please! One of my hands is in my lap now, you will notice. It is holding an automatic pistol. I may mention that I am not afraid to shoot, having shot many times before. And now, sir, we'll have a little talk, with all the cards on the table before us, as they say. I intend to learn a few things."

"But —" Brunton gasped again.

"Sit very still! Put your hands on the table before you! I am going across the room to close and lock the door, and if you make a move while I am doing it, I shall shoot!"

CHAPTER III

THREAT OF TORTURE

ALL his life Eddie Brunton had preyed on women, but never before had he met such a woman as this. He was not the courageous type of criminal; in fact, he was not classed as a criminal, but as a grafter. He had had many clashes with the police during his career, but never had served a term in prison. He prided himself that he always played within the law, or else preyed upon those who would have to keep quiet in order to save some one's reputation.

He felt the perspiration spring out on his forehead as Madame Stalman, watching him carefully, got slowly out of her chair. He felt that he should laugh at the situation, should spring up and take the automatic away from her, or assert his rights in some manner, but he seemed incapable of making a move.

She backed to the door, closed it, and he heard her turn the key in the lock. And then she stepped swiftly forward again and sat down on the other side of the table, holding the automatic before her so that it covered him.

"Why did you want this ring?" she demanded.

"But — but this is ridiculous!" Brunton stammered. "What on earth made you think I was after the ring? Don't you realize how ridiculous this is — you covering me with a gun? If you are punishing me for following you, I'll admit I am punished, and leave and not bother you again."

"No doubt you would like to leave, but that cannot be at present," she replied.

"Do you realize that this may cause a scandal?" Eddie Brunton asked. Threats of a scandal, he had found, generally conquered a woman. "I am known here. Harley knows me — there are half a dozen persons in the big room who know me."

"I care nothing for that!" she said. "I want some information, and I intend to have it!"

"I don't know what you are talking about!" Brunton declared.

"I want to know why you are after this ring."

"But —"

"Don't lie! You are after it! You followed me here to try to get it!"

"I don't know anything about the ring!" Brunton said. "I suppose I might as well tell the truth. My friend and I saw you getting into your limousine. We noticed the ring. We made a bet as to whether one of us could get it."

"That doesn't sound very plausible," she replied. "But, even if it happens to be the truth, the question remains — why do you want the ring at all?"

"To win the bet, of course!"

"But why should you make such a bet? Don't you see that is not at all likely on the face of it?"

"Why, this is all so ridiculous!" Eddie Brunton declared again "We just made a foolish bet, that's all. It's nothing to pull a gun on a man for, is it? I never heard of such a thing! Say I am punished for following you — and let it go at that!"

"What is your name?" she asked suddenly.

"Eddie Brunton. Harley knows me."

"And what is your business?"

"I haven't any business. I — I suppose. I am a grafter."

"I thought you'd say something like that. Really you are not very clever. I have been expecting somebody to make an attempt to get the ring — been witching for it for days. Why didn't they send a clever man at least?"

"They?"

"Oh you know to whom I am referring!" she said.

"But I don't!"

"And you expect me to believe it? Don't you give me credit for having any intelligence at all? You don't want to talk, do you?"

"What can I say?" Brunton asked.

"Very well! I fancy that you'll talk later!"

She pressed the edge of the table with her free hand and Brunton heard a bell tinkle in the distance. She was looking at him fixedly. The perspiration was standing out on his forehead again. He felt that he wanted to scream for Harley the proprietor, but something seemed to seal his lips.

He heard a step and glanced up. A door had opened in the wall directly before him, a door that Eddie Brunton had not known was there. Through it stepped a man whose face was well masked. And behind him came a second.

"Not a sound from you!" Madame Stalman warned him.

"But I —"

Two men sprang forward silently, grasped him, choked the words back into his throat. Almost before he guessed their intention, they had lashed him to the heavy chair in which he was sitting, and had gagged him effectually.

The masked men then stood back. Madame Stalman was up on her feet now, and she whispered to one of them, and both men disappeared through the little door, which was then closed.

"Since you will not talk, we must use means to make you do so," she told Eddie Brunton. "I cannot understand why they did not send a cleverer man."

She walked back and forth across the room before him. Now and then, as she turned, the light flashed from the ring on her finger, the ring Eddie Brunton already was beginning to hate as the cause of all his trouble.

Brunton wondered what it meant. She had said she had been expecting somebody to make an attempt to get the ring. She had spoken of "they," and seemed to believe Brunton was telling a falsehood when he said that he did not understand. Had he stumbled into something gigantic by making a foolish wager? Who were the masked men that came immediately when this woman touched a button? And who was this woman, this Madame Stalman that Brunton had supposed was nothing more or less than a society woman who liked to gamble now and then for high stakes, and so patronized this place of Harley's, as did so many other women of that class?

He glanced at the wall opposite again. The little door was swinging open. This time it was Harley himself who entered the room.

Madame Stalman whirled around to meet him.

"Well, we've caught our man!" she said.

"Why, that is Eddie Brunton!" Harley exclaimed. "I supposed he was harmless enough!"

"He probably was sent because you supposed that. I must say that he was not very clever about it."

"You're sure there's no mistake?"

"He followed me from downtown, got a taxicab and trailed my limousine here, came in, walked through the hall and struck up an acquaintance with me. He even admits that he was after the ring, but says something about its being a foolish bet."

Harley walked over to Brunton.

"I'm going to take off that gag so you can talk," he said. "But you behave yourself! One yell out of you, and I'll see that you don't yell again for a while!"

He took off the gag, and Brunton gulped for breath.

"I — I don't know what all this is about!" he said.

"Of course I'm ready to believe you!" Harley sneered. "Knowing you as I do, am aware that you are the soul of honor and honesty. What is this about a bet?"

"Larimore and I were standing in front of the store, talking," Brunton explained. "I said all women were easy to swindle — that the classier they were, the easier it was. Then this woman came out, and we remarked that she was classy. We saw the ring. And I said I'd bet that I could get it. Larimore said he could if I could. And so we both agreed to try to make her acquaintance and get the ring, and the one who got it was to have five hundred and a dinner from the other man. That's all!"

"So Larimore is in this, too," Harley said. "We were looking for thugs, and they sent us a couple of lounge lizards. Well, it seems that you didn't succeed. And now the question is, what are we going to do with you?"

"He's got to talk!" Madame Stalman declared. "He's got to tell us a few things!"

"I tell you I don't know what this is all about!" Brunton protested. "What kind of a game are you playing here? I don't know anything about that fool ring, and, what's more, I don't want to know. I've told you the truth about it — and that's all I can do!"

"My boy, you couldn't tell the truth if your life depended on it!" Harley told him. "You wouldn't know the truth if you met it face to face in the street!"

"Are we going to make him talk?" Madame Stalman asked.

"We are," Harley said.

He pressed the edge of the table, and again the bell tinkled in the distance and the little door in the wall was opened and the two masked men came in.

"Take him to the other room!" Harley commanded.

Eddie Brunton started to protest, but they gagged him again, lifted him between them, and carried him through the little door. Harley and Madame Stalman followed.

They took him through a narrow hall, up a flight of stairs. Brunton had thought that he knew this house, every part of it, but he discovered now that he did not. They made a turning with him, went up another flight of steps, and into another room.

Eddie Brunton gasped when he saw that room. It was large and furnished lavishly. There seemed to be no windows, and only the one door. A ventilating fan worked in one corner near the ceiling. In the center of the room was a long mahogany table, with a dozen chairs grouped around it. There was a silk banner standing in one corner, and on it a device similar to that of the ring Madame Stalman wore.

They placed Brunton in a chair at one end of the table, and lashed him there.

"Now you are going to talk!" Harley told him. "You are going to tell us who sent you after that ring, and why. And we are going to investigate and be sure you have spoken the truth before you are allowed to leave this room. What we'll do with you after that remains to be seen. Until you do talk, you get no food — and what is far worse, no water!"

He made a sign to one of the men, who removed Brunton's gag.

"Be sensible now," Harley said. "You do the right thing by us, and we'll protect you, perhaps. When you are ready to talk we'll be ready to listen."

"But I don't know what you want!" Brunton exclaimed despairingly. "I told you the truth! I don't know what this means at all!"

"Perhaps you'll change your mind after a few hours of being lashed in that chair. I hope that you had an excellent luncheon to day, for it is going to be a long time until dinner — unless you talk!"

"Harley, you know me! You know —"

"Precisely — I know you! I wouldn't trust you with a one cent piece. If you were a crook I might admire you, but you're only a cheap swindler who preys on women — compromise and then blackmail. That's how you stand with me. Going to talk?"

"But I tell you —"

"All right!" Harley interrupted. "We'll let you think it over for a time, and if you don't talk then, we'll do something to make you. We've persuaded men to talk before — men with more nerve than you have! There is such a thing as torture."

"Harley!"

"Ah! That gets under your skin, does it? Well, you'd better talk, and mighty quick, or we'll begin work on you. Don't try to run a bluff on us, either. You were sent after that ring, all right and we're going to learn who sent you and why. We'll give you a few minutes to make up your mind — and you'd better decide to open your lips!"

Again he made a sign, and the two masked men left the room. Harley sat down at an elaborate desk in one corner and began looking at some papers. Madame Stalman sat down in front of Eddie Brunton, and her eyes glittered into his like those of some wild animal. She clasped her hands before her. Light flashed from the great green ring. Brunton turned his face away.

"Don't you like to look at it?" Madame Stalman asked. "You were eager to get it, you know."

Eddie Brunton made no reply, there seemed to be nothing to say. His mind was in a turmoil. He couldn't think straight, couldn't reason things out.

The minutes seemed to drag into hours. Finally Harley got up from the desk and walked over to him again.

"Well, are you going to talk?" he demanded.

"Harley, I told you the truth! I don't know anything — don't know what you mean!"

"Still stubborn, are you? Very well!" Harley said. "I suppose we'll have to make you talk!"

CHAPTER IV

WHAT HAPPENED TO LARIMORE

WHEN George Larimore saw Brunton get the only taxicab near the department store, he was somewhat chagrined because he had to go half a block before he could hire a taxi for himself.

When he finally had procured one and made the chauffeur understand what was wanted, he leaned back against the cushions and told himself that he "had a hunch" this was going to be a sorry business. It was an indication of bad luck to the superstitious Larimore that Brunton had beaten him at the start.

The chauffeur had difficulty keeping the limousine in sight, but after they had left the business district behind, the task was considerably easier. Larimore watched while they began creeping up on the limousine. He saw a taxicab a short distance behind it, but did not know whether it was Brunton's.

The limousine turned into a side street, and the taxicab followed. When the one in which Larimore was riding reached the corner and made the turning, Larimore saw the limousine running slowly a short distance ahead. He saw the other taxicab, too, but not Brunton, who was hiding behind the corner of the wall. So Larimore went on after the limousine, not aware of the fact that the woman who wore the great green ring had left the machine.

"Fool bet!" said Larimore, much as Eddie Brunton had done.

Larimore, too, had seen that the limousine was running toward a district where wealth and social position predominated, where there were imposing residences surrounded by stone walls, green lawns, great trees.

"I was right! Neither of us can get within hailing distance of a woman like that!" Larimore told himself. "Do my best, of course, since I've got a bet up. I'll wager we'll both be willing to call it off within twenty-four hours."

He wondered what had become of Eddie Brunton. He supposed that Brunton's chauffeur had lost the limousine in the heavy traffic, or had followed some car that looked similar. Larimore began wondering whether he was following the right limousine himself.

And then he saw it turn into a gateway in a wall half a block ahead. Just inside, the chauffeur stopped the car and got out to inspect the engine. Larimore's taxicab stopped, and he descended from it. The chauffeur of the limousine turned so that Larimore could see his face; he recognized the man as the one called Henri by the woman who wore the ring. And he remembered the card she had handed the chauffeur, too.

"I suppose this isn't her home, since she handed the chauffeur that card," Larimore told himself. "Pretty sure the machine hadn't stopped anywhere else. Have to wait until she comes out, and trail her again, I suppose."

Then he realized that it might look suspicious to keep the taxicab standing there. He decided to take the chance of picking up another when he needed it, paid the chauffeur and dismissed him. Then he walked slowly along beside the wall. It was a low wall, so low that Larimore could see over it. Just as he reached the gateway, he became convinced that the woman was not in the limousine.

"Stung!" Larimore told himself. "But where she got out of the car is a mystery to me. Wonder if Eddie Brunton is on the right trail and I'm on the wrong one?"

He stopped as he came opposite the gateway, and glanced down the avenue as if waiting for somebody. He wished he could strike up an acquaintance with the chauffeur. Perhaps by doing so he could at least find out the name of the woman, and her address.

"In trouble?" he asked.

"Little engine trouble, sir — nothing serious," Henri replied. "These engines are mighty sensitive at times."

"Some car you have there!" Larimore said.

"Yes, sir."

"I haven't seen many like it."

"There are only a few in the city, sir," Henri replied. "They are very expensive and need the attention of an expert mechanic. As delicate as a watch, sir. This is Madame Stalman's car."

"Madame Stalman? And does she live here?"

"Yes, sir. She is very rich — and very cranky at times."

"I suppose all employers are that," Larimore told him.

"She rebuked me downtown this afternoon because I did not get to the curb quick enough to suit her."

"Come to think of it, I believe I know Madame Stalman when I see her," Larimore said. "Tall, well-dressed woman about thirty, isn't she?"

"Yes, sir."

"I think I have noticed her wearing a peculiar ring."

"Oh, have you noticed that, sir?"

"Sort of a freak ring, isn't it? Never got a very good glint at it, of course, but it looked to me as if it was jade set with emeralds. Very large, too."

"It is jade and emeralds, sir, and very large, as you have said. I fancy she just wants to wear something different from other women; or perhaps she thinks it is a good-luck ring, or something of the sort."

"I've got a little friend out in California who goes in for things like that," Larimore said. "Wish I could get one to send to her, but I suppose Madame Stalman's is the only one in existence."

"I've seen others just like it, sir."

"You have?" Larimore gasped. It was not beyond him to win the bet with Brunton by getting a replica of the ring and making up some story as to how he had acquired it.

"She has another just like it herself, sir," Henri went on to say.

"And she gave one to her maid, who is a very good friend of mine. I dare say they are not expensive rings."

"I'd give a hundred dollars for one," Larimore said.

"You would, sir? Honestly? I might —"

"Might what?" Larimore asked, as Henri hesitated.

"I was going to say I might get that one from the maid. She would be glad to get the hundred, and she really dislikes the ring. If Madame Stalman happened to notice she did not have it, the maid could say that she had lost the ring."

"Good! Fix it up!" Larimore said, taking a roll of bills from his pocket and allowing Henri to see them.

"Perhaps I can fix it up, sir, if you'll be good enough to come to the house with me."

"But Madame Stalman —"

"Oh, she is not at home, sir. I left her at the residence of a friend, and am to drive there for her this evening when she telephones. There is nobody in the house now, sir, except the maid. The other servants have the afternoon off."

"Well, we'll try it!" Larimore said.

Henri started the car, Larimore sprang up beside him, and they drove up to the house.

"We'd better use the servants' entrance, sir," Henri said, and started to lead the way.

Larimore was jubilant. He would buy the ring from the maid, show it to Eddie Brunton, tell some story about stealing it, and claim the five hundred. Then he would have the bet over with and clear four hundred by the transaction.

They went into a little hallway, and, from that, Henri led Larimore into a small room that was evidently some sort of servants' sitting room.

"If you will wait here for a moment, sir, I'll find the maid," Henri said.

"All right, I'll wait."

Henri left the room. Larimore sat down on a divan in one corner. He'd have the laugh on Eddie Brunton! He'd make up some story of his own cleverness that would make Brunton green with envy. He wondered where Brunton was, and whether he had discovered that he had lost the limousine.

Larimore did not hear a sound in the house. He began to feel a bit nervous. If Madame Stalman came home unexpectedly and found him there, how would he explain his presence?

And then he heard steps in the hall, and Henri opened the door and stood before him.

"Here is the gentleman who wishes to get the ring!" he said.

He stepped aside, and there entered — not the maid Larimore

had expected to see, but two men of evident size and strength.

"W-what?" Larimore gasped.

"Sit down — and shut up!" one of the men behind the chauffeur commanded.

Larimore gasped and sat down. The man who had spoken was covering him with a revolver.

CHAPTER V

SURPRISED

AS far as his method of making a living was concerned, George Larimore was as despicable as Eddie Brunton, but he was no coward. He was tall and broad-shouldered and kept himself in physical trim.

Larimore sensed at once that he had been led into some sort of trap. The three men stood in front of him; the one who held the revolver, in the middle. Their attitude was menacing, like that of three thugs about to fall upon their prey.

"So you want to get a ring, do you?" Henri said, after a time.

"Well, what about it?" Larimore asked. "You said that the maid had one she wanted to sell. And instead of going and getting the maid, you got a couple of your fine friends. I suppose you'll knock me on the head now and take my roll!"

"So that is the way you look at it, is it?" Henri said. "Why, you poor fool, I played a little game to get you into the house, where you could be properly handled. You were following the limousine in that taxicab! I spotted you a long way back. Nice way you thought you had of pumping me about the ring, eh? You can bet I was wise to you all the time!"

"You're talking like a crazy man!" Larimore exclaimed.

"Not much!" said Henri. "So you are eager to get a ring, are you? You have to have a certain kind to send to your little friend in California? And you know blamed well that there's only one ring like that in the world! Either you thought I'd steal it from madame and sell it to you, or you just wanted to get into the house here and have a look around. Smooth? You? Not much!"

"What's all this about?" demanded Larimore, sneering. "Do I have to listen to a speech before you hit me over the head and make away with my roll?"

"Why did you want that ring?" Henri demanded.

"Oh, just a fool notion, I suppose!"

"And who sent you to get it?"

"Nobody sent me to get it!" Larimore exclaimed. "Are you insane, man? I can't understand your line of talk at all!"

"And why did they send you?" Henri demanded.

"Say!"

"Oh, we're wise to you, all right!" Henri declared. "Don't think that you can pull the wool over our eyes! I have an idea that certain persons will want to get some information out of you, young man! And I guess they'll get it, too!"

"We always strive to please," said Larimore, sneering again. "Now, suppose that you explain this little melodrama. If this isn't a den of thieves, then what is it? If you are not going to rob me, just what do you intend to do?"

"We are simply going to detain you here until we receive further orders," Henri told him. "And I guess that there are enough of us here to hold you!"

"But why?" Larimore asked. "What does it all mean? You are talking in circles, man, as far as I am concerned. Explain!"

"You don't happen to need any explanations!" Henri retorted. "You wanted to get a certain ring, didn't you? That's the answer! There have been more than one after that ring, but none of them ever got it. And you're a fizzle, like all the others!"

"This must be a private madhouse!" Larimore declared. "Does it happen to be a crime these days to want to get a ring that you admire — or another just like it?"

"There isn't another just like it in all the world, and you know it, too!" said Henri. "Save your breath — you can't fool us! Now we're going to put you in a room where you'll be safe. If you step along quietly, there'll not be any trouble coming your way just now, but if you try to start anything, you'll find trouble a-plenty."

"Well, you've got a gun on me so —" Larimore began.

"Yes, and we're going to see whether you have one in your pocket," Henri replied.

As he spoke, the two men rushed forward and grasped Larimore by the arms. They searched him swiftly; he made no resistance.

"No gun," one of them reported.

"Bring him along, then," Henri said. "And keep your eyes on him. He might be a smooth customer, after all. We can't afford to take chances in a case like this. If he got away, we'd never hear the last of it from the boss."

Larimore glared at them, but allowed them to urge him into the hall and toward the front of the house. Resistance was useless at present, he knew. He could not handle three men, any one of them a match for him physically, especially when one held a revolver and had the appearance of a man who would use it if called upon to do so. So he merely glared and kept his eyes open as they marched him through a suite of rooms and into another hall.

There were stairs to climb now. They reached the second floor of the house and went toward the rear. Henri, who was walking ahead, opened a door, and they conducted Larimore into a small room.

"I guess you'll be safe here," Henri said. "There is a window, but it is some distance from the ground, and we'll have a man outside watching it. This door is the only one in the room, and it's a pretty heavy door. We'll just turn you loose in here, but the door will be locked, and you can bet you'll be met if you do happen to open that door and get out!"

"But I'd like to know what it is all about!" Larimore protested. "This crazy business is beginning to get on my nerves!"

"There'll be something else get on your nerves when the boss arrives!" Henri told him. "Unless you give up the information that's wanted you'll be due for a lot of trouble!"

They thrust Larimore into the room, slammed the door, and he heard the key turned in the lock. He glanced around the room quickly. It appeared to be a sort of den. There was a desk-table; there were a couple of easy chairs, a divan, some books and magazines, a reading lamp.

Larimore slipped across to the door and listened. He could hear Henri and one of the other men talking at the head of the stairs.

"Watch that door from the hall, and shoot if he tries to get away," Henri was saying. "I'll telephone the boss about it."

"Where is the boss?" the other asked.

"Harley's place. If this bird can be made to talk, there ought to be a reward in it for us," Henri declared.

Larimore heard the other man grunt an affirmation, and then Henri hurrying down the stairs. What was this mess into which he had plunged himself? Larimore began wondering. What information did they expect to get from him? And the boss? Did Henri mean Madame Stalman? Harley's gambling house, eh? Larimore knew it well, but never had seen Madame Stalman there. There must be some mistake, he decided — these men had taken him for somebody else.

He hurried across to the window and glanced out. It was a long drop to the ground, too long to be attempted unless a man wanted to risk a broken limb or crushed skull. Moreover, one of the men who had been with Henri was standing beneath a tree a short distance away, watching the window.

"Can't get out that way!" Larimore told himself. "No chance getting out by way of the door, either, I suppose. This is a pretty mess! Wonder what it all means?"

Larimore was not the sort of man to admit defeat easily, however. He glanced around the room again and saw a telephone on a tiny table in a corner.

"So they forgot about the telephone, eh?" Larimore mused. "Well, there may be a chance!"

He went silently across the room to the instrument. He took down the receiver and put it to his ear. Henri was just calling a number — the number of a private telephone in Harley's place.

"This is Henri, Madame Stalman's chauffeur," he heard the man say presently. "I must speak to Harley or Madame Stalman at once."

There was a wait of fully a minute, and then Larimore heard a voice he recognized as Harley's.

"What is it, Henri?"

"I've got the ring man!"

"What's that?"

"I say that I've got the ring man. He was in a taxicab and he followed madame's limousine. Then he began to talk to me and tried to pump me. Said he had noticed the ring and wanted to get it. I managed to entice him into the house, and the two boys helped me nail him. We have him locked up and under guard."

"Know who he is?" Harley asked.

"No, sir. He is a man about thirty, well dressed, and had a roll of money."

"Well, we thought we had the ring man here," Harley said. "Perhaps they're working in pairs now. You'll have to watch him until Madame Stalman gets there. And be sure he doesn't escape, Henri. We are just starting to make our man talk now. He's a stubborn brute — says he doesn't know anything, but was trying to get the ring on a bet. Stupid gang, to think we'd swallow a story like that!"

"Yes, sir!"

"Henri, I am going to give you another private telephone number. In case of necessity, call it. I'll be there with Madame Stalman, trying to make our man talk."

He gave the number, and George Larimore repeated it to himself, impressing it upon his mind. Then Henri and Harley discontinued the conversation, and Larimore hung up the receiver.

His heart was pounding at his ribs now, and his breath was coming quicker. So Eddie Brunton was a prisoner at the Harley place, was he, and they were trying to make him talk? Larimore asked himself for the hundredth time what it could mean. If Brunton was in trouble, Larimore wanted to help him. And he wanted to get free himself, of course. He was beginning to feel a little fear.

He went across to the door and listened again, but could hear nothing. He stood before the table, trying to think what to do. He knew that he could telephone the police and have them raid the place and rescue him, but George Larimore did not care to make the acquaintance of the police. Moreover, his story was a peculiar one. He could not very well tell the police that he was a prisoner and in trouble because he had made a bet that he could steal a woman's ring before another man did.

He remembered the number Harley had given Henri — the private number to be used in case of emergency. He supposed Harley and Madame Stalman, and perhaps Eddie Brunton, were in the room with the telephone that had that number.

"This is a pretty mess!" he told himself again. "And what it is all about is more than I can guess. I wish I'd never made that fool bet!"

Crossing to the telephone he sat down before it, reached for it, then withdrew his hand.

A faint tapping came to him, on the wall in front. Larimore listened. The tapping continued, and he stepped closer to the wall. Mice playing, he thought at first, but decided the next instant that such was not the case.

The tapping continued. Was somebody trying to give him a message? Larimore wondered. He put his knuckles against the wall, tapped twice himself, listened again. The sound from the other side ceased instantly.

Larimore heard a soft click, and a section of the wall before him started to turn as if on hinges. A girl stood in the opening.

CHAPTER VI

TERROR

STEPPING back a pace Larimore regarded her in amazement. She put a finger to her lips, cautioning silence, and nodded toward the hall door.

"We must listen well. I dare not be caught by Henri or one of the others," she said.

She stepped into the room and smiled at him. She was not young, but she was small and dainty.

"Do not be so surprised," she said. "I am madame's maid. I have been placed here by — well, you know. I used to be in service here years ago. Nobody in the house at present, except me, knows of this passage. My master of years ago was a politician, and he used this way to admit men to conferences — when he wished nobody to know they had visited him. You understand? It was very difficult for me to secure the position of madame's maid, but now I am glad that I succeeded. You walked right into a trap, didn't you?"

"I guess I did!" Larimore said.

"Well, perhaps I can get you out of it. That is what I was put here for. I tapped on the wall a long time before you answered the signal. I wonder whether we'll ever get the great green ring."

"It seems a difficult job!" Larimore admitted.

He sensed that he would have to be on guard against this girl. It was evident that she took him for a friend or co-worker of some sort, and unless he made her suspicious she probably would aid him to escape. He would have to pretend that he understood everything she said, pick up information that would solve the mystery — if he could — and do his best to aid Eddie Brunton.

"Can I get out of here that way?" he whispered.

"Of course! I imagine Henri and the others will be some surprised to find you gone."

"We'd better hurry," said Larimore. "One of those men might take a notion to come in and have a look at me."

"Get into the passage, and I'll close the door."

Larimore stepped through the little opening. The maid followed him, pressed against the wall, the door closed, and they were in darkness.

"Put one hand on my shoulder and follow me carefully," she directed. "I know every foot of this way. Be sure you do not stumble. If any of them hear a noise, they might become suspicious and investigate."

Larimore did as he was directed. It was pitch-dark, stifling, and the air was bad, but he did not care for those things, if the passage led to freedom.

After a time they came to a flight of steps and went down them cautiously. And then they followed another narrow passageway, and finally came to a small room. The girl struck a match and touched it to a candle.

Larimore blinked his eyes and glanced around. The room had no windows, and only two doors — one that led to the secret passage, and the other at the top of a short flight of steps.

"We must talk in whispers to be safe," the girl said. "This room is under the garage. From that other door you can go into a passage about fifteen feet long. At the end is a door that opens into the alley at the rear of the garage building. You cannot go, of course, until it is dark."

"But I'll roast to death in here, or die from the impure air," Larimore protested. "And I have work to do. A friend of mine — he also is after the great green ring — is being held a prisoner."

"Perhaps he will be helped, as you have been," she said.

"I'm afraid not. I listened over the telephone and heard Henri being told all about it. You see, they've got my friend at the Harley place — Harley and this Madame Stalman — and they are trying to make him talk. Understand?"

"But he will not talk, of course!" the girl declared. "He would not betray — well, you know!"

"What is your name?" Larimore asked suddenly.

"You may call me Jeannette," she replied.

"Well, Jeannette, I owe you a great deal."

"You owe me nothing, sir. I am but doing my duty, you see."

"Yes, I know," said Larimore. "Just the same, I feel that I owe you a lot. But I've got to get out of here at —"

"Not until dark!" Jeannette interrupted. "You may be seen."

"But the man at Harley's —"

"He must do the best he can, must he not? Can we endanger everything for the sake of one man? Why are you men so stupid? One by one you walk into traps that a woman wouldn't enter blindfolded."

"Accidents will happen, my dear, even to the cleverest of men," Larimore told her. "And I am not the cleverest of men. In fact, I am beginning to fear I am a sorry dub."

"I don't think so," she said. "It is a very difficult thing to get the ring. And consider the persons we are fighting. But some fine day we shall succeed, and then —"

"Then?" Larimore echoed, hoping she would say something that would give him an inkling of the truth.

"Then everything will be all right, of course," said Jeannette, smiling up at him.

"Well, this conversation isn't getting me out of here!"

"You would not dare to try now!" she said. "The door is a small section of the rear garage wall. And the alley — there always are persons passing through at this time of the day, delivery wagons and peddlers. Some of them would be sure to see you. What would they think if they saw a door open where no door should be, and a man sneak out?"

"I suppose it would arouse some suspicion."

"And sooner or later, madame or one of the others would hear of it. Then they would investigate and find the passage, and then we never could use it again. You see, it is a way of escape for me in case I should be suspected and have to get away quickly."

"I see. I never thought of that."

"Madame trusts me, but they are all very careful not to say anything when I am near. But they often talk in the little den, where you were a prisoner, and I can hear easily through the wall."

"Well, what am I going to do?"

"Remain here in this little room until it has grown very dark. I will come here then and show you how to get out."

"You'll remain with me, keep me company?"

"Oh, I could not do that! I have my duties. Madame would ask where I had been — and what could I say? I must leave you now, and hurry back. It will be dark in two hours. I can come and let you out while they are at dinner."

"Something might happen to prevent you," Larimore said; "and then what would happen to me? I'll tell you — show me how to work the door, and then, if you don't return after it is dark, I can get out by myself."

"No! No!" she said. "I know — you would try to go out before dark, and would risk everything. It would not be fair to do that. I'll come back — I'll surely come back!"

"But —"

"It is the only way!" she declared, "We do not want to make a fatal mistake, do we? The time is growing so short, you know!"

Larimore sat down in a rickety chair against the wall. Jeannette already had slipped back into the dark passage, and he could not even hear her footsteps.

He was more puzzled than ever. First, because, having started out to get a ring on a bet, he had been decoyed and made prisoner and given a lot of mysterious talk. And then this girl had appeared before him, had helped him to get away, and had given him much more mysterious talk.

"I'll be going mad if this keeps up!" George Larimore told himself. "I can't see any sense in it! A man would think that green ring was some sort of heathen idol, or something like that, protected by an army and with another gang trying to get it. That's it! One gang is trying to get that ring from another, and Eddie Brunton and I have stumbled into something that doesn't concern us! Well, it surely concerns us now. That's what I call rotten luck!"

He got up and walked around the little room. He went up the short flight of steps and opened the door, lifted the candle and peered into the short hall. He even walked to the end of it, but could find nothing that looked like a door, could see no button to touch.

Again he went back into the room, put the candle on the table, and sat down in the rickety chair. He supposed he would have to wait for the girl, Jeannette, to come and let him out. At any rate, he told himself, he was glad to be out of that little den of a room on the second floor of the big house. He didn't care for big Henri or the other two, who looked to be thugs, and he didn't know how many others would be there later.

He began thinking of Eddie Brunton again. What was happening to him in Harley's place? If only he, Larimore, could get free, he could telephone something to Harley that might cause him to let Brunton go. Or he could telephone to the police and get them to raid the Harley place, and so release Brunton; but that might get Eddie into serious trouble, too.

"Nice mess!" Larimore growled again.

He told himself that he would feel more comfortable if he had some sort of weapon. He got up and went around the little room again, but found nothing that would serve. Then he thought of taking the candle and inspecting the passage through which Jeannette had led him from the room above.

He looked at his watch. The girl had been gone for an hour, and he did not suppose she would return for an hour more. He picked the candle up, shaded the flame with one hand, and stepped into the narrow hall.

He found that the passage was lined with masonry and had a concrete floor. Nowhere was there so much as a niche in a wall. He followed it until he reached a flight of steps, and started to climb. Now and then he stopped to listen, especially after he had reached the top of the flight and knew that now he was inside the big house. He hoped to hear conversation through the walls, something that would give him an inkling of the truth.

Suddenly he stopped. Before him the passage was divided into three others of the same width, and he could not decide into which of the three to turn. He had not known of these before of course, for the girl had led him through the hall in darkness. He was afraid of running into a network of secret passages, losing time, getting lost, not being able to get out at all. The thought thrilled him with horror. Suppose something happened to prevent Jeannette returning, and nobody else came, and he could make nobody in the house hear him or find an exit himself?

He felt the perspiration standing out on his forehead. He walked a few feet into one of the passages, hesitated, started to turn back. Then he forced himself to stand still, told himself that there could be no real danger, tried to control himself. He whirled around to look down the passage again. The candle flickered and went out.

"Nice mess!" Larimore muttered once more.

He walked back to where the three passages met, bumped against a wall, became confused, got into the mouth of another passage. He forced himself to control his fear for an instant, put the candle between his feet, and fumbled in a pocket for a match.

"Nice mess!" he repeated. "Next time I make a bet, I'll —"

His search became frantic. He went through pocket after pocket. Evidently he had forgotten to put his cigarette lighter in his pocket. And he could not find a match!

Clutching the candle he leaned against a wall and breathed heavily. The silence, the darkness, the dead air of the passage spoke terror to him. He began to gasp. Again he forced himself to search his pockets, but without success. He started down the passage. He didn't know whether he was going into the house or toward that little room beneath the garage. He began to run, feeling of the walls with his fingers. Finally he stopped. He should have reached the stairs long before this, he knew!

A cry of horror came from his lips. The heat was stifling, it seemed that the foul air almost choked him, the silence and the darkness overwhelmed him. He dropped the candle, went down on hands and knees to search for it, and could not find it. He scratched at the floor until his fingers were bleeding. Once he thought that he had kicked it, but he could not find it again.

"Nice — mess!" Larimore sobbed.

For a time he remained stretched on the floor, panting, exhausted, the dust filling his eyes and nostrils and mouth. Then he forced himself to sit up, held his head in his hands, finally staggered to his feet. Once more he started along a passage. On and on he went, and at last stumbled on a flight of stairs. But the steps before him were going up — not down!

CHAPTER VII

COUNTERPLOT

LEAVING Larimore, Jeannette hurried back through the passage, feeling her way, went up the flight of steps, came to the maze of branch passages, turned along one of them, and finally stopped at a turning. With her ear against the wall, she listened for a time, then pressed against the wall. A tiny door opened. She slipped through the door, and was in a servant's room.

Hurrying to the dresser, she arranged her hair, brushed a powder puff across her face, and made sure that there was no telltale dust on her waist or skirt. Then, humming a bit of song and looking as if she had just finished an afternoon nap, she stepped into the hall and hurried down the stairs. Henri was on the lower floor.

"Madame has not returned yet?" Jeannette asked.

"No," the chauffeur replied. "She was to telephone when she wanted the limousine."

"I suppose dinner will be late again. Has the cook come in?"

"Yes."

"What a bear you are this afternoon, Henri!"

"I have had an adventure."

"Well if it has this effect, let us hope you do not have another soon. What was it?"

"I am not at liberty to tell. It has to do with the business of madame."

"Oh! Such a mystery!" she said, smiling at him.

The telephone rang, and Jeannette started toward it.

"I shall answer!" Henri said.

"But that happens to be my business!"

"It undoubtedly is madame!"

He lifted the receiver and spoke.

"At once, madame!" the girl heard him say. "Yes, madame, I understand the instructions perfectly. Alone — yes, madame."

He slammed the receiver on the hook and faced the girl again.

"It was madame," he said.

"I gathered that much."

"You must not be angry because I answered the telephone. I guessed it was madame. And, if I am a bear, do not be angry — there is great business on hand."

"You frighten me!"

"There is nothing to be frightened about. You will tell the cook that dinner is to be served in about an hour. You perhaps will notice a man on guard at the head of the real stairs — do not molest him or ask him questions. I placed him there."

"You appear to be running the place," Jeannette said. "I was under the impression that you were the chauffeur."

"I am the chauffeur — and other things! Do not bother your pretty head with matters that do not concern you. Madame most certainly would not like it!"

And then Henri grasped his cap and hurried toward the rear of the house.

Jeannette walked on through the rooms, still humming the song. She glanced up the rear stairs, and saw the man on guard there, and smiled. She made sure that the cook was in the kitchen. And then she hurried into a small boudoir and went to the telephone.

She sat before it, listening, making sure that nobody was near. Finally she rose and closed the heavy door, and then went back to the instrument, lifted the receiver, called a number. Almost immediately she was answered.

"This is Jeannette," she said, speaking in a low voice. "Be at the garage entrance in about an hour. There is something funny going on."

"Funny?" queried the voice of a man at the other end of the wire.

"Henri and the others caught a man some time ago — a man who was asking questions about the ring. They placed him in the little den under guard and notified madame by telephone. She is at the Harley place, where they caught still another man who was after the ring."

"What's that? None of our —"

"That is what I feared! This man gave me a knock signal, but afterward he failed to answer two cue words, and so I began to suspect him. I rescued him from the little den and left him in the room beneath the garage. He cannot get out, of course. Come in an hour. I'll meet you and let you in."

"What sort of man?"

Jeannette described Larimore.

"No such man working with us! We'd better look into this! I think we'll end the whole thing tonight. If others are after that ring, we can't afford to take chances. We can use the passage, of course, and nobody will know afterward how it happened."

"Madame will be home soon — Henri has just gone to get her," the girl went on. "Do as you think best. I'll let you in."

"She is wearing the ring?"

"Always!"

"Anything new about the Harley place?"

"I haven't heard a word for several days, but she goes there frequently," Jeannette replied. "I shall have to stop talking now, or somebody may overhear."

"All right! In about an hour! Ring off now!"

Jeannette hung up the receiver, listened for an instant at the door, then opened it and went into the adjoining room.

For the next hour, she was the perfect maid. She heard the limousine arrive, and met madame at the door. This was a peculiar household, and the duties of the maid were varied.

"Dinner in a few minutes, Jeannette," Madame Stalman said. "I have some friends with me. We are to talk confidential business, so you will kindly remain away after serving dinner."

"Yes, madame."

"You are a sensible girl, Jeannette; you do not ask questions and do not talk about what does not concern you. I shall have to give you better wages."

"Thanks, madame!"

"We brought home with us a gentleman who took too much wine. You understand? Henri and one of the other men will put him in the little den above for the time being. You are not to go there."

"Certainly not, madame!"

"Dinner for four, tell cook. Henri will help you serve, so that we may attend to our business early."

"Very well, madame."

Jeannette hurried toward the kitchen. Madame Stalman looked after her.

"That girl is almost too good to be true," she mumbled. "I wonder if — Nonsense! The little thing is all right! She simply has learned the art of attending to her own business!"

Madame went to her boudoir.

In the limousine there had arrived Harley, the two men who had been masked at his house, and Eddie Brunton, the last in a state of unconsciousness.

Eddie had been undergoing certain experiences. Lashed to the chair in that peculiar room in the Harley place, the perspiration standing out on his forehead, he had watched Harley leave the desk and cross the room to stand before him.

"For the last time — are you going to talk?" Harley demanded.

"What do you wish me to say?" Eddie Brunton gasped.

"Who sent you to get the great green ring? What instructions did you receive concerning it? Where were you to take it when you got it? And why does the person who sent you want the ring at all?"

"I'm telling the truth, Harley, when I say I don't know what you are talking about! Please believe me! I can't tell you something I do not know — not even if you kill me! I made a bet with George Larimore and —"

"Rot! Very peculiar that you should make a bet about this very ring, isn't it?"

"I don't know anything at all about that ring, I tell you! We just happened to see it on the woman's finger, and we had been talking about —"

"I don't care to hear all those lies again!" Harley interrupted. "You are not even a good liar!"

"I tell you —"

"Will you answer my questions?"

"I can't Harley — I can't!" Brunton protested.

"He may not be a good liar, but he is a fine actor," Madame Stalman put in. "He almost convinces me of his innocence. But his story is absurd!"

"Of course it is!" Harley said. "Shall we force him to talk?"

"We must have the information; you know that!"

"Very well!" Harley said.

He hurried from the room.

Eddie Brunton turned his head quickly and encountered the glittering eyes of Madame Stalman. Also, he could see the green ring that she seemed purposely to flaunt before him.

"I — I have told the truth!" he gasped. "I know nothing!"

"Bah!" Madame Stalman said. "As if a man of your sort could tell the truth — a grafter and swindler!"

"I know nothing about the ring! Nobody sent me after it!"

"Don't waste words on me! We want information, and we intend to get it!"

She turned away toward a corner of the room. Eddie Brunton opened his mouth to speak again, but Harley came back, followed by the two masked men.

Without a word being spoken, one of the masked men hurried across and picked up the gag from the table and affixed it.

"Sorry, but it is necessary, Brunton!" Harley said. "You might be inclined to howl for mercy in a very few minutes, and you might do so loudly enough to be heard in the street."

The perspiration was streaming down Brunton's face and neck

now. His face was white. Fear clutched at his heart. He had no courage, and he never had been able to endure pain to a great extent. But he knew that he would have to stand it now.

One of the masked men opened Brunton's collar and shirt and bared his breast. The other disappeared for a moment, and when he returned he carried a brazier filled with burning charcoal, into which a chisel had been thrust.

"When you reach the point where you are ready to talk, Brunton, let us know by nodding your head rapidly," Harley told him. "But be prepared to talk, and not merely speak lies. If you nod your head merely to escape a few minutes of torture, we'll simply double the punishment afterward."

Eddie Brunton strained at the bonds that held him, and squirmed on his chair. But he had been lashed there securely; the bonds held. His torture had begun already — a mental torture. In fancy he could feel the white-hot chisel applied to his breast. He seemed to get the odor of scorching flesh in his nostrils. He strained at his bonds again, and then relaxed, dropped his head forward, fainted.

"Why, he hasn't the nerve of a rat!" Harley exclaimed. "Bring him back to earth!"

The two men removed the gag and threw water into Brunton's face. He revived immediately, without being taken from the chair.

"I'm — telling truth!" he gasped. "Don't — don't —"

"Not as much nerve as a rat!" Harley sneered.

The telephone buzzer sounded. Harley motioned for the others to wait, and went to the instrument. He spoke at length, put up the receiver, and faced the others.

"That was your chauffeur speaking, madame," Harley said. "He says he has captured the ring man. Fellow about thirty and well dressed, he says. He followed the limousine, and Henri decoyed him into the house and had him overpowered and put into the den."

"What does it mean?" Madame Stalman gasped.

"It probably means that they are working in pairs now, and that two of them started to follow you from the store this afternoon. One we have here. The other undoubtedly failed to see you leave the limousine, and followed it to your house."

"That's Larimore!" Eddie Brunton gasped, his voice low and hoarse. "Don't you see that my story is true? I got the taxi first, and Larimore followed. It was all a bet, I tell you! We don't know anything about the ring! I can't tell you what you want to know — and if I don't you'll torture me!"

"I am beginning to think there may be something in this wager story," declared Madame Stalman.

"I doubt it," Harley said. "It is more probable that both these fine gents are after the ring for an entirely different reason. It is coura-geous of you to wear it, madame, but it seems foolishness to do so when you are shopping. Many a man would slit your pretty throat to get it!"

"Not while I have an automatic in my handbag!" Madame Stalman declared.

"Madame, you are wonderful!" Harley declared. "But it is best to be careful, for all that. Shall we go ahead and try to force this fellow to talk?"

"I believe that he is telling the truth," Madame Stalman said.

"Then what have you to suggest?"

Madame Stalman beckoned Harley to a corner and spoke in whispers so that Brunton could not hear.

"Render him unconscious," she said. "We will call the limousine and take him to my house. Put him in the room with the other. Listen while they talk. Perhaps we can get at the truth of this. At any rate — even if it was only a wager — they perhaps both know too much now to be trusted. We shall have to do something to —"

"When it comes to that, leave it to me," Harley said. "I think that your idea is an excellent one, madame."

He turned away and spoke to one of the masked men, who picked up the brazier immediately and carried it from the room.

"We have decided to learn whether you are speaking the truth, Brunton," Harley said. "We will postpone the torture for a short time. But if we find that your story is false, you will suffer doubly, you may be sure."

"It's the truth!" Brunton declared. "Give me a chance and I can prove it! You've known me a long time, Harley. I've made money for you, steering customers your way."

"This happens to be something so big that I can't trust my casual friends," Harley replied.

The masked man returned to the room. He fastened Brunton's shirt and collar. And then, suddenly, he bared Brunton's wrist and brought a hypodermic needle into play. Before Brunton could so much as gasp, the needle had been driven home in his wrist. The drug seized upon his faculties; his head dropped forward; he was uncon-scious.

"All right! Unbind him and put him on the couch, and watch him," Harley directed the two men. "Madame, call your chauffeur!"

Madame Stalman called and gave Henri the necessary directions. Eddie Brunton was unbound and carried to the couch, and one of the men sat down upon it beside him.

"You two men will have to go along," Harley said. "So take your masks off and get ready. Madame Stalman is telling the chauffeur to drive the limousine into the alley. It is almost dark now, and we can get this man into it easily without anybody seeing us. Madame will be kind enough to give us a meal at her house."

So it happened that, some fifteen minutes later, the two men carried Eddie Brunton, unconscious, down the stairs, through the rear of the house, and put him into the limousine. Then they got in, together with Madame Stalman and Harley, and Henri drove rapidly through the streets in the gathering darkness, to the Stalman residence.

Madame Stalman went into the house immediately. When she had taken Jeannette out of the way for a few minutes, the two men of Harley's, under Henri's direction, carried the unconscious Eddie Brunton into the house and up the rear stairs. At the head of the stairs, the guard was sitting.

"Any move?" Henri asked.

"Haven't heard a sound," the man replied. "Been sitting here smoking and haven't taken my eyes off the door."

Henri pulled a revolver from his pocket, unlocked the door, and threw it open.

"Stay where you are, you, until I snap on the lights!" he exclaimed. "There are three or four men behind me, if you want to try to escape."

He stepped inside, on guard against a sudden attack, found the electric switch and turned it. Lights glowed in the room. And Henri gave a cry that startled the other men at the head of the stairs.

"He's gone!" he shouted. "You fool, you let him bribe you!"

"Don't talk that way to me!" the guard retorted. "Nobody has come through that door!"

"He's gone — and the window is locked on the inside. There is nothing else but the door! You — you —"

The others brushed past him and carried Eddie Brunton in. They put him on the divan in the corner. Madame Stalman came hurrying up the stairs.

"What is it? What has happened?" she asked.

"Our prisoner is gone!" Henri replied. "Madame, he was in there when I left, and this dolt, this fool —"

"I tell you he never came through that door!" the guard interrupted. "I have been sitting here smoking all the time."

"You let him bribe you!"

"Don't say that again, Henri! Bribe me? When madame would give us each ten times as much as the poor fool had on him? Are you insane, man?"

"But he is gone!" Henri said again. "There are only window and door, and the window is still locked on the inside!"

"Wait!" Madame Stalman commanded. "Henri, you are sure he was in here when you locked the door?"

"Yes, madame. And I placed this man on guard at the head of the stairs, and the other beneath the window. The window is still locked on the inside, and so how —"

"There is something very mysterious about this," Madame Stalman said. "If we find a traitor, we shall know how to punish!"

"Before Heaven, madame, I am innocent!" the guard insisted. "I have not moved from this spot! I swear it! I had hoped for a reward, if this man was the one you were looking for."

"Well, let us calm ourselves," Madame Stalman interposed. "We shall talk more about this after dinner. In the meantime, we have another prisoner here. I want that door locked, and I'll take the key. Henri, you shall sit out here with this man, and both of you shall act as guards. You understand?"

"He shall not escape, madame," Henri promised.

"He will be unconscious for half an hour yet, and we shall be here again within an hour. I expect to find that man inside the den, Henri, after dinner."

"He shall be there, madame!" They locked the door, and Madame Stalman took the key. Henri and the guard, each suspicious of the other, sat down at the head of the stairs. Madame Stalman and the others went down to the dining room.

A smiling, dimpling Jeannette, who had heard most of the conversation at the head of the stairs, served the soup.

CHAPTER VIII

FOES IN THE HOUSE

BECAUSE Henri was forced to stand guard with the other man, Jeannette served the entire dinner. She had expected to get away long before the end, but, because she could not, she did not betray her disappointment.

"You may go now, Jeannette," Madame Stalman said when the coffee had been served.

Jeannette left the room quickly, but remained in the one adjoining long enough to ascertain that Madame Stalman and the men had begun to discuss their affairs. That meant that they would be occupied for some time to come. Moreover, Jeannette heard Madame Stalman call the cook and order that sandwiches and coffee be sent up to Henri and the other guard, which meant that those in the dining room had no intention of interviewing their prisoner for at least half an hour or so.

Jeannette hurried up the stairs to her own room, being careful that she was not observed. She closed the door, crossed to the opposite wall and pressed her hand against the wainscoting. Once more the door opened in the wall, and Jeannette slipped into the secret passage and closed the door behind her.

It was but a short distance along the passage to the door that opened into the den. Just outside this, Jeannette stopped to listen for a time, and then she opened the door cautiously and glanced inside. Eddie Brunton, still unconscious, was stretched on the divan. There was nobody else in the room.

Jeannette darted to the other door and listened. She could hear Henri and the other man talking a few feet away, and knew that they were eating the food Madame Stalman had ordered for them. She went back to the divan, lifted Eddie Brunton by the shoulders, and pulled him from the divan to the floor.

Then she tugged to get his body into the passage. Eddie Brunton was a large man, and Jeannette was a little woman. Now and then she stopped to rest and to listen. But finally she was at the little door in the wall, and discovery had not come.

Again she tugged and pulled. Finally the unconscious Eddie Brunton was in the passageway, Jeannette touched the panel and closed it.

But her work was not yet done. She could not leave Eddie Brunton there. When he regained consciousness, the darkness and silence might cause him to scream for help, and if anybody was in the den, his screams might be heard. She took him by the shoulders again and pulled him along the passage. When she had gone a distance of half a hundred feet and had reached a place in the passage opposite a room that was seldom used, she concluded that she had done all that was necessary. She stretched Brunton out and then hurried back through the dark.

Regaining her own room, she brushed the dust from her clothing and rearranged her hair, hurried down the stairs, and went from the house by a side entrance. There was not the least hesitation in her manner. Discovered, she merely had to say that she was having a headache and had stepped out to get some fresh air.

She walked along the side of the house, keeping well in the shadows. She crossed the lawn toward the garage, and after a time stood at one end of it, listening.

She opened the gate in the alley wall and gave a peculiar whistle. There was an immediate reply, and a man came to her out of the darkness.

"Well, Jeannette?" he asked.

"It is even better now than when I telephoned you, Mr. Carster," the girl said. "They have brought the other man here from the Harley place. He had been drugged and was unconscious. They put him in the den, and I have just managed to get him out and into the passage. I could not drag him to the little room below, because he is too heavy. And maybe it would not be right for the other man there to see him just yet."

"Jeannette, you are a wonder!" said the man she had addressed as Carster.

It was Carster to whom she had sent the telephone message — a giant of a man with a cruel face and eyes that gleamed, with a voice that could be wonderfully soft or wonderfully harsh, as occasion demanded. Now he stepped close to the girl and patted her on the shoulder.

"How many are here?" he asked.

"Harley is in the house, Mr. Carster. His two men came, too, to help care for the unconscious man. And there is Henri, of course."

"Four, eh? And there are six of us!"

"So many?" The girl gasped.

"We intend to finish the thing tonight, Jeannette. We may never have another chance like this. Without doubt, they will gather in the den to discuss the mysterious disappearance of the two prisoners, and then we can act. Madame had on the ring when she returned?"

"Yes, Mr. Carster; I was particular to notice that."

"Can you let us in immediately?"

"Yes, sir; in about ten minutes. I shall slip back into the house and to my own room, go through the passage and open the door in the garage wall. The man they took prisoner here is in the little room, and perhaps will follow me to the door. He will think that I have come to let him out. I told him I could not do so until it had grown dark."

"I understand, Jeannette."

"In case madame should want me for something, I may be delayed; but I shall open the door just as soon as I can."

"Very well," said Carster.

"And you will be ready, please, to handle this man?"

"You leave that to us, Jeannette. When it comes to handling men, we are past-masters! And we'll take care of you, too."

"Thank you, sir."

"Better hurry back now, Jeannette — and open the door just as soon as you can. Do not worry about candles or anything of the sort — we have a supply — in case we have to wait in the underground room very long."

He patted the girl on the shoulder again, and she hurried back to the house, went along it to the side veranda, and entered without being observed.

She ascertained that Madame Stalman and the others were still in the dining room, talking, and so went up to her own room, closed and locked the door, and hurried through the entrance and into the dark passage.

She walked quickly now, and presently came to the flight of steps and descended them. She looked ahead, but could see no light.

"His candle has burned out!" she thought.

On she went, until she was at the door of the little room under the garage. There she stopped and listened; no sound reached her.

"Where are you?" she whispered.

And then she spoke the words in a louder tone, and, getting no reply, struck a match, and held it high above her head. She saw that the little room beneath the garage was empty.

She struck another match, hurried up the steps and through the short hall, listened there a moment, and then pressed her hand against the wall. The door in the rear wall of the garage swung open.

"Mr. Carster?" she whispered.

"Here, Jeannette!"

"Be quick! He is not here in the room! He must have wandered back through the passage and —"

Carster growled something and thrust her aside. He entered, five men slipping in behind him, and Jeannette closed the door in the wall. Then Carster flashed an electric torch.

"Lead us to the little room!" he commanded.

Jeannette led the way, and they entered and closed the door. Two other men flashed their electric torches.

"Now, tell us!" Carster said. His voice was harsh now, instead of soft, and the girl recoiled as if she had been struck.

"I — I left him in here a little more than two hours, sir," she said. "He had a candle. He could not get out, of course."

"Sure of that?"

"Yes, sir. He begged me to let him out then, but I would not, saying that somebody would be sure to see him and learn of the secret passage."

"Very peculiar! If you are playing us false —"

"Mr. Carster!"

"There, there! I see by your manner that you are not!"

"He probably walked back through the passage, sir, and is somewhere there now. He certainly could not get out. There is a maze of passages in the house, and probably his candle went out and he became lost. We can find him before long. And the other man — the one who was unconscious — he will be conscious again soon, and may cry out or make a noise."

"Can't we get him and bring him to this room?"

"Yes, sir."

"We'll do that, then. I want to question him. Take an electric torch from one of the men and lead us to him. We can find the other man later."

Jeannette turned on the torch and led the way swiftly through the passage, up the stairs, to where she had left the unconscious Eddie Brunton. He was still unconscious when they found him, and two of the men picked him up and carried him back.

When they reached the little room, they propped him up in a chair, and Carster pulled back the lids of one of his eyes.

"Doped — and with some strong drug!" he said. "But I imagine he will be coming back to earth in a very few minutes. One of you men go some distance down the passage and listen for a sound of the prisoner we think is somewhere in the house. Keep your torch dark. If you run across him, see that you bring him here at once."

One of the men left to carry out the instructions. Carster, Jeannette, and the other four men watched Eddie Brunton.

In a few minutes, Brunton groaned, opened his eyes, shuddered, and lifted his hands to his head. The nausea past, he raised his head and regarded the scene, blinking his eyes in the glow of the electric torches.

"What is this — more torture?" he asked, in a weak voice.

"Been tortured, have you?" Carster asked.

"No. They were going to, but — Why! Who are you? I didn't see you before. And you other men! And a girl! What are you going to do with me?" Brunton shrieked.

"Lower that voice of yours!" Carster commanded. "You are in the hands of an entirely different crowd now. All we want you to do is answer a few questions."

"I don't know anything! I told Harley and Madame Stalman that! It was just a fool bet! We saw the ring — and each bet that he could make her acquaintance and get the ring."

"Try to calm yourself!" Carster said. "Try to be a man, can't you?"

"They were going — to burn me with —"

"This isn't a torture chamber, you fool! You've been drugged, and the drug is still working. Just take it easy for a few minutes, and maybe your head will be clearer. You'll be a nervous wreck if you do not!"

"I — I'm all right now."

"Then pay close attention. Harley and Madame Stalman thought you were after a certain great green ring, didn't they?"

"Yes."

"Were you?"

"Yes — I was."

"Well, why?"

"Just — a fool bet. A friend of mine saw Madame Stalman the same time I did. We had been talking about society women being fools, and we thought she was a society woman. We bet five hundred as to which could get the ring from her. I told Harley that, but he wouldn't believe me."

"Well, it probably didn't sound very good to them. Do you know anything about that ring?"

"No — no!"

"As a matter of fact, I think you are speaking the truth. I fail to see how you could know anything about it, unless you are in league with Harley and Madame Stalman, and you evidently are not, since you have been treated as you have. You have stumbled into something that does not concern you. At present, you know too much. We'll have to decide later what to do about you."

"But what — is it all about?" Brunton asked.

"Asking a few questions yourself, eh?" said Carster. "I'm sorry, but I must decline to answer. Just try to calm yourself, now. I am going to keep you here for a time, until we attend to certain things, and I'll leave one of my men with you. You'll be all right as long as you don't attempt any tricks. If you do, my man probably will shoot first and consider the case afterward. You understand?"

"Yes — yes! Why not — let me go away? I've had enough — of all this!"

"It appears that you have, but we can't let you go at present, my fine young man. Behave yourself, and everything may be all right after a time."

Eddie Brunton held his head in his hands again. It seemed to him that his brain was reeling. He had experienced so much since he had made that foolish bet in the afternoon — his surprise at the attitude of Madame Stalman, his session in Harley's torture chamber, and now — this! He kept telling himself that he could not endure it much longer. And the mystery of it seemed to clutch him, too.

Carster made a sign to one of the men to act as guard. That left five, counting Carster himself and the man in the passage. He motioned to Jeannette, and she touched the button of the torch she held, and led the way into the dark passage again.

They picked up the man on guard, and went up the flight of steps. They crept along the narrow hall silently, stopping now and then to listen for sounds. They came to the maze of passages.

"That first man — he is probably down one of those," Jeannette told Carster.

"He has no weapon?"

"No. Henri and the others searched him before they put him into the den."

"Well, we need not bother about him for the time being, then. You are sure that he cannot get out?"

"Absolutely sure, Mr. Carster."

She led the way again, and presently she stopped and made a sign for silence. They could hear voices now, voices raised in anger and argument. Jeannette listened, with her ear against the wall.

"This is the entrance to the den," she whispered to Carster. "They are in there, sir. They have just discovered that their other prisoner is missing."

CHAPTER IX

THE CAPTURE

THE discussion in the dining room had been completed.

"Well, suppose we go up and have a talk with our prisoner, and investigate the disappearance of the other," Madame Stalman said. "If we can make this man talk, or get some idea of the truth —"

"I still think Brunton was sent after the ring," Harley declared. "And I don't like this about the other fellow disappearing."

"Perhaps the explanation will be easy enough after we have made an investigation," Madame Stalman said.

She led the way up the wide stairs, and so they came to Henri and the other guard. Madame Stalman gave Henri the key, and he unlocked the door. Harley drew an automatic from his pocket and stepped up beside Henri.

"He may be fighting mad," Harley explained. "You never can tell how that drug is going to work."

Henri threw open the door, and Harley sprang inside. Henri and the guard, and the two men who had come from the Harley place, followed at his heels. Exclamations of surprise came from them.

"Gone!" Harley shouted.

"What?" Madame Stalman cried out, pushing past them to the center of the room.

"Brunton's gone! And he was unconscious!" Harley said. "I want an explanation of all this!"

"Before Heaven, madame, both of us watched the door continually!" Henri protested. "And you had the key, and the door was locked just now when you came up the stairs!"

"But how can he be gone — and where?" Madame Stalman asked.

"The window is locked on the inside," said Harley. "And there isn't a place a man can hide, much less two men!"

Madame Stalman collapsed in a chair.

"I don't — understand!" she said. "Why — it is impossible, and yet it has happened!"

"I don't like the looks of this," Harley said gloomily.

"Are you beginning to get suspicious of me?" Madame Stalman demanded angrily.

"I am not saying anything about you, madame. But this thing certainly needs an explanation, does it not?"

They searched the room again. The search did not take longer than an instant. There was no place where a man could hide, except under the divan, and no man was there.

"Let us go down to the dining room and discuss this thing," Madame Stalman said. "Henri, you and one other search the upper part of the house — every room — and then do the same downstairs!"

"Yes, madame!"

"Make your search a thorough one! But I do not see what can come of it. That man certainly was in here; he didn't go out through door or window — yet he is gone! This thing is commencing to get on my own nerves."

She led the way down the stairs. Henri and the guard began searching the upper floor. Harley's face was black as he followed Madame Stalman, and his two men were exchanging glances that meant volumes.

Those in the secret passage had heard the conversation in the den. Jeannette turned to Carster.

"I shall have to go," she said. "They will want to search my room, and I must pretend that I was lying down. This is how you are to open the door — see? Do not enter until you are sure Henri and the other man have gone to the lower floor. And you are to protect me, please remember."

"Have no fear of that. We shall treat you as an enemy," Carster said. "You are too valuable to us to be placed under suspicion. You are a great help, Jeannette."

"Thank you, sir."

The girl hurried back through the passage and gained her room just as Henri knocked upon the door.

"Who is it?" she asked.

"It is Henri. We are to search your room — orders of madame. You must open the door!"

She unlocked and opened the door, and confronted him.

"Search my room!" she exclaimed. "Is it that madame suspects me of being a thief?"

"No — no! The sick man we brought from the Harley place — he has wandered out of his room and is somewhere else in the house."

"I do not have men in my room!" she declared angrily.

"Do not spit like a little cat! It is the orders of madame, I said."

It did not take a moment to search the room, and they turned to go below.

"You are to remain in your room until called," Henri said at the door. "That, also, is the order of madame!"

Jeannette smiled at herself in the mirror after they had gone and she had closed and locked the door again. So the sick man had wandered some place about the house, had he? And she was to remain in her room? That made certain matters very simple. She waited until she heard Henri and the other man descending the stairs, then went into the passage again and hurried to where Carster and the four men were waiting.

"They have gone below — now is the time!" she whispered to Carster. "Wait until I hurry back — for madame may ring."

Then she dashed back to her room and closed the tiny door again.

Carster listened with his ear against the wall, then touched the button that released the spring and opened the door. Revolver in hand, he led the way into the den. When the four men had followed, he went to the door that opened into the hall.

"There must be no mistake!" he whispered. "Use force if it is necessary. We want to get all of them. After we have the ring, we can bind and gag them and leave them here, and get away through the secret passage. The girl will help us out. There can be no come-back; not through the law, at least. Eyes and ears open, now, and watch out for that big Henri and the man helping him search the house."

He opened the door, and they filed silently into the upper hall. Each had a handkerchief knotted around his neck, and now these handkerchiefs were raised so that they masked the lower parts of the men's faces.

Silently they crept down the stairs and to the hall below. There they stopped to listen. They could hear the voices of those in the dining room. Henri was reporting to Madame Stalman.

"We have finished the search, madame, and have found nothing."

"As I expected," Madame Stalman said. "Here is a mystery that will have to be explained before I shall feel easy again."

"That's what I say!" agreed Harley.

"It is something that does not suit me at all. It makes a man feel shaky."

"Are you afraid?" Madame Stalman asked. "Do you suppose it does not make me feel shaky, too? But we know, at least, that we have been dealing with people who want only this ring I wear."

"And I'll take that, please, madame!" said a gruff voice at the door.

The woman and the five men sprang to their feet. For five strangers with handkerchiefs over their faces had sprung in upon them, each with a leveled weapon.

One of Harley's men fired, and one of Carster's shot in reply, the bullet breaking the wrist of the man who had began active hostilities.

"Hands up!" Carster commanded. "We'd be pleased to shoot if it is necessary! We are not here to play cards, or anything like that, remember! You men — turn your backs and place yourselves against the wall! And keep your hands up. We are five men against five men, and we have the advantage of position. Let us have no bloodshed if it can be avoided!"

"You mean five men against five men and a woman!" Madame Stalman declared.

She hurled herself forward like a lioness. Grasping Carster's arm she snatched at the handkerchief and pulled it down from his face.

"So, Carster!" she cried out. "So you are the man who is so eager to get the great green ring! I have suspected you, but was not sure!"

"Well, now that you know, what about it?" Carster sneered.

One of the men had seized her now, and was holding her arms at her sides.

"Carster, eh?" She laughed. "What about it? Perhaps nothing, except that now I know whom I am fighting."

"You mean the man you were fighting! The fight is over, madame, and you lose! Will you hand the ring to me, or shall I be forced to tear it from your finger?"

CHAPTER X

EXPLANATIONS

TORTURED with the horror of the dark and silent passage, George Larimore stumbled and staggered along it, turned now and then into another, tore his fingers against the rough walls — and finally collapsed.

When he regained consciousness, the perspiration was streaming from him, but he was calmer. He forced himself to realize that, sooner or later, he would find the way to the little room beneath the garage. And he was fighting mad!

Once more he began walking through the passages, going slower, feeling his way carefully, trying to get some sense of direction, but finding it impossible. And then, just as despair was clutching at him again, he found the flight of steps that led downward.

He almost allowed a cry of delight to escape him. If these were the steps he sought, he soon would be in the little room again. And then there came to him the fear that perhaps the girl had been there, had found him missing, had gone back and would not return. Was he to remain a prisoner in this maze of passages until starvation claimed him?

Then, as he made a turning, he saw the gleam of a light ahead. The girl must be there, waiting for him, he thought. But he went forward cautiously.

He came to where he could look through the half-opened door of the little room. He saw Eddie Brunton sitting in a chair, his head in his hands, and a man on guard.

Larimore crept forward silently, reached the door, looked in again. The guard, his back toward the door, was but a few feet away. Larimore, angry and courageous because of what he had experienced, determined upon a course of action immediately. He grasped the edge of the door, threw it open wider, and sprang!

He crashed against the guard and hurled him to the floor as Eddie Brunton sprang to his feet with a cry.

"Larimore! The gun — get the gun!" he shouted.

Larimore already had it. And he had struck the guard a blow that rendered him senseless. Brunton grasped the electric torch on the table and hurried across the room.

"He's out for a time!" Larimore said. "What has happened? Who is this man? What are you doing here?"

"Don't stop for explanations now, Larimore!" Brunton begged. "I've been through terrible experiences. Let's get out of here!"

"But —"

"I don't even know where we are. I was drugged. There were six men and a girl, and they spoke about going into the house and —"

"This is Madame Stalman's place! There is a secret passage that —"

"Then that is where they have gone. They are after the ring," Brunton said. "If they have gone that way, we can, too. Keep the gun — I'll handle the torch! We must get out!"

"Come!" Larimore said.

Six men or sixty, it was all the same to Larimore now. He was ready to fight his way out, if it proved to be necessary. He directed Brunton how to go, and followed at his heels, the guard's revolver held ready for instant action.

Through the passage and up the stairs they went, and came to where the passage split up into three. But this time there was a gleam of light ahead to direct them. They crept forward until they came to a door. Brunton snapped off the torch.

They saw a scene that surprised them. Carster and his four men had made Madame Stalman and her five men prisoners. They were bound, gagged — all except the woman. They had been placed on the divan and on the floor. Madame Stalman was standing in a corner, one of the men grasping her by the arm.

"And now, madame, the ring!" Carster said. "Hand it over, or I shall use force to obtain it! We have spent time enough here already. You have guessed at the secret passage, eh? One should know well the house one leases, madame. Look at Henri trying to tear at his bonds! No use, my big bully! The ring, madame!"

"I fail to see how I can prevent you and your four thugs from taking it," she said, with scorn in her voice. "But do not imagine that this ends everything. What are you going to do with me?"

"Having received the ring, madame, we shall be forced to bind and gag you, of course. But I give you my word that I shall telephone the police as soon as we are safely away from here, and direct them to come to release you. Will not that be an excellent jest — to telephone the police? There will be some great explanations for you to make, eh? We shall bind and gag you, as we have the others, and go back through the secret passage."

"If I had one man to help me —" Madame Stalman began.

"Ah, but you have not! Even the big Henri is a prisoner!"

In the secret passage, Larimore pulled Brunton back for a short distance.

"We're up against it again!" he whispered. "If they come back through the passage, they'll find us. That man I rapped on the head will be regaining consciousness, and they'll know from his story that we are somewhere in the house."

"What are we going to do?" Brunton asked.

"Fight our way out!" said Larimore.

"I've got a gun! I'll try to take them by surprise. There are five of them, but they are off guard now."

They went back to the door again.

"Put up your guns, men!" Carster was commanding. "We do not need them to handle madame."

The men obeyed, and Carster slid his own weapon into a pocket. Larimore touched Brunton on the arm. It was going to be easier than they had expected.

"Don't you dare touch me!" Madame Stalman was saying. "Since I am powerless to resist, I'll hand you the ring! If only there was one man free to help, what a reward he'd get!"

Larimore sprang into the den.

"Hands up!" he ordered.

Brunton hurried in behind him. Larimore fired one shot, which, added to the surprise of his entrance, had the effect of causing the five to put up their hands immediately.

"I am after that reward, madame!" Larimore said. "Don't make a move, you men!"

"Quick! One of you untie Henri so he can help!" Madame Stalman cried.

Brunton sprang across the room and did as she had asked. Henri lunged forward and caught Carster; whirled him around, threw him on the floor, tied him with the bonds he had been wearing himself.

"The others!" madame commanded.

"Brunton, untie some of those other chaps to help!" Larimore said.

"No — nobody but Henri!" Madame Stalman insisted. "Work swiftly, Henri!"

Henri did. He hurled the men to the floor one at a time, and lashed their hands together. He took their weapons and tossed them at Larimore's feet. Brunton picked one up and went to the door to watch.

"One of the gang in the passage," he explained. "Don't want him sneaking in on us, of course!"

"All done, madame!" Henri reported.

Larimore lowered the weapon he held.

"I am glad to have been of service," he said.

"And I hope that madame will understand it was only a bet on our part," added Brunton.

"I can believe that now," she said smiling, "since you have helped capture the man I thought sent you to steal the ring."

"What about me and my two men?" asked Harley, who had managed to slip the gag out of his mouth. "Untie us, Henri! These cords are cutting my wrists."

"But you are not to be untied," Madame Stalman said. "You are to remain so until the police come."

"The police! Are you insane?" Harley asked. "What on earth do you mean, woman?"

Madame Stalman sat down beside the table, smiled across at him, lifted her hand and regarded the great green ring.

"The explanation probably will shock you," she said. "You know me as Madame Stalman, of course, but my real name is Corrine Stahl."

"Corrine Stahl, the —"

"Precisely, sir! Corrine Stahl, an operative who has helped do something in Europe to run crooks to earth. I have been three years on this present case, and thank Heaven, it is ended now."

"I don't get this!" Larimore muttered.

"Three years ago it was ascertained that there was a gang of criminals working in this country," she said. "The police could make no headway, so they sent for me. I located the headquarters of the gang. But the organization had been perfected in such a manner that a great amount of evidence was necessary. Why, they did everything! Blackmail, robbery, swindling — it was all the same to them. I managed to become a member of the band. I gained the confidence of the leaders, and became a leader myself.

"And then there was trouble. Some left the organization. The faction headed by Harley here was the one with which I remained. I believed at first that Harley was the big man, but just as I was going to call in the police, I ascertained that the real leader was unknown to us. It was necessary to capture that man, of course, if we were to succeed thoroughly.

"By means of this green ring, a member of the band could carry orders to any other member, and they would be obeyed. No big plan could be put through without the ring. We found out that this unknown leader was trying to get the green ring. If he succeeded, our faction would be powerless. So we were on guard, were eager to discover the identity of this unknown leader. Harley wished to do so in order that the man might be removed. I wished to do so because my work was not done until the chief of the band could be taken into custody.

"You two men understand, now, why we tried to force information from you. And tonight Carster, one of the men I suspected, came to get the ring. He would have succeeded, had it not been for you two. Now I shall telephone for the police. Henri, you go into the passage and secure the man there. Plans are made for rounding up the entire gang, and when they are in jail many persons will be able to breathe more comfortably. You two have helped me more than you can guess. What men you could be, if you stopped living as grafters and swindlers! Why not change before it is too late? After all, you are little more than wayward boys."

"Perhaps we shall," Brunton said.

"And the green ring, Madame Stalman?" said Larimore. "We have a bet up, you know!"

"It would be unfair to give it to either of you, since both of you have suffered and have helped. I intend to keep it as a souvenir of my three years' work. But you shall be rewarded — never fear. Now I shall telephone for the police!"

THE ONLY WAY

CHAPTER I

BEWILDERMENT

THE jovial fat man laughed and whirled around to slap one of his companions across the shoulders, and once more I saw his coat tails fly back, saw the fat wallet in his hip pocket, saw that it protruded such a distance that it would not be difficult to remove.

I am not a pickpocket, and lifting "leathers" was no more my business than it is the business of a brick mason to work at a lathe. But a man must have bed and board — and poets have been known to wash dishes in some greasy, cheap restaurant for that reason.

My lips felt suddenly dry. I licked at them, and glanced around at the crowd. The Avenue was thronged. The parade had just passed that corner, and the jumbled mass of men and women was making an attempt to right itself. Everybody seemed to be wanting to go in a direction opposite to that chosen by everybody else. You know how it is on a corner after a parade has passed.

I had stopped there to view the parade because I intended crossing the Avenue, and could not do so until the procession had passed. I was cold and hungry and disgusted, the more so because it was all my own fault. Three nights before I had cracked a crib that had netted me almost five hundred dollars. And because it had been some time since I had enjoyed prosperity, I was not man enough to endure it long. I had returned certain small sums I had borrowed, and then had repaired to a gambling den — and had walked out with a single five-cent piece in my pocket.

It was my own fault, of course — yet a man must live. Far down a street on the other side of the Avenue was a man who would give me a meal and a dollar or so. But I had boasted in certain safe quarters about my good fortune on my last job, you understand, and I had a certain amount of pride, though that may sound peculiar to you. I could not ask a loan without giving some kind of an explanation where my wealth had gone.

And then I saw the fat, jovial man — and the wallet. If I could get that wallet, and it contained a bundle of bills, I'd be in funds again and would not have to resort to my friends. I realized, of course, that the job was not in my line. I appreciated the fact that a first-class burglar, as I was known to the underworld, descended from his caste when he turned dip. Nevertheless —

Such a thing should not be difficult, I told myself. I knew several pickpockets — furtive-eyed, shifty fellows — who seemed to be of a low order of intelligence. And surely, if they could lift leathers and do it without detection, a man like myself should encounter no difficulty doing so, I know better now — everyman to his trade.

I shall not bother you with a long recital of the affair. It was merely the prelude to the real adventure, after all. Suffice it to say that I edged nearer the fat man as he walked between his two male friends, and awaited an opportunity. It was not long in coming.

At the corner we were jammed together in such fashion that none of us scarcely could move. The people there were surging backward and forward, and seemingly getting nowhere. The throng gave this way and that, and for a time I was unable to do my work. For I realized that I never could succeed in making a getaway in that jam, if I happened to be detected. I did not anticipate detection, of course, but a good criminal always prepares himself for all emergencies.

Then the crowd surged again, and there was an opening. The fat man and his companions moved forward, and I moved close behind them. Once more the tails of his coat flew back, and I made my attempt.

Was it my fault that my foot slipped at that moment on an apple core that some thoughtless girl had tossed away? I lurched against the fat man, almost bowling him over, and in turn he lurched against one of his friends. They whirled around instantly. They saw me — and the wallet in my hand. I had not had time to slip it into one of my pockets.

I dropped it instantly, of course, and turned around to spring toward the curb. But the fat man raised an outcry, and one of his friends, a man much younger, sprang at me.

In that flash of time, I realized that I was facing a term in prison. I had been there once, for a year and a half, and the mere thought of going there again made me shudder. I was penniless, and could not engage a good attorney, and the few real friends I had were almost penniless. My predicament was by no means a pleasant one. Flight was all that remained to me. I darted into the street and across it, in front of automobiles whose chauffeurs turned white in the face and cursed me as they applied the brakes of their machines. One of the fat man's friends pursued me. A policeman who had been helping handle the crowd at the corner took after me.

I darted through the crowd when I reached the other side of the street. There was confusion, of course, shrieks and cries, and I knew that few persons there really knew what had happened. The fat man was shrieking "Stop thief!" at the top of his voice, but there was so much noise that few persons understood him.

I was compelled to run down the side street, because the crowd on the walks of the Avenue was so dense. Two policemen were pursuing me now. One of them was yelling for me to halt, but neither of them dared fire at me, for fear of hitting some bystander.

Finally, I managed to dart through an alley, running between the trucks and drays, and so I came to the next cross street and turned up it toward the Avenue and the welcome throng again. I was wearing a reversible coat, and I darted into a doorway for an instant and changed it. I tossed my hat away, and took a soft cap from my pocket and put it on my head.

But I lacked the courage to remain there and watch the chase go by. I was not certain, you see, that one of the policemen would not know me. And the fat man's friend, if he remained in the pursuit, would be almost certain to recognize me, for he had had a good look at my face.

So I hurried on to the Avenue and turned uptown. Once more ill fortune attended me. The crowd had disappeared as if by magic, now that the parade had passed.

I could do nothing but go on, of course. I glanced over my shoulder and saw that the two policemen were following me, looking up and down the street, searching for me. My coat was gray now, whereas it had been black before, and I wore a cap instead of a hat, yet I dared not face them. The best thing, I decided, would be to continue walking north up the Avenue, hoping that they would turn around and give up the chase, believing that they had missed me several blocks back.

I was half a block ahead of them, and gradually I made the distance greater. And suddenly, around a corner before me came a headquarters detective I knew. Moreover, he knew me. He had been instrumental in sending me to prison that time before.

He would stop me, question me, of course, for that was his way. As he questioned me, the policemen behind would come up. They would learn that I was a criminal. Perhaps one of them would recognize me. I would be taken to the station, and the fat man and his friends would identify me.

I am willing to admit that I was in a panic. It was dangerous to go forward, dangerous to go back. If I attempted to cross the street, there in the middle of the block, I would attract the attention of the detective, and he would recognize me. There was but one thing to do — and I did it.

Before me was a mansion. I knew it only by sight — did not know what particular millionaire lived in it. There was a tiny lawn, and a high fence of heavy bronze, and an ornamental gate that stood open.

I turned and walked through that gate deliberately, went up the walk to the steps, up the steps to the front door, and lifted the knocker. From the corners of my eyes, I saw that the detective glanced at my back and then turned away. He had failed to recognize me. But he would meet the two policemen in a moment, now.

My plan was a simple one. Under some pretext, I would remain at that door until the detective and the two policemen went back down the street, and then I would make some excuse and go out and walk up the Avenue, and so to safety.

The knocker fell, and it seemed to me that it made noise enough to be heard for blocks above the din of the traffic. I saw that the detective had met the policemen and was talking to them, and that all three were looking up and down the street.

The door opened, after a time, and a butler stood framed in it. In that moment, I failed to wonder why it was not a maid or a second man. I realized only that danger was not over and the coast clear yet, that I'd have to remain at that door a few minutes. If I returned to the street, the detective might call to me, stop me, start to question me — and then I would be lost.

"Sir?" the butler said.

He was a gigantic butler with eyes that seemed to glitter, an imposing fellow.

"Does Mr. Traymore live here?" I asked.

"He does, sir."

That statement almost unnerved me, as you shall see in a moment. I gulped, and tried again.

"Mr. John Xenephon Traymore?" I asked.

"Yes, sir. Step in, sir?"

I looked at him, astonished, bewildered for an instant. That unusual and peculiar name — John Xenephon Traymore — *was one that I had invented on the spur of the moment!*

CHAPTER II

A WOMAN AND A WARNING

ALLOW me to say that I am a fairly well educated man, but I have never investigated the deeper problems of learning and existence as they know of them in universities. I do not know much about the law of averages and coincidence, but I think that nine hundred ninety-nine times out of a thousand there would fail to be any such coincidence as this. I had stumbled, it appeared, up the thousandth time.

I had invented a name, and had spoken it at a door. Out of a city of several million persons and hundreds of thousands of habitations, I had spoken it, so it seemed, at the very door of the man by that name. Do you wonder that I was badly startled for a moment?

But I have presence of mind to a degree. The detective was still speaking to the two policemen, and I was afraid to leave the door just yet. It would look peculiar to the butler, too, that I had asked to see a man and then turned and run away without seeing him.

I thanked the butler, removed my cap, and stepped inside the house. It was very simple. I told myself. I could say, when I met Mr. Traymore, that I had been misdirected, that he was not the John Xenephon Traymore I wished to see. I could say that I had met a gentleman who said his name was that, and that he had promised to get employment for me if I would call at his residence, at this address. Mr. Traymore would believe that one of his friends was playing a joke on him, and upon me, too, of course. The principal thing was to remain in the house until the detective and policemen had left the neighborhood.

The butler showed me into a sort of reception room and left with the remark that he'd inform Mr. Traymore I was there. He asked my name, and I told him James Dacy. That happened to be my right name, and why I did not give an assumed one, I do not know. It was my *right* name, I say — not the name by which I was known to the police.

So James Dacy sat down and glanced around the room. I may remark that I have seen the inside of several mansions belonging to very wealthy men, but always before now it had been at night, when I was compelled to work with the aid of an electric torch. I trust that you understand my meaning.

But now I could look at magnificence in the bright daylight, and I truly saw magnificence here. It was the magnificence of excellent taste, too. Even a burglar may have excellent taste. I might explain that, before I became a criminal — But, never mind that now!

I twirled my cap in my fingers and waited. Not a sound reached my ears, save the noises that came from the Avenue. Not a drapery stirred. The air in that magnificent residence seemed to be oppressive. I began to have a feeling of nervousness, a feeling that I could not explain. It was as if I was sitting on a high platform, and all around me were persons who regarded me thoughtfully from wide-opened eyes. I seemed to feel that I was under surveillance.

And then I almost laughed. Some servant, no doubt, was watching me from behind a curtain, making sure that I did not run away with the grand furniture and the expensive tapestries that were in the room and all about me.

From where I was sitting, I could look out upon the Avenue, and I saw the detective and the two officers turn around and walk south. The coast appeared to be clear now, as the saying is, and I was eager to leave this place and hurry about my business. But I could not leave until the butler returned. I did not want to arouse suspicion, or anything like that.

Another five minutes passed, and my nervousness increased. Was it the custom in this house, I wondered, to usher a visitor to the reception room and then leave him alone as long as this? Why didn't the butler return and lead me to his master, or tell me that his master was not able to see me just then?

Another two minutes — and then I heard a woman scream. It was a peculiar scream, not too loud, and it seemed to be choked off before it had run its natural course. I think that I sprang from my chair when I heard it. I was already nervous, remember. And then I sank back in my chair again and told myself that I was a fool. That scream probably had come from the throat of some maid who had seen a mouse, or had dropped and broken an expensive vase, or something of the sort.

But my nervousness continued to increase, I got up and walked to the window and looked out upon the Avenue. I glanced at my watch again, and knew that I had been inside the house for more than a quarter of an hour. I had seen nobody since the butler had left me, had heard no sound in the house with the exception of that one scream.

Suddenly, I decided to leave. I stepped across the room and entered the hall. I looked up and down it, and could see no one. And so I went straight to the front door.

But I did not leave the house. The massive door was fastened in some peculiar manner. I could not open it, and I knew a great deal about opening doors and things too. I began to feel alarmed, to wish that I had remained on the street and had taken my chances with the detective and the two policemen.

A voice behind me:

"Do not be in a hurry. Mr. Traymore is engaged at present, but will see you soon."

Whirling around, I found the butler within six feet of me, looking at me peculiarly. I almost shuddered as I looked at him. He was a giant, his face was almost repulsive, he had a sinister appearance.

"Thought you had forgotten me," I said.

"Oh, no! I had not forgotten you, sir!" he replied, and there was some quality in the tone of his voice that I did not relish. I walked back down the hall and entered the reception room again. The butler bowed and disappeared.

Perhaps I had been foolish, I told myself. Traymore was busy, possibly, and the butler had not believed me to be important enough to run back directly and tell me. I crossed the room and sat down in a different chair, and waited again.

I think that it was the silence of that house that got on my nerves as much as anything. I have sensitive nerves, of course — a man in my profession is rarely successful unless he does have sensitive nerves to telegraph to his brain warnings. I believe that the vulgar call them "hunches."

Once more I looked around the room. Within a few feet of me were heavy portieres that apparently concealed the entrance to an adjoining apartment. As I glanced at them, they seemed to move as if stirred by a gentle breeze. I continued to watch them closely, not having anything more important to do. And gradually they parted, and suddenly a woman stood before me.

She was a woman of about twenty-five, I decided at the first glance. She was of slight build, and had beautiful eyes and hair, and pleasant features. One glance at her was enough to decide me that she was a gentlewoman.

I got to my feet and bowed, thinking that possibly this was the daughter of the house. And then I got a better look at her face, for she had stepped out toward me, and the strong light from the nearest window fell upon her.

Never before had I seen such a look of terror in the face of a human being. She seemed to be wild with fear. Now she clasped her hands before her, clasped them until the knuckles showed white. I remembered the scream that I had heard.

"Madam —" I began.

She had been staring at me, breathing in little gasps, and now she rushed toward me, silently, and grasped me by the arm.

"Go!" she said, in a hoarse whisper."Go from this terrible house while you can! If you love life itself —"

"I — I beg your pardon?" I stammered.

There was something ghastly in the way she acted, something terrible in the tone of her voice.

"Go — go!" she whispered, standing close to me. "I am trying to save you! I know that you cannot leave by the door. But, go! Break the front window, and go! If you do not —"

If you want to know it, she impressed me at that moment as an insane woman. I did not want to break an expensive window and then be called upon to pay for it — when I was penniless — or go to jail. I did not care, you may be sure, to create disturbance and have to face the officers at police headquarters. So I hesitated, naturally.

"Madam —" I began again.

"For Heaven's sake —" she implored. "I — I am running a risk in warning you. Go, while there is time, while you have a chance! The window —"

I opened my mouth to reply, but did not. For suddenly, she darted behind the portieres again. I heard steps in the hall. The ugly butler stood in the doorway.

"Mr. Traymore will be pleased to see you now, sir," he said, in polite tones.

CHAPTER III

MR GREGG

I GLANCED at the portieres, but if the butler noticed that they still moved, he gave no sign. I stepped across the room to follow him, wondering a great deal about the woman, but eager more than anything else to see this man, Traymore, and then get out of the house.

The butler led the way through a long hall and up a short flight of stairs. He opened a door there, and stepped aside to allow me to enter the room.

It was a peculiar room. On one side of it was a huge desk, behind which sat a huge man. If the butler was a giant, this man was almost a monstrosity. He had a large head, a high brow, piercing eyes, thick black hair.

"You may go, Blake!" he said, and the butler bowed, closed the door and was gone.

"Sit down, Mr. Dacy," said the man behind the desk, then.

"I — I am afraid that there is some mistake," I said.

"How is that?"

"I asked to see Mr. John Xenephon Traymore."

"Well?"

"But you are not the man, sir," I said. "I met a gentleman who said that was his name, and he instructed me to call on him here today and see about a position he was going to get for me. It —it must have been somebody playing a joke."

The man behind the desk laughed, and then got up and stood before me. He placed his fists against his hips and glared down at me. I began to feel highly uncomfortable.

"There is no such animal," he said, "as Mr. John Xenephon Traymore — and you know it!"

"But, sir —"

"You'll not find the name in the latest city directory, which is there on the desk, if you care to look — and I am very sure you'll find nobody in the city who knows a man by that name."

"But, sir, the butler told me at the door —"

"Why did you come here?" he demanded.

"To see Mr. Traymore," I persisted.

"I know of no Mr. Traymore. My name happens to be Gregg!"

"Then there must be some mistake, sir, and I'll be going," I said. I didn't like the way in which he stood in front of me. He was a gigantic man. He seemed to radiate strength and energy. I felt my flesh creep as he watched me.

And now he laughed, deep down in his throat, a laugh that seemed filled with some sinister meaning.

"One moment," he said, and walked across the room.

The entire wall was fitted with filing cases, I saw, row upon row of them. He opened a drawer and took something out.

"You have been watched from the first moment you entered this house," said the man who had named himself Gregg. "You were left for a time in the reception room so I could ascertain a few things about you before having you up here."

"But, sir —" I began.

"Kindly wait until I have finished," said Gregg. He walked to the desk and opened the big envelope he had taken from the drawer of the filing case.

"You say that your name is James Dacy?" he said.

"Yes, sir."

"Known to the police as Slick Jimmy."

"Sir?"

"Also as James Regan, alias, Jimmy Carter."

"I —" I began again.

"Silence! You once were convicted of burglary and served a sentence. You are one of those chaps the police are watching all the time. Here in this envelope I have the history of your career. Also a photograph."

He tossed the photograph to me. I knew it instantly — a copy of the one to be found in the rogues' gallery.

"It does look a bit like me —" I said.

"It *is* you! I sized you up the moment you sat down in the reception room. I always remember faces. I have thousands of photographs.

"The moment I saw you, I knew I had your photograph, and I came right up here and walked to a certain filing case and got it. I classify faces. There are only so many classes of countenances. You belong to a certain class. It took me less than five minutes to find your photograph, and then read your history."

"I — I fail to understand," I said. "You are making some mistake, of course."

"I seldom make mistakes, young man."

"This is all very interesting, but I came here to see Mr. Traymore —"

"Why continue to play that farce?" he demanded. "You are telling a lie, and I know it."

"At least, I do not intend to remain here and be insulted," I said, angrily. "I care nothing about your classification of faces."

I got up and started toward the door.

"Sit down!" Gregg commanded.

It was a command, not a request — there was no mistaking that point. I whirled around, and saw that he was within a pace of me. As I hesitated, he threw a big hand forward, clutched me by the shoulder, and almost hurled me back into the chair I had just left.

"See here!" I exclaimed. "I don't understand all this, and I am going to get out of here!"

"When I am ready to have you go," he said.

I began wondering whether he was one of those wealthy nuisances who call themselves criminal investigators and go out of their way to send men and women of the underworld to prison, when it is none of their business.

"Why did you come here and ask to see a man who does not exist?" he demanded. "The truth!"

"I met a man who said his name was Traymore and told me to come here today and he'd get me a job."

"Stop your lying!" he roared, "I want the truth."

"Why did your butler tell me, Mr. Traymore lived here, when he does not?" I countered.

"You would have been admitted, no matter what name you mentioned," Gregg said. "I would have looked at you, found out what you were, if possible. Had I decided that I could not use you, I would have asserted that my name was what you said at the door, but that there must be another man with the same name in the city."

"But, why?"

"Just to get you out of the house. But, when I identified you, when I knew what you are — a criminal — I decided that I could use you."

"Use me?" I asked.

"Precisely. I happen to need you. There is a certain experiment in which I am interested —"

He broke off in the middle of the sentence and seemed to be thinking about something important. I began to believe that I was in a madhouse. First the scream I had heard, and then the mysterious woman and her warning, and now the peculiar words of this gigantic man! My nerves were almost at the breaking point again.

I glanced toward the door, I wondered whether I could dash to it, open it, rush down the stairs, whether I could avoid Blake, the butler. I was ready to break a window, now, or do almost anything else to make my escape.

Gregg was turned half away from me. And suddenly I sprang. I heard his raucous laugh as my hand touched the knob.

"You are a good man, if you can get that door open," Gregg said.

I had found it locked on the outside. The first twist of the knob and the attempt to hurl the door open had convinced me of that. At once, I whirled around and faced him again.

Gregg had not moved from where he was standing. He was still laughing at me.

"Maybe this is funny for you, but it isn't for me!" I snarled at him. "What's the meaning of this? I'll have you in trouble —"

"So Slick Jimmy is going to the police and protest, is he?" Gregg said, grinning. "I think not! I imagine you are not eager to see the men at police headquarters. Now, young man, I want to know why you came to the door of my residence and asked for a man who does not exist."

"Are you a detective?" I countered.

"I am not. You may speak freely."

"Well, then, a couple of cops were after me," I said, frankly. "I saw approaching from the other direction a detective I knew. I was afraid he'd stop me and talk to me, and that the cops would come up and recognize me. I'd tried to lift a leather and bungled the job."

"I thought you were a burglar," Gregg said.

"A man is liable to work at anything when he happens to need ready money," I said.

"Oh, I see. Well, your story impresses me, so far."

"So, to dodge the detective and the cops, I ran to your door and knocked," I went on. "I intended asking for some fictitious man and fool around a few minutes until the officers had gone on down the street. I asked for John Xenephon Traymore, and the butler said he lived here."

"And so you decided to wait and see me, and then say that I was not the man? I understand," Gregg said. "Very clever of you, I am sure."

"Well, if you are satisfied, I think I'll be going now," I told him.

"Allow me to ask you a few questions, first," Gregg said. "Do not be afraid — I am not going to hand you over to the police. Have you any relatives?"

"If I have," I replied, "I am not claiming them — and they are not claiming me."

"Black sheep of the family, eh? I thought possibly it was that way. You talk like a man of some education, you know. Have you any close friends?"

"Two or three, though I fail to see how they can interest you," I replied.

"Did any of them know that you were coming here?" he demanded, suddenly, bending toward me.

So he was trying to pick a flaw in my story, was he? I was a match for him there.

"Certainly, nobody knew that I was coming here!" I said. "I did not know it myself until a second before I darted through your front gate. I have told you the truth!"

"That's all that I wanted to know!" he exclaimed, grinning at me again. "So nobody knows you came here! They won't be able to trace you, if they wish to do so. You'll simply — well, you'll simply disappear!"

So that was it! Why hadn't I intimated that somebody did know where I was. And fear began clutching at me as I looked up at Gregg and saw the expression on his face.

"What's that?" I gasped. "What did I understand you to say?"

"You'll simply disappear," Gregg repeated. "The friends and the enemies of James Dacy, the crooks and the police, male and female — none of them ever will see him again!"

CHAPTER IV

A PRISONER

FOR a moment, I merely stared at him in astonishment. What could the man mean? Was this some terrible menace, or was he only trying to frighten me?

But Gregg did not appear to be amusing himself by scaring the wits half out of me. The expression on his countenance was not that of a man amusing himself, but that of a person who entertained some fixed purpose out of the ordinary.

I did not know what to say, or just how to act. He had ceased to grin at me and seemed to be regarding my face earnestly.

"It is going to be interesting — highly interesting," I heard him mutter.

"Don't you think that this has gone far enough?" I managed to ask him. "I must be on my way. Since you are not going to hand me over to the police, why not have the door unlocked and allow me to go?"

"Fool!" he exclaimed. "Haven't I said that I have need of you?"

"Well, what's the idea?" I asked. "You said something about my disappearing."

"Yes — James Dacy will disappear. Nobody knows that he came here, and so he cannot be traced by bothersome persons."

"What do you mean?"

"You'll know in time," he said.

I glanced toward the windows as he turned to his desk, and for the first time I noticed that there was a network of steel bars over every one of them. I was frightened now, badly frightened. I began to think that surely Gregg was a madman, and that I was in his power and he could work his will on me — whatever that might happen to be.

He sat down behind the big desk and touched a button. I heard a step in the hall outside, and the sound of a bolt being drawn. Blake, the ugly butler, entered.

If I had entertained any notion of springing upon him, hurling him aside and bolting through that door, I promptly forgot it now. For I could see plainly that Blake was on guard, as if expecting some such move.

"We can use this man, Blake," Gregg said.

"Very good, sir," Blake said. He looked at me as a cook might look at a fowl intended for the roasting pan. I felt my flesh beginning to creep again. "We'll follow the usual method, Blake," Gregg went on to say. "I put the matter in your charge."

"Very good, sir."

"What does this mean?" I cried. "What are you going to do with me?"

"My dear Mr. Dacy, you'll know all that at the proper time," Gregg said. "Do not be so impatient. You may sleep better tonight if you do not know too much."

"The usual prison room, sir?" Blake said, ignoring me and looking toward Gregg.

"Yes," Gregg replied. "You handle the matter in your own way, Blake. I shall begin thinking on the subject immediately. Never mind taking a photograph — I have a rogues' gallery picture, and it will suit my purpose admirably."

"Very good, sir," Blake said.

He stepped toward me.

"You are to come with me, Mr. Dacy," he continued. "I assure you that an attempt to escape will be futile. I can handle you with one hand."

"I'm not doubting that — but I want to know the meaning of this!" I cried. "Are you going to murder me? Think you've got a right to make me stay in this house if I don't wish to do so? I think you are all insane, if you ask me — even the woman."

"Woman?" Gregg roared.

"Miss Anita, sir," Blake told him. "She found Mr. Dacy in the reception-room and urged him to spring through a front window and make his escape."

"She didn't get a chance to —" Gregg began.

"Not at all, sir," Blake interrupted. "She was with him an instant only, and told him nothing of consequence."

"Very good," said Gregg.

Perhaps you can imagine what I felt during this conversation. I could not fathom the intention of these men. They seemed to regard me about as much as a scientist would a rabbit upon which he intended to experiment. Evidently, I was to be held a prisoner — for what reason, I did not know. Here, in this mansion on the famous

Avenue — this, that had the appearance of being a home of wealth and refinement — I found myself not my own master. I was at the mercy of a whim of a madman, for such I determined Gregg must be.

And the mystery of it seemed to choke me. I scarcely could determine whether there was a menace or whether they were playing a game with me. The scream I had heard, the woman with her warning — these things came back to me now.

Blake stepped to my side suddenly and grasped me by the arm, grasped me so cruelly that a pain shot almost to my shoulder.

He whirled me around as if I had been a child, and without speaking another word, he took me to the door, through it, and closed it behind us.

I tried to twist and struggle, but to no avail. Blake only gripped my arm tighter. He did not even smile. He was still the butler, and nothing else.

"You let me go!" I commanded.

He made no reply to that. He forced me along the hall and up more stairs. I now was on the third floor of the house. Presently we came to a door, which Blake opened. He hurled me inside a room, slammed the door, and locked and bolted it. I was a prisoner.

Everything had certainly been most peculiar and mysterious, to say the least, and I had been as a spectator. But when I heard the bolt shot on that door, a full realization seemed to come to me. I knew, then, that I was in danger, but from what I did not know. I seemed to go half insane. I sprang to the door, wrenched at the knob, threw myself against it. I might as well have hurled my body against a wall of stone.

The door was massive, the casement heavy. No man could hope to break it down without tools, and I was a small man and had no sledge or ax. Yet I continued to pound it with my fists, to kick it, until I was almost exhausted. And then I heard the calm voice of Blake from the hall.

"Didn't even make a dent in it, did you, Mr. Dacy? Better take it a bit easy, sir, or you'll do yourself a harm."

I raged at him, shrieked a curse at him, and then heard him walking down the hall. I turned to the windows. There were four of them in the room, and over each was the network of steel bars. I knew without making a close examination that escape through a window would be impossible.

The room was a large one, with a high ceiling. In one corner there was a bed, with curtains around it. For the rest, the room was furnished as an ordinary living room. The furnishings were expensive. It was such a room as a man would expect to find in such a house.

And I had heard it called a prison room!

I threw myself into an easy chair beside the table, gasping, trying to tell myself that I should compose myself and work this thing out. I had been in close quarters before, often enough. A successful burglar learns to control himself.

There were books on the table, and magazines. But the books were novels, and the magazines those of wide circulation. There was nothing to indicate anything special, like an interest in criminology.

I prowled around the room and investigated everything. There was but the one door that I could see. I sounded the walls, thinking of stories I had read of houses with secret passages and sliding panels, but found no indication of anything of the sort.

Once more I asked myself what it could mean. Gregg had said that James Dacy would disappear, that his friends and enemies would see him no more. Did the man mean to have me murdered? And, if so, why? He never had seen me in his life until I came to the house — of that I felt sure.

But he had my photograph, a copy of the rogues' gallery picture. And those filing cases — they probably contained all sorts of photographs and life histories. Who was this man, Gregg? What was his game? What did it all mean?

I gave up in disgust. Once more I prowled around the room. I opened all the windows and examined the steel bars. No use in planning to escape there, I knew.

My mind seemed to grow numb. It was getting dark outside by this time, and presently the electric lights in the room flashed on, turned on from a switch in the hall, I supposed. I began pacing the floor, clenching my fists, cracking my fingers, beating my breast at times.

The door opened, after a time, and Blake came into the room. He had a tray in his hands. As he entered, he balanced it on one hand, to have the other ready to handle me if I made an attack, I presumed. He slammed the door behind him and advanced toward the table; but keeping between me and the door.

"Your dinner, Mr. Dacy," he said. "And I might say, Mr. Dacy, that it would do you no good to escape from this particular room, even if you could overpower me and do so. If you did, you could not escape from the house."

"What does all this mean?" I demanded. "Are you going to murder me?"

"I do not have the authority, sir, to speak to you of this matter," Blake said. "Your dinner, sir."

And then, despite my entreaties, he went out and locked and bolted the door again.

The dinner Blake had left was an excellent one. I was afraid to taste it at first, afraid that it might be poisoned. And then I told myself that Gregg had not looked like a man who would feed another man poison. And so I ate — not with keen relish, you may be sure, despite the good food, but I ate.

And then I paced the floor again, hour after hour, prowled around the room once more, and failed to find anything new. My nervousness had almost exhausted me. I examined the bed, and finally threw myself upon it. I was determined not to sleep. And in the next moment, I told myself that I need not fear being murdered as I slept. Gregg and Blake were no weaklings. They would not have to attack a man asleep in order to make away with him.

Finally, I got up and turned off the lights, one by one. Then I stumbled back to the bed and fell upon it without undressing. I found that I was going to sleep whether I desired to do so or not. I fought against it, and lost the battle. As I slipped into unconsciousness, it seemed that I heard a woman's scream again, but I was not sure.

CHAPTER V

AN ATTEMPT THAT FAILED

A DREAM — I cannot recall it now — was broken suddenly. I opened my eyes, blinked rapidly, realized that one of the electric lights was burning. I sprang from the bed.

She stood in the middle of the room beside the table, the woman who had warned me the afternoon before in the reception room. She was fully dressed. The look of terror was still in her face, her hands clasped before her again.

"You —" I began.

"Hush!" she whispered. "Oh, why didn't you go yesterday afternoon when I warned you?"

"Who are you — and what does all this mean?" I asked.

"Hush!" she said again. "We must talk in low whispers —"

"You are going to help me out of this?"

"You cannot get out, I am afraid," she said. "I pretended to go to bed, but I did not. I waited until everybody was asleep, and then I crept up the stairs and through the hall, and unlocked your door and came in. Oh, I do wish that I could help you!"

"Why can't I get out?" I asked.

"You might, if you could get down the stairs and break a window. That is the only way. They — they have some arrangement about the doors —"

"Electric alarm signal, I suppose," I said.

I should have rushed out of the room then, but I wanted to know what all this meant. And I did not want to attempt an escape and fail, either.

"How many in the house?" I asked her.

"Blake, the butler, and a woman cook," she replied. "And my uncle and myself."

"Your uncle?"

"Mr. Gregg is my uncle," she explained. "My name is Anita Frawley. And they — they —"

"What does this mean? Tell me in a few words," I begged her. "What do they intend doing with me?"

"I — I don't know," she said. "We live in a very peculiar fashion. My uncle is wealthy, though once he was only a poor college professor. He inherited his wealth. I think that his studies have made him insane. I — I don't know what it is that he does."

"He has had other men here?" I asked.

"Yes — three of them. I think that is why we have only the two servants. Another woman comes on certain days to clean the house. We are using only a few rooms in it, you see. And these other men — They were decoyed here. I don't know what he did to them. I saw them, as I saw you. I heard screeches and screams and moans. And I never saw them again."

The perspiration was standing out on my forehead now. *She never saw them again!*

"And then different-looking men would leave the house," she went on. "Where they came from, how they got in I do not know."

"I heard a woman scream twice — was that you?"

"Yes, Uncle is very strong. He — he doesn't mean to hurt me, but when he finds me where I should not be, he grasps me by the arm and —"

"I understand," I said. "I think that I'd better get out of here."

"I — I hope that you can. And you'll bring the police, please? I want to get away. I — I cannot endure this sort of thing. I have some money of my own, but my uncle will not let me go away. He bought this house almost a year ago, brought me here to live with him. I never have been out of it since."

"Not out of the house for almost a year!" I gasped.

"They let me go up on the roof for sunshine and fresh air, but Blake is always at my side. I never get a chance to call for help. Blake does whatever my uncle wants him to do. I think that my uncle gives him a lot of money."

"Well, Miss Frawley, I'll send the police word that there is certainly something extremely peculiar going on here — if I can get away. I'll tell them to find you — that you are being held here against your will."

"Yes — please. I suppose it is terrible, since the man is my uncle, but I cannot help that. I know he does terrible things. There is a little room that is always locked, and I never have been inside of it. I know he took the other men into that room — and that was where the screams came from."

You may believe that I was properly frightened by now. The unknown terror of the thing was getting on my nerves again. I think I have the usual amount of courage — but no man can be brave in the face of the unknown.

I strode across the room to the door, and Anita Frawley followed at my heels.

"Break a front window and get out that way," she said. "I'll go back to my room. And please have the police hurry — he will know that I unlocked the door for you, and he may —"

She did not finish the sentence, and there was no need of her doing so. There was horror in her voice. I turned and looked at her. I felt pity for her. I assured myself then and there that I'd help her if it was possible for me to do so.

I opened the door. The hall was in darkness, and I darted back and snapped out the one light she had turned on when she had entered the room. Then I hurried to the door again.

"Be careful going down the stairs," Anita Frawley said. "Are you sure that you know the way?"

"Yes. If I had a weapon of some sort I would be —"

"I do not know of any I could get," she said.

"I'll not wait for you to search for one," I whispered. "Good-by — and thanks!"

Our hands met and gripped for an instant, and then I started toward the stairs. And suddenly the hallway was bathed in bright light, and I saw Gregg and Blake standing before me.

"Trying to escape, are you?" Gregg sneered. "It cannot be done, my young friend, even with the aid of my niece. The mere fact that she opened the door of your room defeated your purpose — it flashed an alarm to us. I shall have to punish you for this, Anita. I have told you many times not to interest yourself in things that do not concern you."

"You beast! You beast!" she cried. "You are doing terrible things, and I know it!"

"Do not alarm yourself," Gregg said. "Just attend to your own affairs, my dear."

"You are holding me here — a prisoner. And you are keeping me from —"

"It is necessary for the present," Gregg told her. "I think that I'll take you for a trip in about another month. So try to be patient — and do not make any efforts to aid my prisoners in attempting an escape."

I had been watching them closely, of course My fear gave me strength and daring. Suddenly I launched myself forward, striking and kicking like a maniac, trying to fight my way to the head of the stairs, trying to prevent either Gregg or Blake getting their hands on me for I knew that I would be powerless if they did that.

It was only wasted effort. My rush disconcerted them for an instant, but that was all. Gregg snarled an order, Blake darted forward and drove me against the wall. And then the gigantic butler pinioned my arms to my sides and held me as easily as he would have held a small child.

Anita Frawley had rushed forward, too, as if to hinder them and aid me, but her uncle grasped her by the arms and held her. I could tell from the expression in her face that he was hurting her with his cruel grip.

Gregg growled out another order, and Blake marched me along the hall and hurled me inside the prison room again, and he was none too gentle about it, either. The door slammed, and was locked and bolted. I was a prisoner once more, waiting for — I knew not what.

But I knew that I was waiting with a terrible fear in my heart!

CHAPTER VI

TERROR

THERE was no more sleep for me that night. I tossed on the bed, and tried to think it out.

Was it possible that such a thing could happen in a mansion on one of the most famous streets of the greatest city in the world? I could not imagine what Gregg intended doing with me. His remark that my friends and enemies had seen the last of me was sinister enough. But why should he make away with me? Why should he slay an utter stranger?

I thought of those filing cases again. Why did this man keep life histories and photographs of people with whom he was not acquainted? Was he only a part of some great system? Had I accidentally run afoul of something, the existence of which the authorities did not dream?

Horror and fear numb a man after a time. That is why, I suppose, a condemned man will walk to the electric chair without giving signs of great emotion. As morning came, my mind seemed to be almost a blank. I had ceased to think of the unknown horror that confronted me, except in a sort of detached way as if it concerned a person other than myself.

I paced the floor again, and now and then stood at one of the windows and looked down at the house on the adjoining lot or out at the Avenue where the traffic already was getting heavy. There, within a few feet of me, was liberty, yet I was powerless to reach it.

Soon the door was opened, and Blake appeared. He conducted me to a bathroom and remained in my presence until I had bathed and refreshed myself. He was the butler again — unsmiling, speechless unless addressed.

"Going to tell me what all this means?" I asked him.

"I am not allowed to tell you anything about it, sir," he said.

"I suppose you are going to murder me? Is that it? And I'm not even going to know why I was being murdered?"

"I have nothing to say, sir," Blake declared. "We'll return to the other room now, sir."

He locked me in, and half an hour later he returned with a tray of breakfast. It was the best breakfast I ever had eaten. Oh, yes, I ate! I wanted to maintain my strength, for one thing. A chance for escape might present itself at any moment, I thought.

Blake even offered me cigars and cigarettes and the morning paper, and struck a match and held it to the end of the cigar I had selected.

"They always feed a condemned man before they kill him," I snarled at him.

"So I have understood, sir."

"You're not human, are you?"

"Why, I fancy so, sir," said Blake.

"If this is some sort of a joke, it is a mighty poor one," I told him. "And if it proves to be anything serious, you'll get yours in the end!"

Blake arranged the dishes on the tray, but made no reply.

"Curse you!" I shrieked. "Are you a man or a machine? Have you no decent emotions. I feel like attacking you, forcing you to fight —"

"In that case, sir, I merely shall tie you to the bed," Blake said. "Mr. Gregg was very much annoyed at the scene last night. It disturbed his rest."

"Too bad it disturbed his rest!" I snarled.

Blake backed toward the door. He paid me the compliment of watching me closely as, he did so. And a moment later he was gone and I was alone and still a prisoner.

Then another mood came upon me. I grew frantic again. I opened a window and grasped the steel bars, tried to shake them, to wrench them away, knowing all the time that they would not give the fraction of an inch. I ran to the door and pounded and kicked it as I had done the afternoon before. I beat upon the walls.

And then, exhausted, I fell upon the bed, panting, gasping.

I could not call for help from the windows. The house on that side seemed to have been closed for the season, or else had no tenants, for the windows were boarded. The Avenue was some distance away, and a shriek would not have been heard above the din of the traffic. And the network of steel bars was so close that I could not thrust an arm through and signal. Had I done so, nobody would have paid me the slightest attention. Anybody who saw me probably would think me some servant working at the window. The people of the city had business of their own that claimed their time and attention. They were not looking for mysteries and atrocities, especially in such a section of the town.

After a time I grew quiet, though not entirely resigned. I got up and walked to the chair beside the table, sat down, even made an attempt at reading the morning paper. I smoked another cigar — and waited.

The horror of the unknown was upon me, and the added terror of suspense. I caught myself listening for sounds in the hall. I was at the point now where I did not even attempt to solve the mystery. I was just waiting!

An hour before noon, Blake opened the door again and stood in it, looking at me. I snarled at him.

"Think I'm fat enough to kill?" I asked.

"You gentlemen *will* have your little joke, sir," Blake said, but without a smile.

"Well, what do you want?" I demanded. "Have you come to tell me what all this confounded business means? Talk — talk, if you're a man! Speak up, curse you!"

"I regret it exceedingly if I have displeased you, sir," Blake said — just like that.

Was the man making a mock of me, I wondered? Was he a heartless brute? There are murderers and murderers, you know — some will weep over the bodies of their victims.

Blake disregarded me, and glanced back along the hall. And suddenly he faced me again.

"You are to come with me now, sir," he said.

"Where are you going?" I demanded.

"Merely to another room in the house, sir. Mr. Gregg wishes to see you there."

Then I remembered what Anita Frawley had said — something about a little room that always was kept locked, and from which she had heard screams and moans and other sounds of agony. She had seen men go in there — and never had seem them again —

I sprang to my feet, enraged with terror again.

"No, you don't!" I shrieked. "No, you don't, you brute! I don't go to any other room! Don't put your hands on me — don't —"

There was a vase on the table, and I grasped it and hurled it at Blake. He dodged his head to one side, and the vase was shattered into half a hundred pieces as it struck against the wall.

Anger flashed in Blake's face for an instant, and then he took a step toward me. I backed away from him, threw up my arms as if to ward off a blow, retreated to the wall and stood there, helpless and panting, my heart pounding at my ribs. I was on the verge of hysterics, and knew it.

"Come!" Blake commanded. He did not say "sir" this time.

He stood before me, waiting. And I swear to you that I actually started toward him, as a child might go to its parent to be punished. I tried to fight against the feeling, but could not.

Then thought of my predicament came to me again. I sprang forward with a screech of rage and tried to grasp Blake's throat. He fought for an instant to get me by the arms, and soon was holding me helpless, except that I was kicking at him like an angry boy.

He did not speak again. He forced me to the door and into the hall, and hurried me along it. We made a turning and came to another door. Blake held me with one hand, and opened the door with the other.

I shrieked again as I caught my first glance of the interior of that room. As Anita Frawley had said, it was not a large room. But I never had seen such an apartment before.

There was a chair that resembled a dentist's. There was a table that looked like an operating table. There were white cabinets that held instruments by the score. In one corner was a skeleton. There were perhaps half a hundred skulls scattered around.

And Gregg was there. The man looked more gigantic than he had before, looked terrible. His face was flushed, and his eyes were glowing. He held a long knife in his hand, and was testing the edge of it with his thumb.

I shrieked again as Gregg looked at me and I caught the expression in his face.

Laughter rumbled in his throat as Blake thrust me inside the room, followed me, and closed and locked the door.

"Mr. James Dacy," Gregg said, "your hour is at hand. Take a look at yourself in that mirror. There is James Dacy, alias Slick Jimmy — see him? He is about to disappear — forever!"

I turned madman then, I think. I know only that I screeched and threw myself upon Blake, who was nearest the door. I know that I fought with greater strength than I had before, and made some progress. I believe that I marked Blake's face, at least.

Then Gregg was upon me, too. He had a hypodermic needle in one hand. I felt a sudden, sharp pain as he plunged the needle into my wrist.

Gregg laughed and turned back toward one of the cabinets on the other side of the room. Blake led me weakly toward a couch nearby. I was sobbing a little, I think. I remember that the skulls scattered around that terrible room seemed to be grinning at me, that the skeleton seemed to be dancing.

And then the drug had its way — and unconsciousness came!

CHAPTER VII

A TRICK THAT WORKED

THE dream began — a dream of atrocities and pain. I seemed to be struggling through pitch blackness toward a single gleam of light. Then voices reached my ears, as if coming from a far distance.

It was in this manner that I returned to consciousness. And suddenly I realized that I was experiencing excruciating pain. I seemed to be unable to open my eyes. I felt very weak.

I did manage to open my eyes, finally. I could make out that I was stretched on the operating table, and I could hear Gregg and Blake talking in low tones, but they were back of me, and I could not see them.

And then I discovered that I was helpless from the waistline up. It was as if I was paralyzed, I could not move my arms, for they were strapped to the sides of the table. And my face —

Never shall I forget what I felt when realized that my entire head was in a cast of some sort. I could open my eyes a slit, and that was all. I could not move my jaws. My mouth already was open a bit, and seemed to have been propped in that position, and there was some sort of tube running into it.

My jaws and cheeks pained so much that I almost fainted. It was as if a pressure of thousands of pounds to the square inch had been applied to my countenance.

My terror returned to me. What had Gregg done to me? What did he intend doing further? Was I to be slain an inch at a time? Was this some terrible torture?

I groaned. The voices ceased, and an instant later I could see Gregg and Blake standing beside the table.

"Conscious already," Gregg said. "His nervous condition, I suppose."

"Shall I administer the hypodermic, sir?" Blake asked.

"Not unless we see that he cannot endure the pain," Gregg replied. "Everything seems to be getting along all right."

I tried to speak, but I could not, of course. Sounds came from between my lips, but they were not words.

Gregg bent over the table and grinned at me.

"I suppose it does hurt a trifle, Mr. Dacy," he said, "but it is necessary, I assure you. That's what you get for coming to the door of my house and asking for a man who does not exist. Poor James Dacy — his friends never will see him again!"

He laughed like a fiend and turned toward one of his infernal cabinets. Can you imagine my feelings at that moment? I was certain, now, that a madman had me in his power. There seemed to be no other explanation. Since I never had seen Gregg before entering the house, this was not being done for revenge, and certainly not for gain as far as I knew.

I think that I lost consciousness soon after that. Now and then I heard their voices, and I realized that I groaned a great deal. There were stretches of time when I knew nothing.

Blake came to me later, and fed me through the tube in my mouth.

"Only liquid food, Mr. Dacy, at present," he said. "It is sustaining, however."

I wanted to hurl a thousand questions at him, but could not, of course. I swallowed the condensed soup, and slept again. Later, Gregg administered the hypodermic.

And then started a season of nightmares. I seemed to lose track of time. I could not tell when it was day and when it was night, for electric lights burned in this room continually. Frequently, I was put to sleep with drugs. At stated intervals, I was fed. There were times when my body was racked with pain, and there were times when it seemed that I had no feeling whatsoever.

My mind seemed to be blank. I tried to reason it out now and then, but always gave it up quickly. Here was something that I could not understand. I wondered what they intended doing with me. Was I to be kept like this until merciful death released me? Were there further tortures in store for me?

Now and then I thought of Anita Frawley, too. I remembered the look of horror in her face. I never had paid much attention to women, but it seemed that Anita Frawley had attracted me more than any other ever had. I wondered whether she had been punished by Gregg because she had attempted to aid me to escape.

Day followed day, I could tell that much. Gradually the pain left my body. I seemed to be growing stronger. And then there came a day when Gregg and Blake stopped beside the table and began unbinding my arms.

"We have decided to have you up," Gregg said, grinning like a fiend. "Take it easy, now. The first part of it is over."

The first part of it! Were they going to torture me again? Were they fiends in human guise?

I could not move my arms when finally they unbound. Gregg and Blake massaged them for an hour or more, and gradually some feeling came into them. And then Gregg began working at my face.

I do not know exactly what he did, but I do know that the terrible pressure was removed. I know that he massaged the corners of my mouth, and my lips, until I could open and close my mouth to its full extent. He massaged my entire face then. It seemed to come alive again.

Blake stood at the end of the table and watched him. I saw Gregg look at him, and Blake nodded.

"Very good, indeed, Mr. Gregg, sir," he said. "I should say that it is excellent."

Then they helped me up and led me to the couch.

"Take it easy," Gregg said again. "Get your strength back a bit at a time. I'm going to send Blake for some real food for you, and I hope that you'll relish it. You went through the ordeal very well. It always has been a question with me just how much pain and misery a human being can stand. Sometimes, there seems to be no limit. I believe you are a man who can endure a lot."

Was this maniac trying to see how much I could endure and keep alive? I raised my head and looked at him.

"You fiend!" I gasped.

"Don't try to talk too much just yet," he told me.

Blake got the food, and I ate, slowly, painfully — but I ate. The solid food was good. And then I stretched myself on the couch and slept, for I could not help it.

When I awoke, Blake was sitting in a chair not far away, watching me.

"You are to have more food whenever you wish it, sir," he said.

"I'll take some now, then."

"Yes, sir. A sort of breakfast, sir?"

I told him that would do nicely, and he hurried from the room. I heard him bolt the door on the outside. As soon as he was gone, I got to my feet. I wanted to investigate those cabinets. I wanted to try to find out what they had done to me, what they intended doing. Was Gregg some crazed scientist, experimenting with me? Was he killing me by inches in an effort to make some discovery?

The steel cabinets were locked. All the instruments seemed to have been put away. There was nothing but the furniture, the operating table, the skeleton, and the skulls. There was a ventilating shaft in the room, but not even a window.

I staggered back to the couch just as Blake entered with a tray. Once more I ate. I felt new strength.

"Well, what's the program?" I asked Blake.

"Sir?"

"What are you fiends going to do with me?"

"I am not allowed to talk about such things, sir."

"I supposed that brute punished Miss Frawley because she tried to help me?"

"I believe not, sir, except by confining her to her room for a couple of days," said Blake. "By the way, sir, I am to take you from this room and to your former quarters."

He went across the room and opened the door, and then he returned and helped me to my feet. I pretended to be very weak. I leaned against him, staggered as I walked, moaned now and then as if in pain, and it seemed to cause Blake some concern.

He took me to the other room, and I sat down beside the table.

"How do you feel, sir?" he asked.

"I'm — very sick!" I complained, in a weak voice.

"Just how, sir?"

"I — You've killed me, you fiends!" I gasped. "My heart — I can't stand it!"

Alarm came into his face. He bent over and looked at me, and then rushed for the door and left the room. He slammed the door behind him, but he did not lock or bolt it. I guessed that he had gone for Gregg, that he feared something was wrong.

I was on my feet and at the door almost instantly. I opened it, stepped out, closed it again. I knew in which direction Blake had gone, and I went in another.

Up a flight I went, toward the roof. I reached the floor above, and darted into a room. It was dusty, unused, not even furnished. I heard Gregg and Blake shrieking at each other on the floor below.

I could not hope to escape by remaining on that upper floor, I knew. I'd have to reach the first floor and smash a front window and get out that way. By glancing through a dirt-encrusted window, I made out that it was very late in the afternoon.

If I could only reach the first floor without running into Gregg or Blake, all might be well. I went back to the head of the stairs. My two foes were investigating the second floor of the house by now. I could hear Gregg yelling for Blake to go to the first floor and stand guard there.

I ran down to the lower floor, but did not know where to hide. In time, I came to a rear stairs, and went down it as silently as possible. At the bottom of the stairs, I opened a door.

I found myself in the kitchen, and a middle-aged woman was sitting at a table there, evidently preparing vegetables for dinner. I was beside her before she knew it.

"Not a word!" I commanded, as she looked up at me in fright. "How do you get out of here?"

"Heh?" she shrieked.

I remembered that Anita Frawley had said that the cook was almost deaf. I motioned for her to remain silent. I grasped a long carving knife from the table and hurried to the door.

You must understand that I was desperate now. I was ready to do murder, if it proved to be necessary. I could hear Blake calling something to Gregg, could hear Gregg reply that perhaps I was on the upper floor, and that he would investigate while Blake remained on the stairs and stood guard.

That was all that I wanted to know — the front of the house would be unguarded for a time. I opened the door and looked into the hall, and saw that the way was clear. Once more I motioned the frightened cook to remain silent. I darted into the hall, closing the door of the kitchen behind. Swiftly, noiselessly, I ran toward the front of the house. I ran into the room just to the rear of the reception room.

And I came face to face with Anita Frawley.

CHAPTER VIII

ANITA

"YOU —" she gasped.

"They're after me —"

"Who — are you?"

I stared at her in amazement.

"Why, I'm Dacy! I'm the man you tired to save —"

"Oh! Oh, they've done it — they've done it!"

"Done what?" I gasped. "See here, I've got to get away! Those fiends will kill me! The window!"

"Wait!" She gripped me by the arm. "Have you lost your senses? Look! You have nothing but trousers and underwear — no shoes, no coat or shirt or hat —"

She spoke the truth, but I had not realized that I was not dressed. Breaking the window would be bad enough. Going out upon the Avenue at that hour of the evening, less than half clothed, would cause a small riot. I'd be in the hands of a policeman in a moment — and then there might be explanations that I could not give.

"I can hide you," she whispered. "I know a closet where they will not find you. Smash the window, then come with me. They'll think that you have escaped. I'll get your clothes to you later — I know where they are."

"Maybe I'd better not —"

"Don't you trust me?" she asked.

I nodded.

"Then smash the window — and be ready to run after me."

We went into the reception room. I glanced through the doorway and saw Blake halfway up the wide stairs. I darted back into the room, picked up a heavy chair, crashed it through the big front window, and then turned and ran noiselessly after her as I heard Blake start to charge down the stairs.

We were successful in dodging him. She ran into the hallway, and I followed at her heels. She took me into the basement. There was a large closet, well ventilated, and she thrust me inside.

"I'll lock the door," she said. "I'll come as soon as I can, but it may be several hours."

And then she was gone, and I was alone in the darkness.

I began thinking that I had been a fool. Better by far to have gone through that window when I had a chance, I told myself. Arrest would have been better than what I probably faced. But I had not wanted to talk to the police. What could I have said? Gregg was a wealthy man, and I felt sure that he had some sort of a story ready. I probably would have been arrested for trying to rob his house.

It was stifling in the closet despite the ventilation. The perspiration poured from my face and neck and my arms. It seemed to me that hours had passed. I did not have my watch, of course, and had no way of telling the time.

I thought of going up the stairs and trying to escape, and then remembered that Anita Frawley had locked the door. I did not dare make a noise by breaking it down.

And then I heard a key being turned in the lock, heard her whisper.

"Are you all right?"

"Yes," I replied.

"I have your clothes. They think that you sprang through the window and escaped. And I have sent for the police —"

"Then I've got to get out of here," I said. "I don't want anything to do with the police."

"Follow me. I've got your clothes in my own room. You can dress there. They never come into my room, and I could hide you if they did. But they think you have escaped."

I left the closet, and took her by the hand. She guided me through the darkness. We went up the steps to the first floor, and through the long hall to a room in the rear. We went inside, and she locked the door and snapped on a light.

"Your clothes are behind the screen," she said. "Hurry, please."

I whispered to her as I dressed.

"How did you send for the police?" I asked.

"I wrote a note and wrapped it around two half dollars. And then I watched, and threw it through the broken window as a man passed. He picked it up and read the note. In it, I asked whoever found it to call the police, that a man was being kept prisoner here — and a girl also. He looked at the house after he had read it, and then almost ran down the street."

"How long ago?"

"About fifteen minutes," she said. "They'll be here soon."

I was dressing as swiftly as I could.

"I've got to get away before they come," I gasped.

"I know — you are a burglar," she said. "Why aren't you honest?"

"There is no chance, now. I've served a term in prison," I told her. "I am a marked man. I want to go straight, but they won't let me. Jim Dacy is a burglar and can be nothing else, in their estimation."

"But you can now."

"Can what?"

"Fool them and be straight," she said.

"I don't see how."

"Then you don't know? You don't know what they did to you?"

"I don't know anything, except that I suffered so much my mind ceased to work."

"You've been in this house almost two weeks, you know," she said. "I accused my uncle of being a murderer, and he told me the truth. He used to be a college professor, you know — he thinks that he is a great scientist. His hobby is faces."

"Faces?" I asked.

"He has thousands of photographs and skulls and things. He claims that there are only so many types, or groups, of faces in the world. He tried to explain it to me, but I could not understand — something about basic structures, and all that. He began to experiment years ago with animals — and then, when he got his money, he went insane, I think, and wanted to experiment with men."

"Experiment?"

"He said he could change their faces," she went on. "He couldn't change the color of eyes and hair, of course, but by some scientific method he could change the structure of the face. He can remove wrinkles and put in new ones, makes noses shorter or longer, wider or more narrow. He can change the shape of a chin. That is why I saw men disappear and strange men I never had seen before leave the house. Blake was his first experiment —"

I gasped and came from behind the screen. I ran to a mirror.

I failed to see James Dacy staring but at me. The face reflected there was the face of a man I never had seen before. There were new lines in my forehead and at the corners of my mouth and around my eyes. My nose seemed shorter and wider. My chin was more of the bulldog variety than it had been before. I began to understand that terrible facial pressure.

"Come!" she said. "The police may be here any moment."

"But —"

"I am going with you," she said. "I cannot remain here. And my uncle said that, if the authorities bothered him, he'd blow up the house and kill himself. You are to escort me to some hotel, and I'll remain there for a time. I have plenty of money of my own, and more in the bank —"

I did not wait to hear more. Despite my new face, I wanted to get out of that terrible house before the police arrived. I snapped out the light, and she opened the door.

We went through the house silently, and so came to the reception room, where Blake had spread a blanket over the broken window. I took the blanket down, and looked out.

"A drop of only five feet to the ground," I told her. "Be careful and do not cut yourself on the broken glass."

I picked her up and lowered her through the window. She had put on a hat in her room, and carried a cloak. I tossed the cloak through after her, and then dropped to the ground myself.

But we could not reach the Avenue. The police already were upon us. I grasped her by the hand and darted toward the house adjoining, the one that was closed. We crouched in the darkness against a wall, waiting.

I saw policemen going to the rear of the house, to the other side, saw two officers go to the front door.

"Come!" I whispered.

We managed to get around the corner of the house and finally came to the side street. And then we walked back to the Avenue, and turned down it.

We saw lights flash in the house, heard the police pounding at the door. And then there came a terrific explosion that seemed to tear the building to bits. We were less than half a block away, on the opposite side of the street.

Screeches and screams came to us. Automobiles stopped. A crowd appeared as if by magic.

Far down the Avenue came the fire apparatus, for fire had started immediately. Anita Frawley stood beside me on the nearest corner and watched, her eyes dry.

"He has done it," she whispered to me. "He has destroyed the house and himself. He was mad!"

"I'm sorry — for you."

"Because he was my uncle? You need not be. I had no love for him, and this last year he has been cruel to me. It is like a horrible nightmare that has ended."

"But you'll be alone in the world —"

"I have money, and a woman need not feel alone in the world these days. There is work to be done," she said. "I'll go away and rest for a time, and then find something to occupy my mind. And you —"

"What about me?" I asked.

"James Dacy has disappeared, has he not? The face you have is not the one to be found in the rogues' gallery, is it? You are free — don't you see? You can be honest now. The police will not hound you.

Don't you realize it all?"

I saw. I understood what it all meant. I could take another name, and my best friends would not know me. That maniac of a Gregg had aided me more than he knew.

The fire was raging now. The police had stretched their lines and were fighting back the crowd. The firemen were working to save the residences on either side of the doomed one. There were half a dozen more explosions of a minor nature.

Anita Frawley and I were caught in a jam and urged to the curb. An officer thrust us back, shouted at me to stand behind the line. I knew him well and he had known me well before. But now he looked at me without recognition. Then I realized, fully.

"Come," she whispered.

We got out of the crowd and went down the Avenue. I engaged a taxicab at the corner, because she wished it. I told her that I had no money, but she slipped a bill into my hand.

We drove to a hotel, and I installed her there, telling the clerk that she was my sister, and had come to the city to visit a sick friend and had missed her return train. There was no trouble about it — a single glance at Anita Frawley was enough to tell a man that she was a woman of the right sort.

I walked with her to the elevator.

"Please come to see me about noon," she said, in a low tone.

"Certainly," I whispered. "If there is anything I can do —"

"I may need your help, or advice, you know. And remember — you are to —"

"To begin again," I whispered. "You can trust me to do that."

I left her then. She had insisted that I keep the change from the bill. I went to another hotel and engaged a room for the night. I stood before the mirror there and looked at my new face, then stretched my arms above my head in a gesture that meant I had thrown off shackles.

And that is why the police wonder what became of James Dacy, alias Slick Jimmy. They think he has left the country, perhaps. They never connected him with the destruction of the house on the Avenue, and they never quite solved the mystery of that house and its occupants. The fortune of Gregg remains unclaimed.

For Anita will have none of it. And I think that it is better that way. Anita? My wife now, of course. For I turned straight and made good. I was educated, talented to a degree. All this happened four years ago, as you perhaps will remember. In those four years I have made a man of myself. I am prosperous and happy, and have made Anita happy.

And I lay it all to the name I invented on the spur of the moment — John Xenephon Traymore.

RUN TO GROUND

CHAPTER I

MR. WESTLEY ARRIVES

WELL and unfavorably known to all other members of the metropolitan department as the "dude cop," Police Officer G. William Waltern squinted over the top of his desk and carefully regarded the unusual man who waited on the end of the bench outside the railing. Officer Waltern was a sort of glorified office boy who received visitors for the chief of detectives. No man on the force had uniforms that fitted as perfectly as those of Officer Waltern. The members of the detective branch who were compelled to dress like brokers, and who loafed around the big hotels on the watch for con men and swindlers in general, were not more fastidious than Officer Waltern.

Officer Waltern might have been passed without unfavorable notice had he confined his apparent superiority to his personal adornment and his well-manicured fingernails. But he had absorbed the idea that clothes make the man in police circles the same as in other lines of human endeavor.

For some years now, by lifting a corner of his lip here and dropping a sarcastic word there, he had sought to convey the impression that the general run of detectives and policemen could not be compared to himself, and that he was doing a great favor to the department and the city government by consenting to receive his monthly pay voucher.

There were some unkind members of the force who intimated that the chief of detectives had Officer Waltern assigned to do office work for the simple reason that he was not man enough to do anything else, and not because he had superior brains. But Waltern did fill his particular niche acceptably for the greater part, and so he was endured.

He made a mistake now and then, but, about nine-tenths of the time, Officer G. William Waltern, as he insisted on being known, could separate the sheep from the goats with consummate skill.

Waltern seemed to know at a first glance whether a caller possessed information of importance enough to warrant him getting the ear of the chief of detectives. He could sense when a man or woman wanted something that could be attended to just as well by some subordinate.

But, being susceptible to the charms of women, he had been known to let an ordinary female book agent into the sacred inner office on a day when the chief was not feeling particularly fit. He had never done it a second time. What the chief said was remarked in the presence of about a score of detectives reporting for their daily grind, and the ears of Officer G. William Waltern burned for at least a week thereafter.

It was about ten o'clock in the morning. Officer Waltern rubbed his fingernails carefully, straightened the front of his uniform blouse, glanced down to make sure that there was no speck of dust on his highly polished boots, hummed lightly a little air that he had picked up at a vaudeville show the evening before, and strutted across the room to the railing to accept a heap of mail the headquarters messenger had brought.

He leaned lightly against the railing like a young millionaire plunger at a race course and skipped through the letters, separating the chief's private mail from that of the department in general, and slipping dexterously into his left hand a mass of circulars advertising "wanted" men.

The man who sat nervously on the end of the bench outside cleared his throat in a manner that should have been a warning, but Officer Waltern failed to notice it. There was a short interval of silence, and then the man on the bench got up, grasped Officer G. William Waltern roughly by the shoulder, and whirled him around.

"Say, you!" the man ejaculated. "I've stood for about all of your nonsense that I'm able to stand without gettin' violent! What kind of an officer of the law are you, anyway? Out in my part of the country you wouldn't last as long as a small icicle in a ragin' hot furnace!"

"Sir!" the outraged Officer Waltern thundered, shaking himself free and glaring at the other. "You sit down over there on that bench and be quiet, or I'll call a man and have you ejected!"

"You'll what? You'll have me ejected, will yeh?" the other retorted. "Why, you fresh, foolish, red-faced kid! You ain't got a cop on the force that can eject me without gettin' his clothes all mussed up in the process! You finger-polishin', hair-slickin' dude, you!"

"Sir!"

"Shut up, you he-female!" the other interrupted. "I told you to inform the chief of detectives that Tom Westley of Arizona was out here and wanted to talk to him pronto! And you've been fussin' around like an old woman dressin' for a party!"

"The chief happens to be busy, and I'll take in your name to him at the proper time," Waltern said.

"You're not goin' to take in my name at all!" Tom Westley told him. "If a man wants a thing done right, then he'd better do it himself. You get out of my way!"

The stranger from Arizona thereupon opened the gate in the railing, grasped Officer G. William Waltern by the shoulder and hurled him almost across the room, and strode straight toward the door marked "Private."

"You can't go in there!" Waltern cried.

A couple of police clerks left their desks quickly and hurried forward to be of service.

"I can't go in there?" Tom Westley said with a dangerous glint in his eyes. "Who in time's goin' to stop me? You — dude? You other fellers? You'd better begin to do your stoppin', for I'm startin' here and now to go in there!"

He whirled around and continued deliberately toward the door of the chief's private office. Officer G. William Waltern motioned to the other two, and the three of them hurled themselves forward.

They reached Tom Westley without difficulty, and grasped at him. Then they learned what it means to lay violent hands on a human whirlwind. Tom Westley had faced about and was at them almost before they realized it. Officer Waltern was the first to receive his undivided attention.

He struck Officer Waltern squarely in the chest with a massive fist, and Waltern grunted and sat down suddenly on the floor about ten feet away, after having traveled for that distance through the air. Stepping quickly and neatly to one side, Tom Westley next grasped one of the unfortunate police clerks and hurled him toward a wall.

The second clerk made the fatal mistake of drawing his revolver. But Tom Westley merely kicked the weapon out of the clerk's hand, badly damaging a wrist as he did so, then floored his man with what is known technically in ring and sporting circles as a right hook to the jaw.

By this time three other members of the clerical force had dashed in from an adjoining office, and a couple of detectives, coming into headquarters for a conference with their chief, ran in from the corridor to ascertain the meaning of the riot.

Recognizing additional foes, the man from Arizona gave a whoop and charged forward. The three members of the clerical force were caught at a disadvantage in the doorway. Tom Westley smashed into the first, recoiled against the other two, and for the moment they were disconcerted and out of the fight.

Two detectives had stopped against the railing long enough to gasp at the sight and try to understand the meaning of the situation. Now they decided that it was time for them to be taking a hand in the game.

"Back up, there!" one of them ordered, covering Tom Westley with his weapon. "Come into headquarters and try to start a roughhouse, will you? Trying to clean out the department? What's the main idea?"

"I came in here to see the chief of detectives, and I'm goin' to see him!" Tom Westley declared. "And no fingernail-polishin' dude is goin' to strut around the office before me like a peacock and refuse to take in my name!"

The detective had noticed something. "What's that you've got on your breast?" he asked.

"That's a star, you fool!" Tom Westley replied hotly. "Are you blind as well as dumb? Down in Arizona I'm a sheriff. I came in here on business, and my time is mighty valuable."

"But you —"

"I didn't aim to have to scrap with the whole police force of this town," Tom Westley continued, "but I can if it's necessary! You betcha! And if you want to start anything, you hombres, just start it — fists, knives, or guns! And you — you simp! You're holdin' that revolver like an infant! I could draw from under my coat and shoot it out of your hand before you could more'n blink an eye! I reckon that you city cops don't savvy firearms much. Why, dang your hides —"

"What's all this?" demanded a stentorian voice right behind the man from Arizona.

Tom Westley whirled around to find himself confronted by a big, red-faced man standing in the open doorway of the private office. He sensed that here was the chief of detectives, the man he had been attempting to see.

"You the chief?" he asked. "I'm Tom Westley, sheriff, from out Arizona way. I came in here to see you on business, and this office boy of yours got fresh! I hate to mess up your nice, clean office, chief, and I'm ready and willin' to pay for any furniture you find broken. And if that plainclothes man don't put away that gun he's holdin' on me, I'm liable to take it away from him and ram it down his throat! I'm sorry for you, chief, if this is the kind of gang they hand you to work with. Me, I've got it all over you — I can pick out my own deputies!"

The chief of detectives seemed undecided whether to grin or signal for reinforcements. He surveyed Officer G. William Waltern and the others — and then decided to grin. The detective saw the grin and put his gun away.

"You must be a regular whirlwind when you really get warmed up and started," the chief told Tom Westley. "Your mode of entrance and calling yourself to my attention isn't quite regular, but I'm inclined to overlook it this time. Come into my office, and we'll talk."

Tom Westley reached up, straightened his necktie, and picked up his hat from the floor.

"Well, by gosh, I'm mighty glad to find somebody around here that's got some sense!" he announced, "I'll come right in, chief — thanks! And if any of you other hombres are hankerin' after revenge, you just wait around until I come out! Fists, knives, or guns — dang yeh!"

CHAPTER II
ON THE TRAIL

SHERIFF Tom Westley came to an abrupt stop just inside the door of the chief's private office and stood with his hat in his hand and gazed at the furnishings. The expression in his face indicated amazement.

"This is what I call class, chief!" he declared. "You ought to see my office out in Arizona — barrel stove, two busted chairs, and a battered desk is about all the furniture I got. This office of yours is fancier than the ladies' rest room!"

Again the chief of detectives grinned, and his eyes twinkled. "Sit down, and help yourself to a cigar," he said, shoving the box toward his visitor.

The chief had been studying Tom Westley with those rapid glances that had gained him a reputation. He saw a man of about forty, tall, broad of shoulder, lean of hip, face bronzed by the sun and weather-beaten, cold eyes that could look a man down. The chief knew men, and he appraised Sheriff Tom Westley to be of great value along certain lines.

Sitting down, the Arizona official cocked his feet on one corner of the chief's mahogany desk, lighted his cigar, and puffed in evident enjoyment. His thumbs were hooked into his belt. From beneath the edge of his coat peeped the corner of a holster, and the chief did not fail to see it.

"You wanted to talk to me about some business?" the chief asked in keen anticipation.

"You're right, chief! I want to talk to you about a couple of things. First, I came to the city to take back to Arizona a skunk of a bank cashier who skipped out one night with all the bank's cash and came here to try to clean out the market and be a financial wizard."

"They often do that," the chief said.

"This one was nabbed pronto, but he's hired a gang of lawyers to fight extradition, and so I've got to wait around two or three weeks until they get through with their arguin'. If extradition is refused, I'll just naturally have to kidnap the cuss and take him back with me!"

"That would be rather a high-handed proceeding and might get you into trouble," the chief remarked. "I do not see just how I can help you."

"Oh, I don't want any help in this bank-cashier case, chief!" the man from Arizona said. "I don't need any help at all. I know the skunk, and he knows me! So there won't be any room for argument in case of a showdown. There's somethin' else."

"And what is that?" the chief of detectives asked, lighting a cigar and making himself comfortable in his chair. Heaven knew that he had interviews with tiresome persons often enough, and when a refreshing individual happened to come along, he intended enjoying himself!

"I had a kid brother, John, twenty-eight years old," Westley said. "A few months ago he sold a minin' claim for quite a bit of change and decided that he'd travel across the continent and see the sights of the big town. Five weeks ago, chief, they sent the boy back to me — in a box! And there was a girl home waitin' for him, too."

"John Westley?"

"Yes, sir."

"I remember the case," the chief of detectives said. "I — I am sorry!"

"Thanks, chief! But I didn't come here to shed tears about it, you see," the man from Arizona said. "I've sorrowed about John all I'm goin' to! John was a good boy — full of life and inclined to be a little wild, maybe, but a good boy! And he didn't die a natural death, either. He was murdered!"

"Yes," the chief agreed. "I remember the case very well indeed. The young man was found dead in an alley in a disreputable section of the city. He had been shot in the head. We identified him by some papers he had in his pocket — and I suppose that you were notified."

"Yes! I ordered the body shipped back home, chief. You folks here in the city attended to all those things in mighty handsome shape, and I'm thankin' you right here and now. But there's one important matter, chief, that's been neglected."

"What is that?" the chief asked, sitting forward suddenly on his chair.

"Where is the skunk who killed my brother?" the man from Arizona demanded, "He ain't in jail, is he, waitin' for his trial?"

There was direct accusation in Tom Westley's glance as he took the cigar from between his lips, sat forward in his chair, and pounded on the end of the desk suddenly with his fist. It rather startled the chief of detectives, having the thing put to him straight that way, and he cleared his throat and glanced nervously around the room.

"Mr. Westley," he said, "you are an officer of the law yourself."

"Yes, sir — my third term as sheriff."

"I am glad of that, because possibly you can understand me better. Have you always caught every breaker of the laws in your county?"

"No, sir! But when there's a cold-blooded murderer runnin' around loose, we generally make a sort of special effort," Tom Westley declared, his eyes mere pinpoints.

"You have it rather easy," the chief said. "Your population is small, for instance, and scarcely a stranger can come into town without being noticed. It's easy for you to learn a stranger's business, too. And then, a criminal has few places to hide from a man like you, a man who knows the country thoroughly. You have your canyons, your coulees, your stretches of wild land, but you and your deputies know how to hunt through them."

"That's correct!" Westley said.

"But apprehending a murderer in the city is apt to be more difficult," said the chief.

"You tried?"

"Of course, we tried!"

"And when you couldn't nab your man in a day or two, you just naturally passed up the case and went ahead with somethin' a lot more important!" Sheriff Westley accused. "You didn't aim to get all fussed up about a boy from Arizona who didn't seem to have any high and mighty friends! That it?"

"We always try to do our duty, Mr. Westley," the chief replied. "We did what we could — do in every case. But of course we have hundreds and hundreds of cases —"

"And thousands of officers to take care of them!" Westley interrupted. "Well, chief, I'm here for the purpose of givin' you a little help."

"What do you mean? You have some sort of clue as to the murderer?"

"No clue! I don't know anything about the affair at all, but I aim to know a lot before I get done. I've got to wait around for a few weeks while them lawyers argue and earn their fees, and I don't like to loaf. So I'll just get busy! I'm here, chief, to find the man who killed my brother!"

"And how do you, a stranger, expect to find him when my men, who know the city, could not?" the chief asked.

"I've got a personal interest your men don't have!"

"But the trail is cold."

"It won't be the first time that I've followed a cold trail, chief!"

"Yes, out in your country, where you know every rock and tree. But you'll find that it is vastly different here in the city — vastly different!"

"I can't see it that way, chief," Tom Westley declared. "We've got canyons, sure, and you've got your manmade canyons here — alleys and dives and the like hidin' places. If my man is still hangin' around, maybe I'll be able to get him."

"I wish that I could help you, Mr. Westley," the chief said. "But we know very little — were able to find out very little. The place where your brother's body was found is in a neighborhood frequented by numerous gangsters. Your brother lived down there in a little hotel called Hogan's Place — I suppose because he did not know any better and because it was cheap. They took him for an easy mark — possibly found out that he had some money and — "

"He did have," Westley said.

"The appearance of the body, especially the face and hands, indicated that there had been a fight before he was shot. I suppose somebody tried to rob him, and he wasn't easily robbed. And then somebody got in that one shot, which was enough. He might have been killed two or three blocks from where his body was found — possibly was."

"Sure!" Westley said.

"When we conducted our investigation we could learn little about your brother, except that he was visiting the city and happened to fall in with a bad crowd. We were unable to learn of any particular enemy he had, or of any trouble he'd been mixed up in. He'd been in town only a couple of months, I believe."

"And so you quit!" the man from Arizona declared, his eyes flashing again. "Oh, I'm not blamin' you! I know you've got a lot of work to do. But I haven't quit!"

"I am afraid that you will be unable to do anything," the chief declared. "It is difficult to gather evidence in a cold case when a gangster has done something of this sort. The gangsters will cut one another's throats, but they won't tip off one another to the police. And if you went down to that locality and got to snooping around, you might be handled the same as your brother."

"Yeh? I'll be right there to be handled!" Tom Westley declared. "And when it comes to evidence, the man who did the shootin' has got one thing with him that's safe and sure evidence — he's got a sense of guilt! I don't aim to know how you'd work such a thing with your regular men, but I know what I'd do. I'd announce who I was, maybe, and that I was there to get the man who'd killed my brother. If the guilty man was around and heard, he'd make a move sooner or later, especially if I kept quiet and waited for it. And then — I'd nail him!"

"But I am afraid that —"

"Oh, don't get the idea that I'm askin' your police department to dry-nurse me!" said the man from Arizona. "Nothin' like that at all! I'm not askin' for a bit of help from any of your men. I'm an officer of the law —"

"In Arizona!" the chief interrupted.

"Yeh! But I've got the right to take in, at any place and at any time, a man I know to be guilty! You needn't be afraid that I'll make any false moves. And I ain't even askin' you to protect me. I just want all the evidence you've got, if any — want to know all that you know about the case. And then I'll toot my own horn! Here are my credentials!"

Tom Westley tossed a big envelope on the desk, and the chief inspected carefully the papers it contained, meanwhile considering the situation.

"Of course, I could assign a couple of men —" the chief began after a time.

"I ain't askin' for that! I don't want to put you to any trouble at all! I'd rather handle this, chief, in my own way. And I don't aim to be stopped or bothered any! Understand that? I'm all primed and ready!"

The chief hesitated for a moment, and then touched a bell button. There entered a clerk who looked fearfully at Tom Westley, puffing furiously at his cigar.

"Bring me all the reports and records in the John Westley murder case," the chief directed.

"Yes, sir."

"And tell those officers just outside the door to go back to work. This gentleman is not going to murder me."

The clerk slipped silently from the room, his face red, and closed the door softly behind him. Once more the chief of detectives faced the man from Arizona.

"Officially, I can't have anything at all to do with this — that is, outside the regular channel," the chief said. "And I want to warn you that you are running a risk when you invade the enemy's country. You don't know the peculiar manners and customs. The city isn't at all like the mountains and plains, you know."

"Human bein's are pretty much the same wherever you find 'em," Tom Westley declared. "A murderer is a murderer — don't care where you meet up with him! And a sense of guilt works about the same in a room in the city as in the middle of the desert! A sense of guilt is a terrible thing, chief!"

"I know it, Westley."

"All you have to do is to be ready to grab the man when I fetch him in."

The chief cleared his throat again.

"Officially, as I have said, I cannot countenance this thing," he replied. "But just the same, Westley, I want to shake hands with you and wish you luck!"

CHAPTER III

THE WARNING

SHERIFF Tom Westley left the office of the chief of detectives about half an hour later. Officer G. William Waltern was sitting behind his desk, and when he glanced up his face turned red and he pretended to be very busy considering some official documents.

The man from Arizona walked across the room to him and grinned as he looked down.

"No hard feelin's, son," he said. "You didn't know me or my business, and I reckon that I didn't know the ropes here, either. You can shake hands or decide to scrap it out at some other time. Makes no difference to me. Any time, son — fists, guns, or knives! Which'll it be?"

"I — I'll shake hands!" Officer Waltern said.

The grip that Sheriff Tom Westley gave him almost dislocated a couple of Waltern's fingers, and he winced, but the man from Arizona did not seem to notice it.

"See you later, son!" Westley announced. Then he left the office and hurried through the corridor out into the street.

Officer Waltern gazed at the door through which he had gone, rubbed his chin, and for the first time in his life thought deeply of things other than perfectly-fitting uniforms, fair ladies, and polished fingernails.

Tom Westley hurried uptown to the quiet hotel on a side street where he had a room. There he packed his few things, put his badge of office and credentials in the inner pocket of his vest, buckled his beloved six-gun under his left arm beneath his coat, went down the stairs and paid his bill, and traveled downtown as swiftly as the subway could carry him.

Leaving the subway, he was obliged to walk a distance of three blocks in order to reach Hogan's Place. Without seeming to do so he scrutinized the district carefully.

The street was narrow, littered, and through it swirled little whirlwinds that carried dust and bits of paper and refuse. The shops were dingy and had unwashed windows. Furtive-eyed men slipped past without giving him a glance. Raucous-voiced women chatted in shrill voices to one another. Dirty children played in the street. Washing was flapping in the wind from lines stretched on the tops of the buildings.

Hogan's Place was over a meat market, and there was a battered sign above the door. Tom Westley glanced around, opened the door, and went up one flight of dark, rickety, evil-odored stairs. He came to a little room that seemed to be an office. There was an old counter in it, a dirty register that looked as though it never was used, an inkwell that did not contain ink. From some room near at hand came the sound of quarreling voices. A door opened, and Hogan appeared.

Tom Westley placed Hogan at the first glance as a lazy brute who would rather fight than work, who had been steeped in the atmosphere of crime for so long that crime was a normal condition to him.

"Well?" Hogan asked surlily. His red-rimmed eyes were taking in the newcomer.

"I understood that I could get a good room here pretty cheap," Westley said.

"I can give you a dandy at a dollar a day," Hogan replied, though he was in the habit of renting them for half that, and sometimes even for less.

"Suits me," said Westley. "Never been in the city before, but I understand that livin' comes pretty high here. Have to pay extra for my meals, I suppose."

"Sure!" Hogan said. "I don't serve meals here at all. But right down the back stairs and across the alley, frontin' on the other street, I've got a bit of everything, stranger — restaurant, pool room, billiard parlor, cigar store — everything! It makes it handy."

"Sounds like it!" Westley admitted.

"Where'd you come from?"

"Arizona."

"That's quite a ways!" Hogan said. "That old grip all the baggage you've got with you?"

"Yep!"

"I'll have to ask you to pay for your room in advance then," Hogan said. "That's customary. Want to pay for a week?"

"Might as well," Westley declared.

He dropped his battered grip to the floor and reached into a hip pocket. He extracted an old wallet that had turned green with age, untied the string that bound it, and took out a bill. Hogan, bending over the counter, saw that the wallet was stuffed with bills, and his eyes narrowed.

The bill was a ten, and Hogan made the change out of his pocket. He did not offer a receipt. Then he led the way through a dark hall and threw open the door of a small room. Hogan apologized for the appearance of the place, and said that it would be cleaned and straightened immediately. The bed was not made, the table was littered, the floor was dirty.

Tom Westley put his grip on the wobbly dresser, took off his hat, and glanced around.

"It'll do if it's cleaned," he announced. "I don't aim to be too particular. I ain't goin' to hang around the room all the time, anyway. Rooms is to sleep in."

"That's the boy!" Hogan exclaimed. "Came to the big town to see the sights and have a little fun, did you?"

"Partially," Westley admitted. "But I'm here on a little business, too."

"Buying stuff?"

"Nope!"

"I don't believe I got your name."

"I ain't mentioned it yet," Westley told him. "Maybe that's the reason. Might as well tell you, I reckon. Got to get acquainted. My name's Tom Westley!"

"Westley? Sounds familiar!"

"I reckon!" the man from Arizona said. "My brother put up here with you a couple of months or so ago. His name was John. He — he was murdered!"

Hogan blinked his eyes rapidly and licked at his lips. "Oh, yes! I remember him!" the landlord said. "Nice boy!"

"Yep!"

"It's too bad about him bein' killed! He just got in with the wrong gang, I suppose. You want to be careful about that, Westley. The boys that hang around my place, for instance, are all right. But there are a lot up and down the street who'd kill a man in a minute for less than a dollar. Better be careful, Westley!"

"I aim to be," the man from Arizona said.

"And any time you want a little fun, Wesley, you just come and ask me about it. As long as I know you're all right, I can tip off where you can have all the fun you want. I always take care of my customers."

"That's right nice of you," Westley replied. "Maybe you can give me a little tip, then. I'm tryin' to find the man who killed my brother John."

Hogan looked a bit astonished for an instant, and then he considered the man standing before him, and smiled inwardly at his own fright.

"I'm afraid that'll be a hard job," he said. "The cops didn't seem able to do that. He — he just got into a fight and got the worst of it, I suppose."

"I don't care what the police did!" Westley declared. "I'm on the trail, and I'm goin' to keep on it until I find the murderer. And when I find him, there'll be fireworks!"

"All right! If I'm able to learn anything, I'll let you know," said Hogan. "Now I'll show you how to get across the alley to my place. You'll like it, all right! I'll tip off some of the boys that you're all right, and they'll be real friendly."

"Yeh?" Tom Westley replied.

He followed Hogan down the back stairs and across the littered alley, through a rear door.

There were little back rooms for card games and private conversations, there was a pool hall with a restaurant and cigar store in front, and Westley saw that there was a private office, too.

Hogan made a great show of introducing Westley, announcing

that he was "all right" and was to be extended the privileges of the place. The man from Arizona was the picture of innocence, a consummate actor for the moment. He acknowledged the introductions and sat down to watch a billiard contest, puffing at a cheap cigar. To all appearances he was merely killing time and getting acquainted with his new surroundings, but in reality he was alert. He might be in the city, but Sheriff Tom Westley was right on the trail.

Hogan did not return to the lodging house, but went into the private office instead. A few minutes later Westley saw a rat-faced little man slip into the office and close the door behind him. The rat-faced man was known as "Lefty Joe" Jones.

Hogan was waiting for him, sitting at a roll-top desk and smoking a cigar furiously. He waved toward a chair, and Lefty Joe sat down, not taking the trouble to remove his hat. He was a typical man of the district — cruel, cunning, sneaky. His face was pasty, his lips thin, his eyes narrow and too near together. It would not have been difficult for any student of human nature to catalog Lefty Joe.

"Well, boss?" he asked.

"It's mighty well," Hogan said. "He's here already."

"This man Westley?"

"The same, Joe. And the fun of it is that he came to my place and got a room."

"Maybe he did that on purpose, Hogan."

"Whether he did or not, it puts him where he can be watched — and handled if necessary," Hogan replied. "He's out in the pool hall now."

"That bird in the gray suit sittin' against the wall?" Lefty Joe asked.

"That's the man! He's already told me that he's lookin' for the man who murdered his brother. Maybe he is, and maybe he isn't. He looks like a hick, but a hick can be bad medicine at times. He might have fooled us if we hadn't been put wise. It's a good thing to have a friend around police headquarters."

"What did they say about this bird?" Lefty Joe asked.

"He got peeved because he had to wait to see the chief and almost cleaned out headquarters. Then him and the chief had their noses together for about an hour, and the chief sent out for the reports in the Westley case. This Westley has taken off his tin star, though he admits what he's here for."

"Do all the boys know?"

"Some do, and the others will before long. We've got to handle this thing easy, Lefty. We don't want to make any mistakes."

"There won't be any mistakes. But I think he's just a rube, don't care if he is a sheriff back home. And he'll have a hot time gettin' a line on anything that'd bother anybody down here!"

"That's the way I look at it!" Hogan said. "If we can't handle him, we ought to take to the country ourselves. The boys can handle him if he starts any rough stuff. Meanwhile, there's pickin's."

"Mean to say he's got coin?"

"I got him to pay in advance, so I'd get a flash at his roll," Hogan explained. "He's got a wallet stuffed with currency, and the last time I saw it, he had it in his hip pocket."

"The poor boob!"

"A little poker game might help," Hogan suggested.

"Just give me a knockdown to him, not bein' too particular about it, and let me do the rest," Lefty Joe said. "I hope he's got enough coin to be worth goin' after. But a poker game's slow at that. If he carries it in his hip pocket —"

"Go slow!" Hogan warned. "No dip stuff in this place with this man from Arizona. If you have to touch him, do it a few blocks away from here. He can't make a howl if he loses at poker. And, as far as the cops are concerned, this bird is here on his own. Our man at headquarters reported everything him and the chief said. The chief told him that he'd have to work alone, and warned him he'd better stay out of trouble."

"That makes it real nice!" Lefty Joe remarked. "Let the boob look all he wants for the man who killed his brother. We'll trim him good while he's busy lookin'. Now introduce me to him."

Hogan got up and led the way into the pool hall, but they found that Tom Westley was gone. He had walked back across the alley one of the attendants said, having dropped the remark that he intended changing his shirt and putting on a clean collar, and then eating supper and having some fun.

"We'll catch him when he comes back, Joe," Hogan declared. "You'd better hang around."

Westley, as a matter of fact, had returned to his room to readjust the holster under his left arm, which was not hanging to suit him. He ascended the rickety stairs, found his room, and pushed open the door.

A woman was in the room making the bed. Westley gave her a quick glance. She was about twenty-five, he judged, and might have been pretty if she had been neatly dressed. She had cleaned the room after a fashion, and was finishing with the bed.

"You go right ahead with your work, and don't mind me," the man from Arizona told her. "I just came back to get a clean collar and unpack some of my things."

The girl made no reply to that. She looked at him, and then bent over the bed and worked swiftly. Finally she picked up some soiled towels and hurried toward the hall door. She looked out, peered up and down the dark hall, and then darted swiftly across the room and to Tom Westley's side.

"You want to watch out for yourself if you stay around here!" she whispered. "But don't tell anybody I told you that. They'd — they'd half kill me!"

"Why, what's the trouble, young woman?"

"They'll be after you! They'll get you some way."

"Who?"

"I'm not mentioning names. I'm just warning you to watch out for yourself."

"I ain't got any enemies in this town."

"Don't try to play the boob with me!" she said. "I know who you are — Sheriff Westley, of Arizona!"

"What? How?" Westley gasped.

"And they know all about you, too. I heard them talking about it. Some man at police headquarters is a spy of theirs. You better be careful! It'd be a lot safer for you if you'd stay away from this part of the town!"

Tom Westley changed his manner swiftly. "You seem to know a lot about me and my business!" he said in a tense voice. "Suppose you tell me some more now. Who's the spy at police headquarters?"

"I don't know that."

"Then, who did you hear talkin' about me and my affairs?" Westley demanded.

"I'm not saying! I've simply warned you —"

"And just why did you take the trouble to do that? You've never seen me before!"

"Because — because I don't want them to — to rob and kill you," she replied.

"I reckon I can take care of myself!"

"Against a score of thieves and murderers?" she asked, her lips curling in sudden scorn. "They have handled plenty of men just as wise as you! And how long do you think a hick sheriff would last with them?"

Suddenly, as Tom Westley would have answered her, she darted away from him, reached the door, and hurried out into the hall. The door was slammed shut behind her, and by the time Westley had crossed the room and opened it again, she was out of sight.

CHAPTER IV

THE SHOW-DOWN

THE man from Arizona stepped back into the room, a thoughtful expression in his face, closed and locked the door. Then, from force of habit, he adjusted his holster before he did anything else. After that, he touched a flaming match to the end of a fresh cigar and sat down on the edge of the bed to indulge in some deep thinking for about fifteen minutes.

The girl herself did not bother him much. She belonged to the district, Tom Westley supposed, and so far as her motive was concerned, she probably had given him the information in a wild attempt to "get square" with somebody she hated. Yet, she had mentioned no names.

If the information she had imparted was to be relied on, it was important. Tom Westley felt that he could rely on it, for she had rattled off his name and official position, and the reason for his presence in the neighborhood.

He had to consider that spy at police headquarters. That was the first thing.

He began to feel thankful that he was working alone. The spy had done all the damage he could, for Westley did not intend to have another conference with the chief of detectives. He intended to make no report of any nature until he took in his prisoner.

But he hated the thought of the spy. He had judged the chief of detectives to be a loyal, efficient, and hard-working officer of the law. He disliked the idea of such a man having near him a traitor to the service. Westley decided that he would tell the chief about it later.

One thing he had to guard against — the spy coming down into this neighborhood and playing a part against him, causing him trouble, possibly turning the chief against him in some manner. As to the identity of the spy — Westley knew it might be any man around headquarters, possibly a clerk, but he wondered whether it was Officer G. William Waltern.

The spy must have been in touch with the gangsters before, of course, and serving them. Possibly he simply had reported this affair as he would have reported anything else that might have been of interest to the gang.

So far as the gang was concerned, Westley told himself that it was too early to decide anything. The fact that the girl worked for Hogan did not mean that Hogan was in the gang. She might have overheard that conversation she mentioned at some place down the street. She had been particular not to mention names, though.

At any rate, they knew that he was a sheriff and why he was there! But they did not know that Tom Westley was aware of their knowledge. That would help a bit, Westley decided. For a time he would continue playing the unsophisticated countryman, leading them to believe that he thought he was fooling them.

Then, when he had something upon which to work, he would declare his real self and be a whirlwind of vengeance. He knew the men around Hogan's Place for what they were, but it did not follow that one of them had shot down his brother. Hogan's Place was not the only thieves' hangout in the neighborhood.

He still believed in the sense of guilt! Since it was known what he contemplated, Tom Westley felt sure that the men responsible for his brother's death would get in touch with him soon.

One of several things might happen. They might merely watch him to assure themselves that he did not stumble upon any damaging evidence. Or, they might think it best to attack him at once, remove him, and so make sure of their own safety. Westley intended to force them to show their hands at the earliest opportunity.

"I reckon this is goin' to be some mess," Westley muttered to himself. "And if I ever find out that the finger-polishin' dude I mussed with is the spy, there's goin' to be fireworks!"

He got up and put on a clean collar, made sure again that his holster hung exactly as he wanted it, and then went out into the hall, closed the door, stumbled down the dark back stairs, crossed the alley, and entered the dive on the other side.

He played his part perfectly, too. He loitered around the back room and finally went to the front, where he sat on a stool before the counter of the restaurant and ordered a steak, potatoes, and coffee.

Just as he finished his meal, Hogan came along the counter and slapped him on the back.

"Well, Westley, I see you're fillin' up before tacklin' the sights of the big village!" he exclaimed.

"Yep!"

"Where are you going to start in? Goin' to tackle the Brooklyn Bridge, Grant's Tomb, or the Statue of Liberty?"

"We've got plenty of scenery out in Arizona and adjoinin' States," Westley said. "We've got a natural rock bridge in Utah almost as big as your Brooklyn Bridge, and plenty of tombs in Tombstone, and every man out there is a personal statue of liberty — and don't you forget it!"

"Then there aren't any sights that'd interest you?"

"A lot of 'em!" Westley said. "It's action I crave, though. I can look at scenery when I get old."

"You come along with me to the private office," Hogan said.

Westley followed him as though it were a great honor. They sat down in the private office, and Hogan winked and drew from a drawer of his desk a black bottle.

"Prohibition doesn't stop me treatin' a man I like now and then," he said. "Help yourself."

Westley was an adept at the art of pretending to drink and only wetting his lips. But Hogan drank after him, so he judged the liquor was good. Then the door opened, and Lefty Joe put in his head and started to apologize and back out again.

"Come in!" Hogan commanded. "Mr. Westley, I want to make you acquainted with one of the boys. This is 'Lefty Joe' Jones, and Action is his middle name. Joe, Mr. Westley is here to see the town, and he craves action."

"Wine or cards?" Joe asked.

"I don't likker much lately," Westley remarked. "The doctor says it doesn't agree with me. But I could play a game of cards, I reckon."

"Ever play poker?" Joe asked.

"Some," said Westley. "I'm from Arizona, where, in the old days, they gave babies poker chips to play with instead of their dads' watches. But a man gets stale, o' course."

"There's a little game startin' in one of the back rooms in a few minutes," Lefty Joe said. "I was just going to ask Hogan if he wanted to sit in."

"Not this evening," Hogan replied. "Let Mr. Westley have my chair. But I'd better explain, Mr. Westley, that we have to go slow with poker in the city. Some folks think it is a crime and make laws against it. So — no noise!"

Westley winked and got up to move toward the door. Lefty Joe winked, too, at Hogan, and though Tom Westley did not see the wink, he suspected it. He followed Lefty Joe through the billiard hall to one of the private rooms, where Joe introduced him to three other men.

Westley looked them over carefully as they prepared for the game. Thieves, thugs, and gangsters, he told himself! He wondered whether one of them had slain his brother, and for an instant he almost lost control of himself.

He began to watch their every word and action. He took the old wallet from his hip pocket, extracted half a dozen bills, tied the wallet up again and returned it to his pocket. But every man there had seen that the wallet was still fat with currency.

Tom Westley began playing cautiously. Gradually he became more intimate with the other men, until he was calling them by their first names. But he almost sneered at the crudeness of the game they were working, the old "come-on" game, where the "sucker" was allowed to win at first.

He did not betray that he knew anything of the science of poker. And, after an hour of playing, he sensed the change. They were ready to make the killing now.

"Game's a little slow," Lefty Joe said. "Let's take off the lid — anything goes!"

"All right with me," Westley replied. "When you get too stiff I can drop out."

And then he began to play poker, silently, chewing on a dead cigar, his face inscrutable. They tried to guess him, and could not.

They dropped out, and found that he had been bluffing. They decided to stay in — and discovered that he had a winning hand.

They attempted tricks that almost made Tom Westley smile. But even their crooked dealing could not outwit him, and when it was his deal he dealt crooked himself, and so cunningly that they could not see it.

Lefty Joe and the other three grew desperate. One of them had made a trip out of the room, and Westley guessed that he had gone to Hogan to get more money. But another hour found Westley with the money he had obtained.

"You're mighty lucky, seems to me," Lefty Joe said.

"Luck and science!" Westley answered frankly. "Anything goes, you said. You've tried a few simple little tricks on me, but they didn't work."

"Mean to say you've been cheatin'?" one of the others asked.

"Sure! And so have you! But you don't know the modern methods," Westley informed him.

"I've heard that, out in your country, when a man is caught cheatin' the one who catches him pulls a gun and commences shootin'."

"It's done sometimes," Westley admitted. "But not generally when everybody is cheatin'. However, son, if you want to pull a gun and start shootin', don't let me stop yeh! It wouldn't be the first time I've had a gun pulled on me."

"Bad man, are you?" the other sneered.

"Uh-huh! Plenty bad for this crowd," Westley declared, watching them closely. "If the game's over, I reckon I'll cash in and go take a walk. You can have revenge tomorrow night, if that suits you any."

"Why, curse you —" one of the players began.

Lefty Joe sprang to his feet and hurled the other man back against the wall. "You behave yourself!" he commanded. "Want to make a howl and have us all pinched for gamblin'? You got the worst of it, so be a sport and a good loser. Mr. Westley here is a friend of mine, and nobody jumps him while I'm around!"

"Thanks!" Westley said dryly. "But let him come on, if he wants to! Fists, knives, or guns!"

"He'll not bother you any more," Lefty Joe said, glaring at the other. "I'll cash in your chips."

Tom Westley had quite a pile of currency when the cashing in was concluded. He drew out the old wallet and stuffed the bills into it, then wrapped the wallet with twine and returned it to his hip pocket again. Every man there watched him.

"Thanks for a lively evening, gents," he said. "Now I'm goin' to take a walk and cool off. I always like to do that after a poker session. Nothin' like it!"

He left the room and went through the pool hall and the restaurant. There Hogan stopped him.

"Have a good time?" Hogan asked.

"Tolerable. I nicked them boys for about four hundred, rough guess. They can't play poker at all, Hogan!"

"You — you got away with it?" Hogan asked in amazement.

"Yep! One feller tried to deal off the bottom, but he didn't know the first thing about it. And he wanted to jump me, but that Joe boy stopped him. Joe's a fine lad!"

"He's a good boy," Hogan agreed.

Tom Westley walked on to the street and turned down it, wandering aimlessly apparently. He was thinking again. Lefty Joe had made an attempt to show himself Westley's friend. That was an old game. But he couldn't be sure yet whether these gangsters were only trying to get his money or whether they had more sinister intentions.

He had flashed that wallet purposely, and he expected results. He turned into a side street, and when he came to a dark place he removed the wallet from his hip pocket and tucked it away beneath his vest, and toward the back. Another wallet, similar in size and appearance, was taken from his coat pocket and put into his hip pocket where the first had been.

Then Tom Westley walked on down the street slowly, puffing at his cigar and evidently looking over the district. He turned into another street that ran beside a little park, where it was dark in spots, and where there were few pedestrians.

"It ought to happen some place along here, or I miss my guess," the man from Arizona muttered to himself.

He did not miss his guess. As he reached a dark spot, a form flashed from behind a tree at the edge of the walk.

"Hands up!" came in a hoarse whisper.

Westley saw that the other held an automatic pistol ready.

"Wh-what — —" he gasped, feigning surprise.

"Keep your mouth shut or I'll plug you! There's a couple of us, so you'd better be careful!"

Westley could see another man standing beside the tree in the semi-gloom. He longed to draw and commence shooting, but that was not his present game. He was there to listen and watch.

The man with the automatic advanced cautiously, turned Westley around, and immediately searched his hip pockets. He clutched the old wallet, transferred it to one of his own pockets, and poked Tom Westley in the back with the muzzle of the pistol.

"Walk right ahead and keep goin'!" he commanded. "You as much as turn around before you get to the corner and you're a dead goose! Walk, you simp, and keep quiet!"

Westley continued his acting. He still held his hands high above his head, and he walked down the street toward the corner as he had been commanded. But when he was half way to the end of the block, he dropped his hands and began chuckling.

"They think they got away with it, I suppose," he muttered. "They'll be tellin' each other how easy it is to hold up an Arizona sheriff. They'll be thinkin' that Westerners ain't as bad as they're painted. And that's just what I want 'em to think."

Arriving at the corner, he crossed over to the avenue and made his way back to Hogan's Place. He hurried now, and when he entered he found Hogan in the pool hall.

"Well, I've been robbed!" he said.

"Robbed?" Hogan gasped.

"Yep! I was walkin' along that little park and a feller came out from behind a tree and stuck a gun in my face. He took a wallet out of my hip pocket, too."

"Um!" Hogan grunted. "You goin' to report it to the police?"

"Nope! Served me right for not bein' on the job," Westley replied. "Anyway, they didn't get much!"

"But, you said your wallet! And all the money you had, and what you won at poker —"

"Oh, I ain't exactly a simp, Hogan!" Westley said. "I thought maybe somebody would try something like that. So I put that wallet with the money somewhere else, and I put in my hip pocket on old wallet stuffed with pieces of newspaper."

"You did!" Hogan gasped.

"Yep! And that's all the holdup man got — some pieces of old newspaper. Funny thing, too, Hogan. He never went through me — just went into that hip pocket as if he knew I carried a wallet there."

"Um!" Hogan grunted again, because he did not know what else to say.

Tom Westley's manner changed. His eyes narrowed and flashed. He bent forward and spoke in a tense voice.

"Hogan," he said, "I know the men who held me up! Tell 'em to look out!"

"What do you mean? What have I got to do with them?"

"Oh, I thought maybe you might know them, too! A lot of the boys hang around here."

"I don't want a man around me who accuses me of harborin' thieves!" Hogan exclaimed. "You get out of my roomin' house!"

"Not much, Hogan! You collected a week in advance!"

"I'll give you back your money!"

"I don't want it. That room's mighty handy!"

"You get out or I'll call the police and have 'em throw you out!"

"All right, Hogan! Go ahead and call the police!"

"If I do —"

"But you won't, Hogan! I'm callin' your bluff! Go right ahead and send for the police!"

For a moment they faced each other, eyes glittering dangerously, and there was sudden quiet in the big room. Pool and billiard players stood still, their cues held in the air. Those at the cigar counter turned to watch the scene.

"All right! Stay in the room!" Hogan said angrily.

"I aim to do just that, Hogan!"

"And see what you get!"

"I'm not worryin' much about that, Hogan! And tell any of your friends who might like to know that I sleep mighty easy and awake easier! I'll be ready for them, Hogan, at any time, night or day — fists, knives, or guns!"

"Feelin' strong, are you, Mister Sheriff?" Hogan asked sneeringly.

"Mister Sheriff, eh? How did you know I was a sheriff, Hogan?" Westley asked. "Oh, don't look as if you'd let somethin' drop! I know how you knew — your spy at police headquarters!"

Hogan's face was livid. A look of fear came into it now. This man had mentioned a spy at police headquarters. Was it possible that the spy had been discovered?

Fear and anger made Hogan reckless. He bent forward, and his brute face was within a foot of Westley's.

"Showin' your colors, are you?" he cried. "What do you know about police headquarters?"

"Oh, I was there this mornin' on business," Westley answered. "But you know all about that, Hogan. Your spy reported the whole thing — maybe!"

"What do you mean?"

"Maybe you don't know everything, Hogan! Just digest that statement for a few minutes. It'll give you food for thought, I reckon! And maybe there are other spies besides yours!"

Tom Westley was striving for something, and he could tell by the expression in Hogan's face that he was succeeding. The man who hires a traitor is always afraid of one in his own camp. Westley was watching Hogan carefully now, trying to decide whether Hogan was merely a "fence," protecting his crooks, or whether he had greater crimes for which to answer.

"Do you think for a minute, Hogan," Westley asked, "that those two men could have held me up a while ago if I hadn't wanted them to do it? I went out expectin' to be held up. I had a purpose in it, Hogan! Tell some of your friends that!"

"You're crazy!" Hogan cried.

"I'm not crazy, and you know it! You're thinkin' pretty hard about a few things right now, ain't you, Hogan? You're goin' to think harder, maybe, before long. I'm here to find the man who killed my brother John. And I'm goin' to find him!"

"Why come here to do it?"

"I just wanted to be in this part of town, Hogan. I wasn't much interested in you until you caused me to be. How did you know I was a sheriff, eh? Because your spy reported it to you! And if you're a law-abidin' citizen, why do you have a spy at police headquarters?"

"Cards on the table, eh?" Hogan asked sneeringly. "All right! I thought maybe some of the boys I know might be concerned, and I'm always ready to help my friends. Understand that? I know all about you, Westley! I know you're workin' alone, for instance! And if any-thing happens to you down here, there won't be much fuss."

"Nothin' is goin' to happen to me," Westley declared. "And remember what I said, Hogan — maybe you don't know everything! Maybe your spy wasn't in a position to report everything to you! And how did I happen to know you had a spy? Think about that!"

Hogan was infuriated now. He sprang backward.

"You cursed rube!" he cried.

But Hogan was a trifle slow. Even as his hand touched the butt of the automatic under his coat, he found himself looking into the busi-ness end of a six-gun.

"You're playin' my game now, Hogan," Tom Westley said, smiling a little. "Shucks! When it comes to gun play you're as slow as an old woman! Take out that pop pistol of yours and toss it on that pool table! Do it quick, Hogan! As you pull it out, you can turn it and shoot — if you've got the nerve!"

Hogan was mumbling curses. His eyes glared defiance, but he slowly took out the automatic. For an instant he hesitated, as though about to take the chance of turning the weapon and firing. But he found Tom Westley's stern eyes looking straight into his own, and his courage waned.

He cursed again and dropped the pistol on the table. "Well?" he asked.

"Well, Hogan, we've put up a mighty good little show for the boys here," Tom Westley said. "But they're disappointed a bit, I reckon. I'm sure they expected you to try to shoot. But you were a wise man not to try it, Hogan!"

"Think so?" Hogan sneered.

"Yep! I reckon that we understand each other now, and so we're on a workin' basis, as the sayin' is. This little spat of ours don't really amount to anything. I'm willin' to pit my wits against those of you or any of your friends at any time. If you want to play with me, Hogan, all right! But you know why I'm here, and I don't like to have my mind taken from my job. If you keep on pesterin' me, you see, I'll think you're interested in a big way — say that you're worryin' that I'll accomplish my object. Understand, Hogan?"

"You're crazy!"

"Uh-huh! Nevertheless, Hogan, I'm here to get my brother's murderer! Any gent who raises his hand against me is liable to advertise the fact that he's interested in seein' that the murderer ain't caught! That's plain enough, ain't it, Hogan? Now I think that I'll go to my room in your hotel and get some sleep. And I hope that I ain't disturbed any. I get plumb violent when I'm disturbed at night!"

Sheriff Tom Westley returned his six-gun to its holster and walked through the back room and across the alley, up the rickety stairs and to his room, where he closed the door carefully after snapping on the light.

And, behind him, Hogan neglected to lift his hand to grasp the automatic and fire a shot. Westley had judged that Hogan would not. Hogan would wait and try other methods!

CHAPTER V

TWO INTERVIEWS

TOM Westley prepared for rest that night much as he might have in the midst of his own country when he anticipated a clash with enemies. He removed his shoes and loosened his clothing, put his six-gun handy, snapped out the light, and sat before the one window of the room looking down at the dark alley.

He was thinking deeply.

The unknown woman who had straightened things in the room had mentioned the spy and the fact that he had reported to somebody in the neighborhood. Hogan had betrayed that he knew what the spy had reported. So Hogan was one of the gang, too, or else he had their confidence.

It did not follow, however, that Hogan had killed John Westley or even knew the identity of the man who had. Hogan, being a "fence" and the friend of thieves, might have a spy at police headquarters for business reasons, and that spy might have reported Westley's presence and intentions so that Hogan could notify anybody interested.

And it was possible that Hogan feared Westley was a sort of detective in disguise and was in the district for another reason, possibly to gather evidence against Hogan's fence. Westley could not feel sure that Hogan had been concerned in his brother's murder. He was sure only that Hogan was his enemy now, and that Hogan's friends were his enemies also.

Still, that was as he wanted it! He had made public his intentions. He was playing a daring game, for he wanted the guilty man to grow afraid and attempt to get him out of the way. Westley was daring him to do just that.

He would have to continue watching and listening, trying to get a word or see an action that would give him a clue. He wondered about the identity of the girl who had warned him, and he decided to question her if he got an opportunity.

Westley felt, too, that his actions during the evening had been a bit boyish and unworthy a sheriff of Arizona. He had recognized the two men who had held him up. The man who had taken his wallet had a handkerchief over his face for a mask, but Westley knew that he was the poker player who had wanted to attack him. And the one who had stood back in the shadows had been Lefty Joe, who had pretended to be his friend. The two men had joined forces in an attempt to rob him.

Although Westley had laid himself open to the robbery in an effort to learn something, he was as much at a loss as ever. Lefty Joe might have been inclined to rob him to get some easy money. Westley guessed that it was a common thing for Joe and his friends to play that game. Possibly, he was not on the right track. But possibly, on the other hand, all these men knew the truth about the killing of John Westley, and one of them might give a hint that would help.

Westley did not remain before the window long. He had locked the door, and now he propped a chair under the knob, too. And he did not stretch out on the bed. He tossed the covers into a heap in the middle of it, took one quilt, and retired to a corner of the room, where he spread the quilt on the floor and stretched himself upon it. Tom Westley, who had spent many a night sleeping on sandy ground, did not find the floor particularly uncomfortable.

He slept, too, well aware that the slightest unusual sound would cause him to awake. But nothing happened during the night. His foes did not make a move. That would have been too raw. They would wait. Hogan was not the sort of man to run his head into a noose by having anything violent happen in his own establishment.

Westley washed his face and hands, and dressed as he had the day before, taking care that the six-gun hung properly beneath his coat and under his left arm. He went out of the building by the front entrance, seeing nobody in the office or hall, and walked up the street and around the block. He did not see any of the men who had been in Hogan's Place the night before, but he passed many who glanced at him peculiarly, and he guessed that the district was acquainted with his identity.

He ate a big breakfast, but he did not patronize Hogan's Place to get it. In time, he returned slowly to the lodging house. Hogan was in the little office.

"Feelin' better this mornin'?" Westley asked, grinning. "We had it a bit heavy last night, didn't we?"

"No man makes a fool of me and gets away with it!" Hogan muttered.

"Now, don't get fussed up, Hogan," Westley replied. "Suppose you tend to your business and let me tend to mine. You ain't interested in mine, are yeh?"

"I'm not!" Hogan said.

"It'd be a bad thing, under the circumstances, to admit that you was," Westley told him, his eyes narrowing. "We'll get along fine as landlord and tenant if you don't try to tramp on my toes. But if you want to start anything, Hogan, go right ahead and start it — fists, knives, or guns!"

"I don't want anything to do with you!" Hogan declared. "You came down here lookin' for trouble, and you're liable to find it, and I don't care to be mixed up in it. Understand? I'd be pleased if you'd get out of my house and find a room somewhere else."

"I'll think about that when my week's up, Hogan. Meanwhile, you won't be bothered by me so long as you don't try to bother me. Armed neutrality, Hogan — that's us! But any time you want to declare war —"

Hogan sneered and turned away, and Tom Westley went down the hall toward his room. He found the door part of the way open, and the woman he had seen the day before was busy making the bed. She looked up, startled, as he entered.

"Go right ahead with your work. Don't mind me," Westley said pleasantly.

The woman did not answer, and Westley watched her as she went about her work. She made a trip out into the hall and returned with clean towels, and Westley guessed that she had made sure that Hogan was not outside.

"You goin' to stay here?" she whispered.

"For a week, anyway," Westley replied.

"You're a fool, I guess! You spilled the beans last night, didn't you? Got them all down on you now? Trying to commit suicide?"

"Not exactly!" Westley replied. "I want to ask you a few questions."

"I don't intend to answer any."

"I think it'd be best," said Westley quietly. "You wouldn't want me to tell Hogan about what you told me yesterday, would you?"

"Don't you dare!" she uttered in a hoarse whisper. "If you did —"

"Then you'd better answer a few harmless questions. Thanks for tellin' me what you did yesterday. You ran away before I had a chance to thank you. I just want to know what your interest is in all this. Did you know my brother?"

"He lived here. I tended to his room, of course, and saw him once in a while. But I never spoke to him more than half a dozen times in my life, and then just to say good morning.'"

"Would you mind tellin' me who you are?"

"Why not? I'm Millie Hogan!"

Westley whistled. "Hogan's daughter?"

"No, thank Heaven! I'm his niece," she replied. "My folks died when I was about ten years old, and he adopted me. I've been his drudge. I've worked myself half to death for him and never been able to get away."

"That's a shame," Westley said.

"Oh, a man like you couldn't understand. He thinks that everybody is like him. He imagines I like this kind of life — thieves sneakin' around all the time, decent men bein' slugged and robbed. He thinks it's clever, and that the men who do it are clever."

"Uh-huh! I can understand that!"

"I've tried to keep decent — and I have! But I can't stand much more of it. I've thought of sneakin' away and gettin' a job some place, but then I wouldn't know anybody or have any friends. And now — now he's urgin' me to tie up with this Lefty Joe."

"Lefty Joe ain't a fit man for a girl like you to marry," Westley announced.

"I know it," she said grimly.

"I hate to see a girl like you in a place like this," Westley said. "Gosh, if you were in a place like Arizona, where folks are clean and decent, you'd be a great girl!"

"You might as well say if I was in heaven! Hogan won't give me a cent. He's afraid I'll run away, and then he'd have to hire somebody."

"You ain't got any particular love for him, then?"

"I haven't! He did take care of me when my folks died, but I've more than worked that out."

"Maybe we might make a little deal," Westley informed her. "I reckon you know what I'm after?"

"You want the man who killed your brother."

"Correct!"

"Some of these thieves did it, of course. If not this gang, then some other gang around here."

"I've got an idea you might make a pretty good guess."

"I'm not guessin'," she said.

"Not if I make the right kind of inducement?"

"I don't want to do anything like that! That wouldn't be straight and decent. I did enough to warn you. I — I just wish you'd go away and save yourself. I just don't want another crime around here, I hate to see men like these putting away a good man!"

"I'm here on certain business, and here I stay until that business is done — or I'm done!" Westley declared, his eyes narrowing again.

"You see, I thought a lot of that kid brother of mine!"

"Well — I hope you don't lose out!"

"Thanks," Westley said. "Any time you want to talk —"

"If I do, it'll be to square things with somebody, not to get a reward."

"I understand."

"You'd better get a room some other place."

"Um! I figure this is safest. Hogan ain't goin' to let anything happen to me while I'm in his house — not in here, that is. And this is a handy place, too."

"Then watch!" she whispered. "It'd be a shame — If they got you, too!"

She whirled toward the door and was gone before he could make a reply.

Westley digested that interview and got a little hope out of it, but not much. He slept for a time, and then went out upon the streets, purposely showing himself to any who might be interested, walking back and forth defiantly.

Then night came, and Westley left the district and ate a meal some distance uptown, returning to the district again about ten o'clock. He had given his foes every chance to get together and make their plans. He was alert, cautious, ready for them to make a move that might betray them.

He strode down the street, entered a shop and purchased some cigars, emerged again, and stopped to light one of the smokes. Over his cupped hands he saw a man walking along close to the fronts of the buildings. Westley stepped back into a doorway as he gasped his surprise. The man who approached was Officer G. William Waltern, in civilian clothes. Westley stepped out as Waltern came opposite the doorway, and they faced each other.

"Takin' a little stroll?" Westley asked.

"I was hoping that I'd see you," said the officer.

"Any special reason for wantin' to see me?"

"Well, nothing in particular. But I am — er — interested in you and what you are doing."

"You are, are yeh? I wonder why?"

"Well, to tell the truth, I think you have opened my eyes," Waltern said. "You said some pretty hard things to me at headquarters, you know, and — er — handled me roughly."

"Oh! You've been lookin' for me so we could fight it out?" Westley asked.

"No, sir! I've had all I want along that line," Waltern declared.

Westley looked at him carefully. "It makes me feel suspicious to see you down here." he said. "Before I got down here yesterday, somebody tipped off to certain people hereabouts who I was and what I intended doing. I learned that it was a spy in police headquarters. And now you come prowlin' around."

"I don't doubt it," Waltern replied. "Some of the clerks around headquarters might be doing that sort of thing. Gangsters are kept pretty well informed. Ask some of the detectives who stage raids how many of them are tipped off in advance."

"You don't seem to grasp my meanin'," Westley said. "I said that this visit of yours looks suspicious."

"Do you mean to insinuate that I am the spy?" Waltern demanded. "I may be a little fussy about dressing, and things like that, but I hope I am a loyal officer."

"I hope so!" Westley agreed.

"I know what you are doing, of course," Waltern continued. "And, strange though it may seem, I have a kind of liking for you. I consider that you're a real man!"

"Thanks!"

"I'm not talking foolish!" Waltern said. "I got to thinking about you, and I made up my mind that I could learn a lot from you. If I was out in Arizona, say, a deputy of yours, for instance, and had that sort of experience for a couple of years, I could come back to the city and be a regular man on the force, a man worth something, instead of a fashion plate working in an office."

"I see. You came down here to ask me for a job?"

"You won't understand, I see, Mr. Westley! I — I'm for you! I'm afraid for you down here. I know a few things about these people and their methods, and if I can be of service to you —"

"Thanks, but I'm playin' this game myself," Westley said. "I don't often misjudge a man, I may as well tell you."

"If you doubt my motives, you are misjudging me!"

"Well, I'm doubtin' your motives, but if I find out I am misjudging you, it won't take me more than a second to apologize," Westley informed him.

"I assure you —"

"Time will tell! I'm pullin' off a big fight, you see, and I don't aim to let anybody stand in my way, be he cop or crook! Good evenin'!"

Sheriff Tom Westley turned away without another word and went rapidly down the street.

"I can't quite make that man out," he confessed to himself. "Maybe he is just a plain fool — and maybe he's playin' some sort of a deep game!"

CHAPTER VI

BLOODLESS BATTLE

FOR four days Tom Westley lived in the midst of danger without encountering a show of violence. He seemed to breathe defiance. He glared at men who glanced at him, thrust gangsters out of the way when he came near them, and seemed to be challenging the world to mortal combat.

But it was not all bluster. The real Tom Westley was lurking behind this show of foolishness, watching, always alert, hoping to see or hear something that would put him on the right trail.

He managed to see Millie Hogan every day, and they had frequent talks. Westley found himself beginning to like the girl. He told her tales of the West, and particularly of Arizona, and once he got her to smile. It was not at all a bad-looking smile. But he wanted most to get her to talk.

"I hate to see a girl like you in a place like this," he told her one afternoon. "If you had a chance —"

"That's something I'll never get," she declared. "I've given up hope!"

"No sense in givin' up hope! If you're ready to talk and say what I want you to say, I might see that you get a chance," Westley said.

The girl looked out of the window, down at the filthy alley below and the furtive-mannered men slipping along it like rats scampering to their holes.

"It would be great to be in a place where everybody didn't have to sneak around," she whispered. "I like to see a man who's able to hold up his head. And that — that is why I wish you'd go away. I don't want them to get you!"

"They won't!"

"They will just as soon as they get frightened enough," she declared "It'll be a shot from the dark, maybe. You might as well go away and save yourself — you haven't a chance of getting the man you want."

"There's always a chance — and I thought a lot of John," Westley answered. "It'd be an act of friendship to humanity, I reckon, to send some of these fellers to the chair. How'd you like to go out to Arizona? You'd have friends there, all right, before you'd been there a week,' 'specially if I was to slip around the word that you were lonesome and needed friends. We've got more friends than anything else out there. And clean work and clean living too!"

"Why do you torture me?" she asked. "Why do you tell me such things?"

"You can have it, if you want it. My word's good! I'd see you got along all right."

"I don't doubt your word," Millie Hogan said. "But what chance have I to do such a thing?"

"Every chance in the world!" Westley told her, "Just talk! You could tell me what I want to know, I'm thinkin' — or at least give me a pretty good hint. Of course, I don't blame a girl for wantin' to protect her uncle, even if he is a brute. It wouldn't be nice to have a relative go to the chair."

"Oh, he didn't do it!" she cried.

"Ha!" Westley grunted. "Sure he didn't? Then you must know who did! You talk, girl — talk to me straight! I'll take you out of this hole! I'll take you away to Arizona, and I'll see that you have a good, clean job and a chance to live right — every chance in the world!"

"No — no!"

"Interested in the guilty man, are yeh?"

"I —I hate him!" she said.

"Then you do know who he is? You talk!"

"I — I can't say the word!" she cried.

"Think of my poor kid brother, shot down like a dog!"

"I — I can't talk!" she repeated. "I'm afraid!"

"No need to be. I'll take care of you."

"Oh, you don't know — you can't guess! You can't even take care of yourself if they decide to go after you!"

"Don't you worry about that!" Westley told her. "I've handled quite a few men in my time, and some of them thought they were bad. You just slip me the word, then stand back and watch. Nobody'll know you told."

But he was unable to gain his point. She hesitated, seemed to be on the verge of speaking, but suddenly hurried from the room as she had done many times before. Tom Westley walked through the hall, out of the building and down the street, still alert and watchful, still hoping that something might happen to give him the clue he sought.

He did not think that Hogan was the guilty man, and never had thought so. Hogan was the sort to sit back and take profits while other men did the dirty work. And the girl knew! If he could only force her to speak! He did not avoid Hogan's Place. Rather, he went there frequently.

On this afternoon he went a step farther. He sat down to watch a pool game, careful that he was in a corner with his back to the wall. He knew that his presence there made certain men nervous, but he did not care. He wanted them to be nervous.

Hogan passed and glared at him. Tom Westley stopped him with a hail.

"Hogan!"

"Well?" Hogan whirled around, hesitated, and then walked back.

"Got a bad disposition, ain't yeh?" Westley said. "Can't even answer when a man speaks. I've got a bit of information for you."

"What is it?" Hogan asked.

"Gatherin' facts in this locality ain't so hard when a man knows how to go about it," Westley said, lowering his voice so that only Hogan could hear. "You needn't be fussed up about me any more, Hogan!"

"Got enough? Going to leave this end of the city?" Hogan asked, with some eagerness.

"Nope! But you needn't be afraid of me and what I'm doin', Hogan. I've learned a few things. I know, for instance, that you didn't kill my brother."

"Of course I didn't!" Hogan replied.

"Then we haven't any fight, Hogan. There is just one man on earth that I'm after now — and that's the murderer of my brother!" Westley stepped closer and whispered. "And I'm mighty close after him, Hogan!"

"Close after him?" Hogan repeated. "You mean that — that you know who he is?"

"Yeh!" Westley said. "He's been showin' his hand, though maybe he don't know it. I suppose I could name him to you, Hogan, but I don't aim to do it just now, I want to gather a bit more evidence and make sure, you see. And I want to handle this thing all by myself. You know him, all right! But you won't have many more talks with him, I reckon!"

"I know him?" Hogan gasped.

"You do, Hogan! That's all I'm sayin' just now. I just wanted to let you know that you weren't under suspicion, so far as I am concerned."

Westley went out upon the street again. He had made his point, and he felt that his falsehood had been in a worthy cause. He did not doubt that Hogan knew the identity of the murderer. And Hogan certainly would inform the murderer of what Westley had just said. Perhaps that would frighten the guilty man, cause him to come out in the open and make a move — or else make one from the dark.

Westley was in his room shortly after supper, with the door locked and the shade drawn at the window. He was preparing for whatever might come. He had inspected his six-gun, oiled it, and filled it with cartridges. He had more cartridges in a handy pocket. He might have been Sheriff Tom Westley, back in Arizona, preparing to take the trail of a dangerous man.

There was a knock at the door. Westley went across and unlocked it, then stepped to one side, his right hand near the butt of his revolver.

"Come in!" he said.

The door was opened. Millie Hogan stood in it.

"Clean towels," she muttered.

Westley watched as she hurried across to the washstand. He knew that she had put clean towels there earlier in the day, that this was a subterfuge of some sort. As she went back to the hall she stepped close to him and whispered:

"Watch out tonight! Stay in your room!"

"I've got to go out and get fresh air," Westley complained, also speaking in a whisper.

"Don't be a fool! They're after you," she said. "Something has made them afraid of you. The gang has orders to get you. I — I heard them talking. They never pay any attention to me. They think I'm a stick of furniture, I suppose. They'll get you, kill you, weight your body, and toss it into the river —"

Somebody was coming along the dark hall. Millie Hogan darted out, her towels on her arm, and hurried toward another room. Tom Westley closed the door silently behind her.

She had given him good news. So they were frightened at last! Hogan had passed the word that Westley had said he was on the right trail!

So they were after him! It was a dangerous game he played, but he recognized it as such, and hence was on guard. He would fight it out with them, try to ascertain the identities of his particular foes, and among them find the man he sought.

For an hour or so longer he waited, then left his room and went through the hall toward the front stairs. Hogan was in the little office.

"Stickin' around home, are yeh?" Westley asked.

"I've got a toothache," Hogan declared. "I'm goin' to stay right here until bedtime."

As Westley went down the stairs, he grinned. So Hogan was preparing an alibi! Hogan expected them to make a move tonight.

Westley acted in an ordinary manner as he stepped out upon the street and started for the nearest corner. But he knew that he was watched and shadowed. He saw a man slipping along through the shadows on the opposite side of the street. The word was being passed, he supposed.

He loitered along the street like a man without any destination in mind. He dropped into a cigar store and made a purchase, watching the other customers. By the way in which they glanced at him, Westley knew that word had gone through this crime-infested district that he was to be "got."

He put a cigar between his teeth, but he did not light it, for he wanted no cigar glow to give a target in the darkness. The gangsters would not shoot him down in the lighted street, he reasoned. They would wait for him to get into a place where the deed could be done swiftly.

Coming to the mouth of an alley, he stepped to the curb and hesitated. Just inside the alley two men began quarreling. A few others ran toward them. Tom Westley grinned.

It was an old trick, and he did not intend to be taken in by it. All that was necessary was for him to run to the spot to see what the quarrel was about. And then there would be a scuffle, a knife between his ribs, a scattering, and a story for the police afterward of sounds of a fight and of a man found dead.

Westley crossed the mouth of the alley and continued down the street, noticing with satisfaction that the quarrel stopped as soon as he did so. He came to Hogan's Place and entered.

There was a scattering of men in the pool and billiard room, but Westley noticed that several he knew were missing. Lefty Joe was not there, nor the man who had made the howl on the night of the poker game. Certain others were missing, too. They were outside, waiting for him, Westley supposed.

Despair clutched him for an instant.

Out into the street again he went, and down it to the corner. He turned into the side street and approached the end of the alley that ran behind Hogan's Place. He stood at the curb there for a few minutes and chewed at his unlighted cigar. Then he turned into the alley abruptly, as though he had decided to go to his room.

He slipped along as noiselessly as a cat until he was halfway from the end of the alley to Hogan's back door. Then he stopped, felt around and picked up a tin can, and tossed it far ahead of him. It crashed to the ground, made a noise such as it might have made had a man stumbled over it.

Tom Westley crouched against the wall of a building. From down the alley came a flash of flame, the ringing of a shot. From directly opposite him came another. Westley whipped out his gun, but he did not fire.

He heard men running, heard a soft whistle. He tossed another can, so that it fell some distance from the first. Again there was a shot from down the alley, another from opposite.

Westley's gun roared. The bullet sped toward the nearest flash and crashed against the wall within a foot of his assailant's head. With the flash, Westley changed his position. He dashed for the street. Behind him, automatics spat and revolvers roared.

He came to the street and darted into it. Then he walked deliberately along it, as though not concerned with anything that was happening. He saw a few men running toward the alley, saw in the distance two policemen.

Westley chuckled a bit and walked on down the street, block after block. He had drawn the fire of the enemy and had escaped unscathed. But it had availed him nothing so far, he told himself. It was the aftermath upon which he depended.

He walked about for half an hour longer, and then went back to the lodging house and up the front stairs. Hogan was sitting in the office talking to a man and a woman. His eyes bulged when he saw Westley.

"Nice evenin', Hogan!" the man from Arizona said. "How's the toothache?"

Hogan glared at him, but did not answer. Westley went down the hall to his room and entered it. He remained there for some time, and now he smoked the cigar he had been chewing. He removed the exploded cartridge from his six-gun, cleaned the gun, inserted a fresh cartridge, and put the gun back into his holster.

Then he snapped out the light and crept to the door once more. He opened it softly, slipped out, closed the door behind him, and started toward the rear stairs.

The excitement in the alley had died down. The police had made a short investigation and had reached the decision that some gangsters had engaged in a row without casualties.

Westley went down the rickety stairs quietly and stopped just at the door. He did not want to walk into a trap now. He heard somebody descending after him, and darted quickly to one side to crouch in the darkness. He heard somebody hurrying up the alley, too.

It was Hogan who came down the stairs. He met the other man in the doorway.

"Hogan!"

"Lefty, you fool!" Hogan whispered. "So you didn't get him!"

"He dodged us," Lefty Joe said. "We had boys planted all around the alley, too, and trailed him to it."

"You're a bunch of bungling fools!" Hogan declared. "Understand me, Lefty, I'm out of this from now on. This man Westley is no fool! If I was in the boots of a certain man, I'd be a little afraid."

"Something's got to be done!" Lefty Joe said.

"Then you and the boys go ahead and do it, but I don't want to know anything about it," Hogan declared.

"You turnin' against us?"

"No! I'll help you whenever I can. But I'll have no hand in this thing. I want you to understand that! I don't want anything pulled off near my place, either. Use your wits, if you have any! Now get away from here. I'm goin' across the alley."

"I'll go with you and play pool," Lefty Joe said. "That'll look best."

They walked across the alley together, but Hogan entered the place first, and Lefty Joe waited for five minutes or so before following, while Westley crouched quietly in the darkness and waited, too.

A moment longer he waited, then he crossed the alley himself, opened the door, and walked into the back room.

CHAPTER VII

IN THE PRIVATE ROOM

THE place was crowded now. Groups of men were playing pool and billiards, others were gathered around the cigar counter, others were merely standing around and watching. But every group seemed eager in whispered conversation, and Westley did not doubt that he was the subject of it.

He walked quietly along the wall, and for a time his presence was not noticed. And then he was seen, and a swift change came over the place. Some men slipped away from his vicinity. Others refused to glance at him even. Loud talk took the place of the whispering.

Lefty Joe was playing pool at a table well down the room, and Hogan was standing near, watching, and talking to another man of the district. Westley continued along the wall until he reached the table at which Lefty Joe was playing. He saw down with his back to the wall, saying nothing, pretending to watch the game. His cigar was cocked at a jaunty angle.

Those in the resort could not understand the man or his attitude. He rendered them nervous. Had he threatened them, they would have understood. But he only smoked and watched.

Hogan walked slowly along the wall and approached him. Lefty Joe came nearer as he played his game. Westley glanced up and saw Hogan, and smiled.

"Toothache better?" he wanted to know.

"Yes."

"Scared out of yeh?"

"I don't know what would scare it out of me," Hogan said.

"Thought maybe the shootin' did," said Westley. "Had a little excitement in the alley an hour or so ago."

"Yes?" Hogan asked.

"Mighty poor shootin', if you ask me," Westley said. "Just fool blazin' away! Them boys can't shoot!"

Lefty Joe's face flushed, and some of the other men near growled down in their throats.

"It must have been poor shootin' if there was nobody hurt," Hogan said.

"It didn't worry me any," Westley declared. "If they were shootin' at me, they didn't come very near. And I could have potted a couple of them as easy as not, if I'd wanted to."

"Think you can shoot, do you?" Lefty Joe asked sneeringly. "Shoot off your mouth!"

"Huh!" Westley grunted. "What you firin' up about? I thought you was a friend of mine, Joe. You don't mean to say it was you doin' that shootin', do yeh?"

Lefty Joe realized that he had made a mistake. Westley puffed at his cigar and grinned, as Lefty Joe ignored him.

"Ever play poker any more?" Westley persisted. "I'm ready to give you revenge any time."

He saw the sudden gleam in Joe's eyes, and he knew what Joe was thinking. It might be possible, if they could get Westley into another poker game, to shoot him in cold blood, then fire a shot out of the revolver they knew Westley carried, and say that there was a quarrel over cards, and that they had fired in self-defense.

There was danger in such a course. There would be an investigation, and possibly some of their number would have to go to jail for a time, and even stand trial. But there was another chance, too — the chance of knifing Westley in a private room and later taking his body some distance away, so as to please Hogan.

Westley knew that these gangsters never carried their guns except when they intended to use them. It did not do for them to be caught by the police with such weapons in their possession. Westley judged that they would try to knife him, if they got the chance. And he was offering them the chance.

He saw Lefty Joe glance at Hogan, and he saw the answering look that Hogan gave him.

"Got to be careful about this poker stuff," Hogan said. "I don't want the place raided. But if you want to play, Joe, you go to one of the rooms with Westley, and I'll round up three more of the boys. Anybody you want in particular?"

"I don't care," Joe said. There was no need to mention names, Hogan knew the men Joe wanted.

"Westley will probably clean all of you again," Hogan said, attempting a laugh. "He must be a bear at poker."

"Why not get in the game yourself?" Westley asked.

"I've got some business to tend to," Hogan replied. "I may drop in later."

Lefty Joe put his cue in the rack. "Come on!" he said to Westley; and he led the way toward the rear of the establishment.

They went to one of the private rooms, and Lefty Joe snapped on the lights. Westley gave the place one quick glance. There was only one door and one window, and it was high in the wall. He did not think there was a chance of a shot through the window. They would not shoot if it could be avoided. They would use the silent knife, and then get the body away.

In the center of the room was a table, and there were half a dozen old chairs scattered around. Westley walked around the table and sat down in one of the chairs, leaning it back against the wall. Joe seemed to be nervous. He left the door partly open and stood in it, waiting.

"Same boys?" Westley wanted to know.

"I suppose so," Lefty Joe said.

"Hope you put up a better game than you did the last time. It ain't fun takin' money from infants."

"You were lucky the last time."

"Uh-huh! And I aim to be lucky tonight," Westley said, with double meaning. "Who do you suppose tried to shoot me?"

"I don't know," Joe replied. "You've been shoutin' around that you knew your brother's murderer and was going to get him, so I suppose some of his friends tried to get you first."

"It's likely," Westley admitted. "The boys comin' yet?"

"Yes!" Joe snapped.

He stepped back into the room and sat down near the table. The door was opened wider, and three men came in. Westley glanced at them quickly. Two of them had been in the other game, but the third was a stranger. Westley wondered a bit about him. Was he the man most concerned, or was he merely a professional murderer appointed to do the work?

Westley pretended to be lighting a fresh cigar, while they arranged the chairs and got out chips and cards. They were maintaining a meaningless conversation, such as generally is maintained by men under a nervous strain, but it did not fool the man from Arizona. He watched them coldly.

"Shut the door!" Lefty Joe commanded.

One of the men got up and obeyed, and Westley noticed that he locked the door, too. Then Westley got out of his chair and pulled it forward to the table, as the others sat down. He had decided on a bold move, and he knew just how dangerous it would be.

He remained standing behind his chair, and now he was looking them over coldly, his eyes narrowed, his body tense.

"Sit down!" Lefty Joe ordered.

"There's no hurry," Westley replied. "I've got somethin' to say first."

"Want to make a rule about dealin' crooked?" Joe sneered.

"This hasn't anything to do with poker," said Westley. He cocked the cigar to one corner of his mouth, and suddenly his right hand made a lightning-like movement, and they saw that it held a revolver.

"Sit quiet!" Westley commanded. "Nobody's goin' to be hurt —

just yet. It's just to keep you from gettin' reckless and forgettin' to keep your minds on what I'm goin' to say."

"What fool stunt is this?" Joe asked, some nervousness in his manner.

"I'll tell you quick enough. Everybody around here knows who I am, and why I'm here. We'll let it go at that. There was an attempt made to get me tonight, and it didn't work. I'm not sayin' that any of you boys were concerned in it, and I ain't sayin' that you weren't."

"You're crazy!" Lefty Joe gasped.

"Nope! Now you boys listen to me. I want to know the name of the man who killed my brother. Maybe some of you know it, and maybe all of you do. One man I know does — and he's Lefty Joe!"

"Why —" Joe began.

"Don't lie about it, Joe," Westley said, watching him carefully. "You know — and I know that you know! And you're goin' to tell me right here and now! You boys put your hands on the table and sit quiet. I'm goin' to plug the first man who makes a move. Ready to talk, Joe?"

"You're a crazy fool!" Lefty Joe cried. "Think you can pull off a fool stunt like this, do you? I don't know anything about it!"

"Don't lie to me!" Westley interrupted. "I was within six feet of you when you were talkin' to Hogan by his back door. I followed you over here. I heard everything that you said. You know who killed my brother, and you're goin' to tell me now — and tell the truth!"

"You —"

"I'm doin' the talkin' now! You were in the gang that tried to pot me tonight, Joe! You thought you had me when I suggested a card game. Well, you've got me in here! You'd like to slip a knife between my ribs, and then toss my body some place half a mile away, wouldn't you? You thought you had me when you got me in here — whereas, I've got you!

"Why, you poor fools! I suspect I'm the only man in this room who's carryin' a gun. You are too afraid of bein' caught with a gun on you. And if anybody has a gun and wants to pull it, let him! I can bring down a man with every shot, and I've got six shots, and there are only four of you! And I'm goin' to shoot merry blazes out of this gang if you don't talk! I'm an officer of the law, you know. And I can say I shot in self-defense, if it's necessary. Nobody would kick much if I cleaned out the entire gang!"

"I — I don't know anything," Lefty Joe repeated, licking at his lips.

"Forgotten, have yeh? Then you'd better remember right sudden, boy! The door's locked, remember. I can lay out all of you and reload my gun before anybody can break it in!"

"I don't know anything —" Joe stammered.

"Enough of your lies and nonsense! You other fellers keep your hands flat on the table, or I'll show you some fancy shootin'! Now, Lefty Joe, you talk!"

Westley stepped a short distance around the table and shoved the muzzle of his revolver straight at Joe's breast. The others did not make a move. There was a moment of silence, save for the heavy breathing of the men sitting around the table.

Then there came a knock at the door. Somebody gave a sigh of relief.

"I'm goin' to put my revolver back in the holster," Westley said, "and stand right here at the end of the table. The gent who has the key will unlock that door and see who's there and what is wanted. And at the first funny move, I start shootin'. Unlock the door."

One of the men got up and stumbled across the room. Westley was watching all of them carefully. His revolver was back in the holster, but his right hand nestled under the left side of his coat, and they knew he could draw swiftly.

The door was opened. Millie Hogan darted into the room, shut the door behind her, and stood with her back against it. All looked at her with surprise. Her hair was hanging down at the side of her head. There was a bruise upon her lips, a cut on one cheek. Her eyes were wild, as though she was on the verge of hysterics.

"I — I'm going to tell!" she stammered.

"Get out of here!" It was Lefty Joe who ordered her. "We're playin' cards and —"

"Easy, Joe!" Westley warned. "All you fellers keep quiet now! The lady's got somethin' to say, and she's goin' to say it! And if anybody makes a move to stop her —"

"Playing cards!" the girl gasped. "I know the game you're playing. And I'm going to take a hand in it!"

"You —" Lefty Joe began. His face was livid, Westley noticed.

"Keep quiet!" the man from Arizona commanded. He whipped out his revolver again, and the sight of it seemed to quiet Lefty Joe more than words.

"Mr. Westley!" the girl cried. "You don't know what they did to me! When — when I warned you in your room tonight they heard me. They caught me when I went into the hall. I've stood a lot, but I won't stand being beaten like a dog!"

"What's that?" Westley cried.

"Hogan, and Lefty Joe! They beat me with their fists because I had warned you! I won't stand it any more. You want to know who killed your brother, do you?"

"Millie!" Joe shrieked. "You're crazy! You don't know what you're sayin'!"

But the girl did not even glance at him now. She stepped into the room, panting, weeping, looking to Westley as though for protection.

"Who killed my brother?" Westley asked excitedly.

The girl hesitated for a moment, then new strength seemed to come to her. She did not speak in reply. But she raised one arm and pointed a forefinger straight at Lefty Joe!

"Lefty Joe!" Westley cried. There was a menace in his voice.

"It's a lie!" Joe cried. "She's lyin'! Don't you believe her! She's mad because Hogan wants her to marry me."

Millie Hogan staggered back against the door again. The men in the room were silent. Tom Westley, revolver in hand, stepped forward slowly, his eyes blazing, his jaws rigid, the light of a killer in his face.

"You shot my brother, John!" he accused.

"It's a lie! I didn't!"

"Miss Hogan, please leave the room," Westley said in the same tense voice. "Just wait for me out in the street, please."

She gasped and darted out of the door, slamming it behind her. Tom Westley did not take his eyes from the man before him, save for a quick glance at the others now and then.

"You killed my brother, curse you!"

"No — no!"

"And I'm goin' to shoot you to death a bit at a time!" Westley went on. "I come from a country where men can shoot! Lefty Joe, I can shoot you a dozen times, and yet you'll be alive."

"I — I didn't do it!"

"It's in your face!" Westley declared. "Get ready to suffer, Joe! And you'd better pray that you die quick!"

Westley's revolver exploded. He had not raised it to aim, but the bullet nicked Lefty Joe's left ear.

"The next one will tear through your cheek!" Westley said.

"I — I ain't got a gun!" Joe wailed, "Give me a chance — you coward!"

"Did my brother have a chance?"

"I haven't said that I killed him!"

"But you did, didn't you? If you was man enough to admit it, I might give you a chance. I might shoot it out with you. But you're a liar —"

"All right!" Sudden courage had come to Lefty Joe, the courage of despair. "All right — I killed him!"

"Ah!" Westley cried. "You confess it, do you? That's what I was playin' for, Joe! I wanted to hear that confession. Oh, I ain't goin' to shoot you now! But you're goin' to the electric chair. Day after day you'll sit in your cell and wait, knowin' that you can't fight, can't help yourself! That's what you've got comin' to you, Joe!"

The crucial moment had arrived. The momentary paralysis the gangsters had suffered was at an end. A chair overturned, a man sprang.

Westley's gun roared. All the men were upon their feet. Knives flashed. Lefty Joe cried for help and gave the call of his gang.

Tom Westley sprang back against the wall. He fired again, and a man dropped. He hurled a chair at them as they charged. Outside, he heard cries and pounding feet. The door burst open, and more men charged into the room, Hogan at their head. Hogan had a weapon in his hand.

"Get him!" Lefty Joe was crying, "He started shootin' —"

Westley dodged a thrown knife and fired two more shots. Then they were upon him. Hogan had fallen, he saw, but another man had grasped the weapon Hogan had held. Back in a corner, Westley battled, fearing that they would get him after his revolver was empty. Lefty Joe was behind some of the others. If he saw disaster coming, Westley wanted to save one shot for Lefty Joe!

More men were running from the front room. Westley fired again, whirled away, grasped another chair and hurled it at his foes. Then there was a sudden jumble of men in the room, men who took a part in the fighting, but did not fight against Westley.

He saw the flash of brass buttons. He saw a face he seemed to remember as having seen at police headquarters.

Once more he was in a corner, and they were bearing down upon him. His revolver was wrenched from his grasp. With his bare fists he fought against their knives.

It was the end, he thought, but he had done something toward avenging his dead brother. He knocked one knife aside and saw another descending. But between it and his breast was interposed the body of another man. The knife went home. Westley dropped to the floor, the other man, wounded, atop of him.

A few more shots, curses and shrieks, and then sudden quiet. Westley, surprised that he was not badly injured, rolled the man off him and sat up against the wall. Lefty Joe and the others were wearing manacles. Hogan and others were stretched on the floor, some still, some groaning.

Westley seemed to be dazed for a minute. He turned and looked at the man who had saved his life. It was Officer G. William Waltern!

"You —" Westley gasped.

"Glad to be — of service," Waltern stammered. "I'm not hurt — bad. Clean cut — in the breast!"

"Why, boy, I —"

"Everything's all right," Waltern said. "You've been working alone, but you've been watched and guarded. The chief saw to that. You've done it, Westley — got your man!"

"I — they almost had me."

"Not a chance!" Waltern said. "I was watching. I heard Joe's confession, and so did another man. We were — just outside that window. I whistled for help — and came in. Glad — to be of service."

"Boy, I — I misjudged you —"

"It's all right, sheriff. But — about that deputy's job —"

"You get it!" Westley cried. "Keep quiet now until we can get you to a doctor!"

He staggered to his feet. One of the detectives hurried to him.

"Not hurt?" he asked.

"Only a few bruises," Westley said.

"Hogan's dead, and another man. Good work! Lefty Joe's a safe prisoner! He's whimpering now like the coward he is! One of the men has gone to phone for the wagon."

"Waltern is knifed," Westley said.

"There'll be a surgeon here with the wagon. Waltern's a great kid. Took a fancy to you after you messed up headquarters that day. Talks about you all the time. Changing, too. He didn't even have a fresh shine on his boots this morning."

"Um!" Tom Westley grunted.

"Hogan was a bad egg — glad he's gone," the detective went on. "Sorry for that niece of his, though. Hogan didn't own anything — just ran this place for another man."

"She'll find friends enough!" Sheriff Tom Westley exclaimed "I'm goin' to take that girl to Arizona and give her the chance she wants. And I'm goin' to take Waltern, too — Officer G. William Waltern — and I'm goin' to make him Deputy Sheriff Bill Waltern."

THE OBVIOUS CLUE

CHAPTER I

THE PIPER CALLS

STOPPING abruptly, as he caught sight of the policeman on the corner ahead, Calderton sucked in his breath. Fear smote him, and his heart hammered at his ribs.

In the next instant he realized what he had done and almost laughed aloud. Why should George Calderton, well-known young man about town, feel fear of a policeman who probably did not know him either by sight or name, when a few hours before he would have faced the entire police force with no emotion whatever?

Calderton knew the answer, of course. But he forced himself to be calm, and stepped forward briskly, even going as far as to hum the air of a popular song under his breath. As he passed the policeman he looked at him frankly, and the policeman smiled. So much for that!

It was almost eight o'clock in the evening. Calderton was in a district where wealthy men had their homes, where the big houses sat far back from the street, and the spacious lawns were landscaped with trees and shrubs.

Calderton was due at the residence of Garland Moberg at eight. That was the hour which Moberg's secretary had telephoned, and when Moberg said eight o'clock, he did not mean fifteen minutes after. When he reached there and was admitted to the familiar library — then would come the crucial moment.

"Maybe he doesn't know," Calderton said to himself. "Maybe it is something else."

But he was feeling genuine fear for the first time in his life. He was fashionably dressed, had money in his pocket, and a position in society. Yet the bare thought that he had been found out had been enough to make him forget himself.

"I'm acting like a low crook, a thug!" Calderton told himself. "I'm George Calderton, and that makes a difference. Maybe he hasn't found out — maybe it is something else — something confidential he wishes me to undertake."

He came to the corner nearest the Moberg residence, and unconsciously he slackened his pace. He could not explain to himself why he had walked rather than take a taxi from the club where he had lived. It was not a particularly fine night for walking, and there was not even a moon. Once more he licked at his dry lips, and once more he realized that he was acting like a man afraid.

"Never do in the world!" he muttered to himself. "I've got to carry this thing through in the proper spirit. Suppose he has found out? He'll only give me a lecture and make me pay the money back. It isn't as though I were some unknown, penniless clerk. I am George Calderton!"

As he walked up the street and turned in at the gate before the Moberg residence, he fought to get control of himself, and he hummed the song again and tried to walk in his usual manner, that of a man who enjoyed life and did not have a care in the world.

He hurried up to the steps, went up on the veranda, and touched the bell button. Renkin, Moberg's old butler, answered the ring. Calderton glanced at him shrewdly, but Renkin showed nothing in his manner to lead a man to believe that anything was wrong.

"Mr. Moberg expects you, sir," Renkin said.

"I trust Mr. Moberg is in his usual good health, Renkin?"

Renkin lifted his eyebrows slightly and made reply. He was the perfect servant, but Mr. George Calderton was almost like one of the family, and that made quite a difference.

"I am afraid that he is in a fearful temper, sir," Renkin said in a very soft voice. "He had quite an argument with Miss Margaret, sir, and sent her out to the country place."

"Um!" Calderton felt his anxiety was growing.

"You are to go right to the library, sir," the butler continued.

Calderton walked down the long hall toward the door of the library. He braced himself for trouble. Mr. Moberg's temper, which was a well-known quantity to his associates, might have been directed solely at his fair daughter, Margaret, because of some infraction of household rules such as the magnate always was making. Possibly Calderton was not concerned in it at all. He certainly hoped not!

Yet he hesitated before the library door, and he realized once more that he was afraid. He tried to tell himself that he was man enough to face the situation, even if the worst came to pass. He forced the usual smile to his face and knocked.

"Come in!" Moberg's voice was not reassuring.

Calderton recognized that Moberg still was in his fit of temper. Yet he opened the door instantly and stepped into the library, carefully closing the door after him. Renkin was an old and perfect servant, but even old and perfect servants can be curious at times.

"You sent for me, sir," Calderton said. "The appointment was for eight, I believe."

"Yes, and you are on time!" Moberg returned grudgingly. "Whatever else I may say of you, I'll always admit you are a stickler for punctuality. Sit down!"

Moberg indicated a chair at the end of the library table, and Calderton crossed the room slowly and sat down. He glanced furtively at Moberg as he moved across the room. There could be no denial of the fact that Garland Moberg was in an awful rage. But Calderton hoped that he was not the cause of it.

"Punctual!" Moberg grunted. "George, your father was an associate of mine, and I loved him. Because of a foolish investment he died poor. Then I decided to take you into my office, give you a chance to do what your father had failed to do — make a fortune."

"Yes, sir," Calderton said.

"I told you several things that day when you entered my office — things I demanded. One of them was punctuality. You have remembered that — and have forgotten all the others!"

"Sir?" Calderton exclaimed in simulated surprise.

"You are a thief!" Moberg said. He did not thunder the sentence, rather he spoke it in a low tone, as though it was something that he could not understand.

"Sir!" George Calderton repeated.

"Oh don't be an ass!" Moberg continued. "Don't try that indignation stuff on me! I was judging men before you were born. You've been found out!"

Calderton hung his head and clasped and unclasped his hands nervously, ashamed to look at his employer and his father's friend.

"What in the name of Heaven is the matter with the present generation?" asked Moberg thunderingly. "Have all of you gone insane? You, my old friend's boy, betray the trust I put in you. My daughter defies me. And Morgan Snade —"

He ceased speaking, as if his anger choked him. He got up and took a turn around the room and sat down again.

"Well, George, what have you to say for yourself?" he demanded. "There can be no question. You have been under suspicion for some time. Your books have been examined. You have been stealing systematically for more than a year. You did it cleverly, but you have been found out. A thief always is found out sooner or later. He cannot escape forever. The law of retribution doesn't work that way."

The young man made no reply. He sighed deeply once, and then he looked across the library toward the French windows that opened to the veranda. One of them was open a few inches, and the soft breeze was fluttering the curtains. Calderton wondered that he could notice such a trivial thing at such a time.

"You have stolen more than nine thousand dollars!" Moberg said, and his voice grew even sterner. "What have you to say for yourself?"

"I — I am sorry, sir."

"Sorry! The criminal is always sorry when he is found out, when he faces punishment for his crime. And it is not alone the money, George. There remains the fact that you have betrayed my trust in you. Where would you be today, but for me? Working in some firm's shipping room, possibly. But, for your dead father's sake, I gave you every chance. I paid you more than you were worth, I prepared to give you a chance, a little later, to stand on your own feet. I even looked with delight upon the growing friendship between you and my daughter. I even hoped that you would marry Margaret and be my son.

"And you have thrown all this aside by being a thief. Why did you, George?"

"A — a man can't live on air — not the way I live."

"I grant you that it was necessary and right for you to live like a gentleman. You had the right to have decent quarters, to dress properly, to have your clubs, to take your place at social affairs, despite the fact that your father had lost all his money."

"And I couldn't do it, sir, on my salary," Calderton said. "I began taking small amounts, and they grew larger. I — I am sorry, sir. I'll try to do better — to make amends in some way."

"I know of nothing you can do that will wipe from my mind the knowledge that you are a thief," Moberg said. "And you have added to your infamy now by being a liar as well!"

"Sir!" Calderton exclaimed.

"Had you stolen to maintain the position of a gentleman, I might be inclined to try to save you," Moberg declared. "But you did nothing of the sort. I have ascertained that you could have maintained your position properly on your salary. It would have paid all legitimate bills and left a few dollars over. I say legitimate bills."

"What do you mean, sir?"

"I mean that you spent money recklessly — stolen money. You are a gambler. You have posed, not as a gentleman, but as a cheap sport! You have tried to make men believe that you have a fortune. You wasted money on unworthy companions. You stole for vicious reasons."

"Are you sure of that, sir?" Calderton asked. "It would not surprise me to learn that an enemy of mine has been getting misinformation around to you. I wouldn't put it past Morgan Snade, for instance. He thinks, with me out of the way, that he would have a chance with Margaret —"

"That's enough!" Moberg replied, "I am receiving revelations this evening regarding your character. Now you would attempt to blacken Snade, whose only fault is that he looks higher than he should; at least, he is honest. I have not been listening to stories about you or any other man. My time is entirely too valuable for that. What I have told you are facts that have been given to me by two different private-detective agencies."

"Those fellows are the greatest liars on earth!" Calderton said.

"They gave you those reports because they supposed that was the sort you wanted."

"Pardon me, but they knew distinctly I would be gratified to find myself wrong," Moberg declared. "I almost begged them to show me that there was some mistake, that you were the right sort of man. And the investigation has been going on for more than two months. You have been watched during that time. I discovered two months ago that you were a thief. I made sure of my facts before I called you before me."

"Perhaps I can explain —"

"You cannot explain the money you have wasted over the gambling table."

"I was mad, sir — I gambled in an effort to win and pay back what I had taken."

"What you had stolen, you mean. Do not come to me with that old story and explanation. Did you expect to get the money to pay me back by giving a dinner for cheap sports? Don't lie again, George. Try to be a man in part, at least."

"I — I do not know what made me do it," Calderton said. "After I started, it was easy to keep on stealing. But I'll straighten up. I'll work hard and pay you back."

"I hope you do straighten up, George, for your dead father's sake. This has been a terrible blow to me. I did not want Margaret to know — and so I sent her out to the country place for a few days. I did not want her to share your disgrace. I do not know how far things have gone between you —"

"There is no understanding, sir. I was waiting until my financial condition was better."

"I am glad of that. It is the first thing that has pleased me today. She will not be heartbroken, then."

"Is it necessary for her to know at all, sir — for anybody to know? I'll straighten up, pay you back — —"

"Do you think things can be as they have been?" Moberg interrupted. "Certainly not! Do you think I'd overlook this, let you marry my daughter — a thief marry a Moberg?"

"But —"

"Can't you understand that you must be punished for this? I do not intend to compound a felony."

"You — you mean that you are going to prosecute me?" Calderton asked.

"That is for the district attorney to do. I merely make the complaint."

"Don't do that, sir! Give me a chance!"

"No! You're vicious — bad, and you must be punished. Theft is never pardonable, to my way of thinking, and certainly theft for an unworthy purpose is not."

"You'd send me to prison?" Calderton demanded.

"You have sent yourself there, if you go. I have had nothing to do with it. I gave you every chance in the world, and you threw everything aside for a riot of what you call fun. You have danced — the piper remains to be paid!"

Calderton began to beg. Moberg turned from him in disgust.

"Don't be a coward, too," Moberg said. "Take your medicine like a man. Pay the bill! Now get out! I'll give you twenty-four hours to put your affairs in order. But do not try to leave the city. You are to be watched, commencing with tomorrow morning. If you run away tonight, I'll have them catch you, if it takes years, and I'll punish you the more because of your cowardice! Twenty-four hours to get ready, Calderton! The bail will be heavy, and you'll never be able to raise it. Your freedom will end with your arrest. So take one day to part with your friends, have one last good time, if that is your idea. Get out!"

"If you will listen —"

"No!"

George Calderton knew that further argument would be futile. He knew Moberg well, and he realized that there would be no change of heart. He was doomed! As Moberg had said, he had danced, and the piper remained to be paid.

He got up, straightened his shoulders, sighed, and looked once more at his employer. Moberg was not even looking at him now — he was staring across the room.

"At least, I'll show you that I can take my medicine like a man," Calderton said. "If you wish to send to prison your old friend's son —"

"Ah!" Moberg exclaimed. "So you have to make that last whine, do you? You cannot stand on your own feet. You play on my friendship for your dead father!"

"Pardon me, sir, but I play on nothing," Calderton said. "I can take my medicine — and I can remember you when I come out."

"Threats now, eh?"

"Call it what you like," said Calderton. "I can go down laughing, at least!"

In a spirit of bravado Calderton stalked across the room and opened the hall door. He turned and smiled peculiarly at the older man, who still sat beside the table. He bowed ironically, and the white left his face, and the red flooded it.

"Good evening, Mr. Moberg!" he said. "I hope that you get a good night's rest!"

That moment of bravado almost sent an innocent man to the electric chair.

CHAPTER II

NOBODY KNOWS

WITH that smile still upon his face, as though it had been frozen there, Calderton stepped briskly along the hall and came face to face with old Renkin. The butler glanced at him questioningly.

"He's all right," Calderton said. "Just a bit huffy at something that has happened."

"I hate to see him excited, sir," said the butler. "His heart isn't any too good, I am afraid, sir."

"Bosh! I don't believe that he has a heart!" Calderton replied, with a nervous laugh. He did not know why he acted in this manner, unless it was to make everything appear ordinary — to prevent an inkling that there was trouble.

Calderton went on toward the front to get his hat and coat, and the old butler kept at his heels. In a little reception room near the front door another man was waiting. Calderton saw, with surprise, that he was Morgan Snade.

Snade was a young man of promise who had come up from nothing and was rapidly making a name for himself in the financial district and in Moberg's employ. Calderton always had hated him, because he recognized Snade's superiority as a man of business, realized his cleverness and ability. He had presumed to make an attempt to patronize Snade, to look down upon him because of his humble birth. Snade had about as much money as Calderton, but he had not had a distinguished father, did not have the entrée to exclusive clubs, and was a mere beginner in the social game.

And then Morgan Snade had met Margaret Moberg and fallen in love with her. Nor was he to be easily thrust aside. Even Margaret resented Calderton's slurring remarks about Snade. She seemed to think that he was honest, sincere, hard-working, and possessed of those qualities for which men of fashion seldom take the trouble to look.

Accordingly, Snade and Calderton were always at swords' points, though Calderton tried to tell himself that it was ridiculous to think of Snade as a suitor for Margaret Moberg's hand. As they met face to face in Moberg's home, each wondered what had brought the other there. There was quick suspicion between them.

Snade was in the act of lighting a cigarette. He put his gold cigarette case down upon the table at his elbow as Calderton stopped to get his hat and coat, crumpled the cigarette in his fingers, and bowed courteously, but frigidly.

"Evening!" Calderton remarked with bad grace.

Old Renkin feared a scene, and he detested scenes. "Mr. Moberg will see you now, Mr. Snade," he said. "Just step into the library, please."

Snade glared at Calderton and brushed past him to go down the hall. He had forgotten the cigarette case. Calderton sneered at his back and allowed old Renkin to help him on with his coat. Then Renkin turned to get the hat.

Calderton found the cigarette case at the tips of his fingers. He picked it up quickly and slipped it into his overcoat pocket. Then Renkin let him out.

Why he had taken that cigarette case Calderton could not tell himself. It was as if his mind and muscles were being guided by somebody other than himself. His brain was in a turmoil. He was making an attempt to appear natural, and all the time he was thinking that he had but twenty-four hours, that, at the end of that time, he would be behind bars. Moberg had spoken truly — he would be unable to give bail. He would have to remain in jail until his trial, then go to prison to serve his term.

He shivered as he walked down the steps and started toward the distant street. Prison seemed near to him then. He knew nothing of prisons, but he had a horror of them. It was the fear of incarceration that bothered him more than the disgrace. How did a man in prison bear up under the dull routine? Did he cease to be a man, and turn into a mere human machine?

His thoughts changed. What was Snade doing at the Moberg house? Had his visit been at Moberg's command? Did it have something to do with Calderton's affairs?

Calderton remembered the open window on the veranda. He circled across the dark lawn and made for it. A thousand intangible ideas seemed to be galloping through his brain. He was not Calderton now — he was a man over whom a prison sentence was hanging.

At the end of the veranda he was glad to find that it was dark. He drew on his gloves and then crept over the railing carefully, so as to make no noise. Along the wall of the house he slipped until he came to the open French window.

There, he found, he could remain in the darkness and yet see into the room. He could hear well, too. Morgan Snade was just seating himself in the chair at the end of the table, the one in which Calderton had been sitting when he had heard his doom.

It was evident from Snade's actions that he had been summoned to the house, but he did not seem to be at all nervous about it. Moberg often called his clerks there to given them confidential orders or to ask them to carry out confidential missions.

"I was on time, Mr. Moberg, but I was kept waiting," Snade said.

"You had another visitor."

"That's all right!" Moberg replied. He still was angry and unable to conceal his anger, or else he did not care to do so.

Snade was waiting for his employer to speak. He picked up a heavy, sharp paper knife from the table and toyed with it while he waited. Moberg suddenly bent forward and, though he spoke in a moderate tone, Calderton, out on the veranda, could hear every word that was said.

"Snade, possibly you may not like what I am going to say to you," the financier began, "but you've got to hear it, whether you like it or not. You're a good man in the office. I've been watching you for some time. You work hard, you have a natural ability, and there is no reason so far as I know, why you should not succeed."

"Thank you, sir," Snade said.

"I'm having quite a time today. I'm straightening out a few little affairs that I find need straightening. I'm making a clean sweep. I've dealt with a few persons already — and you are the next and the last!"

"I hope that I have done nothing to merit rebuke, sir," Snade said, a note of alarm in his voice.

"Not a thing — in the office," Moberg said. "I am glad, Snade, to pick up a worthy young man of no family or position, let him enter my employ, and prove that I am a good judge of men, and that a man can succeed by his own merits alone. If he makes good, I'm very much pleased. But, whereas I am willing to take a man in that manner into my office, I might not be willing to take him into my family."

"Sir?" Snade visibly paled.

Moberg bent across the table again. "I don't mix business and family affairs," he said. "I'll be glad to have you continue with the firm, and I hope you'll win a managership some day, with all that implies, but I want you to discontinue your attempts to interest my daughter!"

Snade's face went livid, and he seemed about to choke. He gripped the sharp paper knife until his fingers bled.

"Pardon me, sir," Snade said, restraining himself with difficulty, "but I am sincerely interested in your daughter. I do not mind confessing to her father that I love her deeply, that I'd be the happiest man in the world if I could win her for my wife. Surely, sir, you did not think that I was trying to arouse your daughter's interest merely to use her for getting into society?"

"No, sir!" Moberg fairly thundered. "I give you credit for your sincerity, young man. I realize that you love her and want to marry her. That is why I have sent for you to come here tonight. I sent her away this afternoon, and things are going to be settled before she returns. Understand, Snade, now and forever — you are to stop seeing my daughter!"

"You mean —"

"I mean that she is not to marry a nobody!"

"You are insulting!" Snade sprang to his feet.

"Possibly. I'm talking straight and hard, as I always do. I want you to understand this thing."

"You mean that I am not worthy of her? My folks were poor, but they were honest —"

"Never mind that talk!" Moberg said. "No argument, now! I have decided, and I'm boss in this! Go ahead at the office if you wish, but stay away from Margaret! As an employee you're all right, but not as a son-in-law. Matter of fact, you'd never win her. But I don't intend to let you try. I don't want it said all over town that I'm letting a clerk try to marry my girl and get his fingers into the business!"

Calderton, on the veranda, started at Moberg's words and the tone he used. Moberg was more insulting than usual. Calderton supposed it was because of the series of events that had troubled him during the day, his own affairs among them.

Morgan Snade had sprung to his feet, unconscious of the sharp knife that was still cutting into his fingers. In a towering rage he tossed the knife to the table and shook his fist in Moberg's face.

"Take your job!" he said. "I wouldn't work for you another day for half a million dollars! You're not human! You're an insulting brute! I'm more worthy to be your daughter's husband than you are to be her father."

"Snade!"

"I've had my say, and I'll take no more abuse from you. I don't care if you are Garland Moberg!"

Snade's outburst subsided, and a moment of quiet ensued. The two men glared at each other. Then Snade hurried out into the hall, slammed the door after him, and almost collided with old Renkin.

"My hat and coat! I want to get away from this accursed house!"

Like a maniac he grasped the hat and coat which Renkin offered, jerked open the front door, and hurried toward the street, where his taxicab was waiting.

On the veranda, in the darkness, Calderton grinned evilly. He had rather enjoyed the scene he had witnessed. Somebody besides himself was getting a tirade from Moberg. His rival was a rival no longer.

Then Calderton remembered that it would avail him nothing. Twenty-four hours he had, and then he would be in prison and in disgrace. The fat financier who sat in the chair a short distance from him would see to that.

Calderton guessed that the shortage was known only to Moberg. The books which he had doctored had been those that dealt with some of Moberg's private investments — not those of the firm. If

Moberg failed to act, nobody but Moberg could prove the shortage. Detectives might say that they had been watching Calderton at Moberg's orders, but that in itself would be nothing. There was scarcely a clerk in the office who was not watched at one time or another.

But there was no hope, Moberg had said that he would make the complaint, and undoubtedly the complaint would be made. Inside twenty-four hours Calderton, who liked and abused freedom, would be a jailbird. He had expected to marry Margaret Moberg and inherit through her the wealth Moberg would leave. He had anticipated a life of abundance, with money to gratify every whim. Now he was doomed to a life of ruin. If only Moberg would die tonight!

His heart almost stood still at the mere thought of it. All the evil impulses of his nature had surged to the foreground in his hour of peril. If Moberg should die he would not go to prison, and possibly he could marry Margaret by playing on her sympathies.

Through the window he could see that Moberg was sitting with his back to him, his head bent on his breast. The two scenes had almost exhausted him.

Then the diabolical plan surged into Calderton's brain. He told himself that some evil power must be guiding and guarding him. In his pocket he had Morgan Snade's cigarette case. On the table was the heavy, sharp paper knife, undoubtedly with Snade's fingerprints all over it. Snade had rushed from the room after hurling maledictions at old Garland Moberg!

Calderton was like a beast now. His eyes were burning, his face felt hot, his mouth was dry. He made sure that his gloves were on, and he felt in the pocket of his light overcoat to make certain that the cigarette case was there. Like a shadow he slipped still nearer to the window, reached out, and opened it wider. Moberg made not the slightest move. Like a cat he crept through the window onto the thick rug. If Moberg turned Calderton could say that he had returned to beg mercy.

But Moberg did not turn. Calderton reached the table and grasped the knife by the handle, careful not to soil his gloves with the stain that had come from Snade's fingers.

Another swift step he took. His left arm went around Moberg's neck, and his right hand drove the knife into Moberg's heart.

Panic seized him as the knife went home. He sprang backward and reached the window. He tossed Snade's cigarette case to the floor. Outside he darted, and there crouched in the darkness for a moment.

Moberg had slumped forward in the chair, and he had ceased breathing. The deed was done! Moberg could not have Calderton arrested now. And, if the detectives who had been watching him made a move, Calderton could say that it was the usual espionage.

He hurried to the end of the veranda and dropped to the ground. He started across the lawn, keeping to the shadows until he reached the side street. Here the darkness of the giant trees cut off the light from the arc lamps.

As the first drops of rain hit his face, Calderton almost laughed aloud. Even the elements were working for him. If he had left footprints at the end of the veranda or on the soft places in the lawn, the storm would obliterate them.

CHAPTER III

PETER NOGGINS

"SEND Noggins!" said the chief of detectives.

Detective Peter Noggins asked for and obtained the services of a man from the fingerprint department, engaged a taxicab, and started for the residence of Garland Moberg.

When he came to the detective department three years before, Noggins had created a sensation on the day of his arrival. The sensation was not because he solved some deep mystery, but because he looked more like an overworked bookkeeper than a detective.

But Peter Noggins, for all of his quaint appearance and mild ways, had proved his worth. Now he was admitted to be the best man on the homicide squad.

"Garland Moberg — think of that!" the fingerprint man said.

"No use thinking of it," Peter Noggins said. "When we get there we'll find out all about it. If he's been murdered, it will be up to us to find the murderer. That's all there is to it."

Peter Noggins yawned and looked through a window at the wet streets. The rain had ceased, but everything was dripping.

"It's a bit cooler," Noggins observed.

"Say, do you realize who it is that's been shuffled off?" the fingerprint man wanted to know. "Garland Moberg! One of the richest men in town."

"What about it?" Noggins asked. "Probably easier to find the murderer of a rich man than of some poor devil nobody knows. Stop fussing about it. Wait until we get there."

The fingerprint man grunted and clasped closer to his breast the box he held. If you asked him, Peter Noggins wasn't human. He never got a bit excited. You couldn't impress the man. They called him "the common-sense detective."

That nickname had been given him a year or more before when he had solved a particularly puzzling murder case and had declared to the newspaper boys that there had been nothing to his work except the application of common sense to the knowledge he had acquired concerning the crime.

Noggins' method of work was canny, according to the other men in the department. He waited until all the fuss was over, and then he pointed out some little thing that nailed his man. The little clues that other men overlooked were the ones upon which Peter Noggins built his success and his reputation.

The taxicab reached the Moberg residence, and Noggins and the fingerprint man entered quickly. They found a doctor there and a man from the coroner's office and old Renkin, with a white face. Noggins looked at the doctor and the coroner's man and raised his eyebrows.

"Stabbed through the heart," the doctor reported. "Death was instantaneous. Nothing has been touched. A glance was enough to assure me that Mr. Moberg was beyond all help."

Noggins followed them to the door of the library, and the others stood in the hallway and allowed him to enter alone. Watching Peter Noggins at work was nothing to give a person a thrill. He approached the body, looked at it from a distance of four feet away, then glanced around the room. He noticed the open window and walked over to it. He leaned out and flashed his electric torch on the floor of the veranda, and came back into the room again.

Once more he looked at the body, once more he glanced around the big room. Then he took a glove from his pocket, put it upon his right hand, grasped the hilt of the knife, and withdrew it from the wound.

He grunted to the fingerprint man, and the fingerprint man understood. He approached the table, opened his box, and began working on the knife. Peter Noggins looked around the room again. On the floor, some six feet from the body, at the edge of the rug, was a gold cigarette case.

Noggins carefully picked up the cigarette case and carried it to the table. Engraved across the face of it was a name — Morgan Snade!

Then he went back to the hall entrance and explained that he wished to talk in the small reception room at the front, and that they would leave the fingerprint expert to do his work. The doctor, the coroner's man, and old Renkin followed him.

"What has been done?" Noggins asked.

"I sent the servants to their quarters, sir, called the doctor, and sent word to the country place, where Miss Margaret went this afternoon. This is terrible, sir!" Renkin replied. "I have been in his service for more than twenty years. He —"

"Softly!" Noggins instructed. "Let us get at this thing right. Who discovered the crime?"

"I did, sir," said Renkin, "Mr. Moberg had two visitors this evening. After the last visitor left he did not call for me, and that was unusual. He generally had me prepare medicine for him at a certain hour."

"Medicine?" Noggins asked.

"He had a bad heart," the doctor explained quickly.

"No question but what that knife caused death?" Noggins asked.

"None whatever," the doctor replied.

Noggins grunted again and motioned Renkin to be seated. The old butler sank into the nearest chair, and Noggins looked him over carefully.

"Now, we'll get at it," he said. "Go ahead with your tale."

"Why, I went to the library, sir, and knocked. There was no answer, and that surprised me. I opened the door and peered in, and I — I saw him, sir."

"Just as he is now?"

"Yes, sir," said Renkin. "I rushed inside, and I saw the knife in his breast, and that he was dead. I — I must have screamed, sir, for some of the servants came running from the rear of the house. Then I sent them back, telephoned the doctor, and sent word to the country place."

Noggins glanced at the doctor.

"I notified the coroner and the police," the physician said, in answer to that glance. "Nothing has been touched."

"As far as I am concerned, the body may be removed at any time," Noggins told the coroner's man. "But be careful that nothing else is disturbed. Now, butler —"

"Renkin, sir."

"Thank you. Now, Renkin, we'll go back a bit. You say that Mr. Moberg had two visitors this evening?"

"Yes, sir."

"Who were they?"

"The first was Mr. George Calderton, sir, and the second Mr. Morgan Snade."

"Who are they?"

"Both have positions in Mr. Moberg's office, sir. Mr. George Calderton is of an old family. I believe that his father and Mr. Moberg were great friends. His father died poor, and Mr. Moberg looked after Mr. Calderton."

"And this man Snade?"

"An employee of some sort at the office. I believe that Mr. Moberg thought a great deal of his ability."

"Mr. Calderton called first?"

"Yes, sir."

"Mr. Moberg was all right before he called?"

"Yes, sir," said Renkin. "But he had been in a temper, sir, all day. He went to the office at nine o'clock, but he returned about noon. Miss Margaret was here then, sir, and they had a scene about something. He ordered Miss Margaret to go to the country place, and she went by motor."

"Know what the trouble was about?"

"No, sir. If I may say so, sir — though it seems dreadful to say it now — Mr. Moberg was something of a tyrant in the house, and often rebuked Miss Margaret for breaking some little rule he had made, though he loved her deeply."

"Very well. What time did Mr. Calderton call?"

"At eight, sir," Renkin answered. "Mr. Moberg had told me that he was to call, and for me to show him to the library immediately. And Mr. Snade would call a little later, he said, and he gave me the same instructions regarding Mr. Snade."

"That's all he told you about it?"

"Yes, sir. When Mr. Calderton called, I admitted him myself. The second man is ill, and I had excused him for the evening. I directed Mr. Calderton to the library."

"Anything said?"

"Mr. Calderton asked after Mr. Moberg's health, and I remarked that he was having a fit of temper."

"Wasn't that rather an impertinent remark for a servant to make to an outsider?"

"Pardon me, sir, but Mr. Calderton is almost like one of the family — like a son. It is my impression, sir, that a marriage was intended between Mr. Calderton and Miss Margaret."

"All right! Go ahead with your story," said Noggins.

"Mr. Calderton remained about twenty minutes, I should judge, sir. Then he came out. I heard him wish Mr. Moberg a good night's rest, sir. In the meantime, Mr. Snade had called and was waiting. Mr. Calderton and Mr. Snade met at this doorway, sir. I — I was a bit afraid of a scene, and so I hurried to get Mr. Calderton's coat. But Mr. Snade hurried down the hall to the door of the library."

"Why were you afraid of a scene?"

Noggins asked.

"Mr. Calderton and Mr. Snade do not like each other, sir, I have observed. I believe, too, that Mr. Snade has been paying a great deal of attention to Miss Margaret, and Mr. Calderton did not like it."

"So Snade went to the library?"

"Yes, sir. And Mr. Calderton left the house."

"How did Calderton act?"

"Why, about as usual, sir. He seemed a bit huffy to find Mr. Snade calling, but he greeted him respectfully."

"He didn't seem excited, or anything like that?"

"No, sir."

"Renkin, you didn't accidentally happen to overhear any of the conversation between Mr. Moberg and Calderton, did you?"

"No, sir."

"Haven't any idea what Calderton was here about?"

"Not the slightest, sir. He often calls of an evening. But this was business, I am sure, sir. Mr. Moberg used to have one of his young men up here, now and then, in the evening, and outline special work he wished them to do, I believe."

"I understand. Get ahead with your story."

"As Mr. Calderton prepared to leave the house, sir, Mr. Snade went directly to the library, entered, and closed the door. I walked along the hall a few minutes later, and I heard high words, sir."

"From whom?"

"From both of them, sir. I hope that you will not think I'd eavesdrop on my employer, sir. They were talking so loudly that I could not help hearing."

"Talking about what?" Noggins snapped.

"I gathered, sir, that Mr. Moberg was telling Mr. Snade that he did not wish Mr. Snade to pay further attentions to Miss Margaret. He — he used some harsh language, sir. And then Mr. Snade grew angry. I heard him declare that he had been insulted, and that he would not work for Mr. Moberg any longer. And I heard him say distinctly, sir, that he would endure no more abuse, even from Garland Moberg!"

"He said that, eh?"

"He did, sir. And a moment later he came tearing into the hall, sir, slamming the door of the library behind him. He shouted for me to get him his hat and coat. 'I want to get away from this accursed house!' he exclaimed. He grasped his hat and coat, jerked the front door open himself, and hurried out to the curb, where a taxicab was waiting for him."

"Exactly! And he was in such a confounded hurry," said Detective Peter Noggins, "that he left his cigarette case behind! Where is the telephone?"

"There is one right here, sir," Renkin said.

A moment later Detective Peter Noggins was using it. He was telephoning headquarters to have George Calderton and Morgan Snade picked up as soon as possible and brought under police escort to the Moberg residence. Then he went to the library and held a whispered conversation with the fingerprint man.

CHAPTER IV

BEFORE PUTTING ON HIS GLOVES

THERE was no doubt that Calderton was a finished actor. Detective Peter Noggins watched him carefully from behind the portieres as Renkin told him of the tragedy. Calderton appeared to be horrified. He said just the right things, and he did not overdo his excitement or horror.

Then he was ushered into the reception room and told to wait a moment, that an officer wished to question him, and Noggins stepped out and consulted the detective who had picked Calderton up and conducted him to the house.

"Where did you find him?" Noggins asked.

"At his club. He was playing billiards with some of his friends. He expressed surprise, but came willingly enough."

"Act peculiar?"

"Not a bit," said the detective. "He seemed to be puzzled, but that was all."

"All right!" Peter Noggins said.

He went to the reception room and introduced himself to Calderton and sat down before him, while the other detective stood in the doorway. Renkin and the doctor were excluded from this interview.

"This is terrible!" Calderton was saying. "I do not seem to be able to realize it. Poor Mr. Moberg! He has been like a father to me. This will almost kill Margaret."

"Sudden death always is terrible," Noggins said softly. "I must ask you some questions, Mr. Calderton. In a case like this we try to get at the facts as quickly as possible."

"I understand," Calderton replied. "I'll gladly answer your questions, sir, if I can aid in bringing Mr. Moberg's murderer to justice. But I do not know that I can be of much help."

"You called here this evening?"

"At eight o'clock, sir."

"And remained?"

"About twenty or thirty minutes — not longer than half an hour. I saw Mr. Moberg in his library."

"Then you left?"

"Yes, sir, and returned to my club. It was there that the other officer found me."

"You went directly to the club?"

"Yes, sir."

"Taxicab?"

"No," said Calderton. "I walked from the club to the house and walked back after my interview with Mr. Moberg. I believe the doorman at the club could tell you what time I returned there, sir."

"I see. When you left Mr. Moberg he was all right?"

"Yes, sir. He — he was in a bit of a temper, if you'll pardon me for saying so."

"How do you mean?"

"He was angry when I came," said Calderton. "Something had displeased him. Renkin, the butler, whispered to me that his master was having a fit of temper."

"Angry at you?"

"I must confess," Calderton replied, "that he was displeased with me. But he must have been angry at something else, too. As soon as he had finished with me, I left, telling him I hoped he would get a good night's rest and be himself again. It was just a mild rebuke, sir, for which I am sorry now. It was the last word I spoke to him."

"Care to tell me why he was angry at you, and what he wanted with you here?" Noggins asked.

"I suppose it would be best, sir, though I hope you will keep it confidential if it has no bearing on the murder."

"You may be sure of that."

"Very well," said Calderton. "I — I am like a lot of other young men, I suppose — want some fun now and then. My father and Mr. Moberg were great friends, and Mr. Moberg has done everything for me. It was rather understood — though nothing had been settled — that I was to marry Miss Moberg."

"I understand."

"And I — I have been a bit wild, I suppose. I believe that Mr. Moberg had some private detective watching me. He called me here last evening and remonstrated with me. He had learned that I had been gambling at the club. He rebuked me for my conduct, and I promised to behave myself in the future."

"How did he take that?" Noggins asked.

"He seemed much pleased, sir," said Calderton.

"You parted in a friendly manner?"

"Absolutely, sir. I gave him my word to do better, and that pleased him. Yet something else was troubling him, sir. I could tell by the way he acted. He was trying not to show it. It was something that had nothing to do with me, I presume, and naturally I did not question him."

"Meet anybody as you were leaving?" Noggins asked.

"Mr. Morgan Snade was waiting to see Mr. Moberg. He went to the library as I left the house."

"Speak to him?"

"I believe I wished him good evening. We — we are not on very good terms, sir."

"How does that come?"

"We never did like each other, it seems," Calderton admitted. "And Mr. Snade has been bothering Miss Margaret with his attentions, I believe. He seemed to dislike me because I am more prominent socially, and, I suppose, because he thought Mr. Moberg wished to see me married to Margaret."

"Any idea what Snade was doing here?"

"No, sir. He works in the office. He might have been summoned on office business," Calderton replied.

"Very good," said Noggins. "You'll go to the room adjoining, please, and wait there for me. I expect to interview Mr. Snade. He has arrived, I think."

Calderton arose and bowed and stepped into the next room. Peter Noggins looked after him. Calderton had carried himself well, and he knew it. He did not make the mistake now of grinning or looking relieved. He seemed to be shocked by his employer's death.

Noggins ascertained that Snade had arrived, and had him ushered into the reception room. He spoke with the man who had brought Snade in.

"Where did you get him?"

"At his rooms, Noggins. He seemed to be a bit dazed — nervous as the deuce. He scarcely could talk — either angry or scared. And his waistcoat and the bottom of his dress shirt are soiled with crimson stains."

"Um — thanks!" Noggins hurried into the reception room and sat down before Morgan Snade. Snade had been made acquainted with the tragedy, and he seemed to be shocked, also. He was nervous, as the officer had told Noggins, and his face was the color of ashes.

"This is a terrible business, Mr. Snade," Noggins said. "I sent for you because I was informed you had called here this evening. In fact, I believe you are the last person known to have seen Mr. Moberg alive. Are you ready to answer my questions?"

"Yes," Snade said.

"I believe that you reached the house a little after eight. Mr. Calderton was closeted with Mr. Moberg, and you were forced to wait a few minutes?"

"Yes."

"Then you went into the library?"

"I did."

"Tell me what happened there, please."

"We — we had a scene," Snade admitted.

"Do you care to tell me about it?"

"It is necessary, I suppose. Mr. Moberg was very angry with

me — and unjustly so. I — I love Margaret Moberg. Mr. Moberg had noticed that I was paying her a great deal of attention. He told me that I was all right in his business, but that he did not care for me in his family."

"That made you angry, I suppose?" Noggins asked.

"It made me furious," Snade replied frankly. "He as good as called me a gutter pup! I tried to reason with him, but that could not be done. He would hear no argument. Both of us grew furious."

"What was the result?"

"I told him that I would not continue in his employ. I told him that I had been insulted enough, that I would endure no more. Then I left him."

"You did not kill him?"

"Good heavens, no! What would lead you to believe such a thing?"

"You quarreled with him," said Noggins. "You were furious at him, you admit."

"But I would not have harmed him for the world. Though he was unjust, he was Margaret's father, you see."

"I see," said Noggins. "This is yours, I believe?" He took the cigarette case from his pocket, handling it carefully. It had been wrapped in tissue paper by the fingerprint man, and Noggins removed enough of the paper so that Snade could identify it.

"Yes — it is mine." Snade's face wore an expression of bewilderment.

"It was found in the library near the body," Noggins declared.

"Found in — I — I never left it there!"

"It looks rather bad, Mr. Snade."

"I — I remember now. I was lighting a cigarette when Mr. Calderton came from the library and Renkin said I could go in. I had put the cigarette case down on the table. I — I do not like Calderton, and I hurried down the hall to the library. I must have left the cigarette case on the table. I have not missed it."

"Then you have not wanted a cigarette from that time until this? You do not smoke much?"

"It isn't that, I was terribly upset. I hurried back to my rooms and was pacing the floor. I never thought of smoking. So I never missed the case."

"How do you suppose it came into the library?"

"I do not know," Snade replied. "I am sure that I left it on the table."

Detective Peter Noggins was silent for a moment. Then he stepped to the door, called the fingerprint man, and summoned Calderton from the adjoining room. Calderton and Snade glared at each other.

"Gentlemen," Noggins said, "the murder was committed with a heavy, sharp paper knife. On that knife fingerprints have been developed. I am going to ask you gentlemen to let this man take your fingerprints for the purpose of comparison."

"Certainly!" Calderton said promptly.

"I — I—" Snade began stammering.

"What is the trouble with you?" Noggins asked.

"I handled that knife," Snade declared. "I was playing with it when Mr. Moberg began talking to me. My fingerprints must be all over it."

"Ah!" Noggins exclaimed.

"But I did not kill him!" Snade exclaimed.

"How about that crimson stain on your waistcoat and shirt?" Noggins asked suddenly, pointing accusingly.

Snade looked down aghast. He had not noticed it before. He wore a dark waistcoat and Tuxedo, and on the top of the waistcoat was a dried stain. On the edge of the shirt, just where the waistcoat covered it, was another telltale stain.

"I — I—" Snade gasped in astonishment.

"Snade, you murderer!" Calderton exclaimed.

"Don't you call me that!"

"Quiet — both of you!" Peter Noggins commanded. "We'll take the fingerprints now."

Save for Snade's heavy breathing there was no sound in the little room. The fingerprint man did his work swiftly and well and then went out into the hall again. Noggins followed him and handed him the cigarette case.

"Take care of all the evidence," he directed. "Let me know as soon as you have made the comparison."

Noggins stepped back into the room. Snade and Calderton were sitting opposite, their hatred of each other showing plainly in their faces.

"We seem to be getting down to the bottom of things," Noggins said. "I always have said that no man can commit a murder and get away with it forever. There is always a clue left behind. Sometimes it is an obvious clue, such as that cigarette case. Sometimes it is a little thing that a man might overlook while making an investigation. The most careful criminal makes his little slip and is caught."

"I never killed him!" Snade said again "Why, I — I couldn't do such a thing!"

"Of course you never killed him, Morgan," said a soft voice at the door.

The three men were upon their feet instantly. Margaret Moberg, just returned from her father's country place, stood there. Though they could see that she was suffering, yet she was calm. Noggins offered a chair, and she seated herself.

"I have been listening," she said. "Mr. Noggins, do not make this terrible thing still more terrible by accusing an innocent man of my father's death."

"My dear Miss Moberg, I have accused nobody yet," Noggins said. "When I do accuse a man, he will be the guilty one. I have merely pointed out the obvious clue. Mr. Snade visited your father, had a quarrel with him, left the house unnerved. Your father was found dead, and beside the body was Mr. Snade's cigarette case."

"Morgan Snade could not have done this," she declared. "He is an honest, sincere man. I quarreled with my father this morning because he ordered me to see no more of Mr. Snade, and I declared that I would not obey him. He sent me to the country place, and said he would tell Mr. Snade that he must keep away from me. I obeyed my father and went to the country place, thinking that it would all come out right in the end."

"And Snade killed your father, Margaret!" Calderton said. "That is the kind of man he is! The evidence —"

The fingerprint man came to the door and beckoned Noggins. The detective excused himself and hurried into the hall, and those in the reception room were quiet for a time. Then Detective Peter Noggins returned; he sat down and looked at all of them in turn, as though trying to read their thoughts.

"We have examined the knife, and we have examined the fingerprints of Calderton and Snade," he said. "We fail to find any fingerprints on the knife except those of Morgan Snade."

Margaret uttered a cry of horror.

"Of course you found my prints," Snade said. "I was handling the knife, I remember, as Mr. Moberg talked to me. In my anger I gripped it and cut my fingers. You can see the cuts. That accounts for the stains on my shirt and waistcoat. I didn't kill him! Can't you believe me?"

"We have the obvious clue," Noggins said, "Your fingerprints are on the knife with which Mr. Moberg was slain, your cigarette case was found beside the body, you had quarreled bitterly with the victim. You had the motive, the opportunity!"

There was silence for a moment. Here was an innocent man caught in a web of evidence that might destroy him Calderton would have smiled had he dared. Everything was perfect. He had left Mr. Moberg in peace, according to Renkin, and Snade had left him in anger — afterward. The fingerprints on the knife, the cigarette case — they were enough to convict Snade!

"He never did it — never did it!" Margaret Moberg declared. "I would stake my life on his innocence."

Noggins watched her carefully, and then he watched Snade again as the latter was comforting Margaret Moberg. Then he glanced at Calderton.

"While we are at it let's make the evidence as conclusive as possible," Noggins said. He took from his pocket the cigarette case, which the fingerprint man had returned to him.

"Snade, in the presence of witnesses you admit that this case belongs to you?" he asked.

"Yes. My name is engraved on it."

"You can identify it, Miss Moberg?"

"Yes," she replied. "I have seen it hundreds of times. But it means nothing to me. I know Morgan is innocent — I feel it."

"I am afraid that a jury would ask for something more than that," Noggins said quietly. "Now, Mr. Calderton —"

"Sir?"

"Can you identify the case also?"

"No," Calderton said. "I don't believe I ever saw it before."

"Take a good look at it," Noggins said, putting it before his eyes.

Calderton pretended to look at it carefully. "It is an ordinary gold case," he said, "with Morgan Snade's name engraved in script across the face of it. But, when you come right down to it, I can't declare that it is his. I never saw it before."

Calderton imagined that he was showing a kind heart there. Margaret would think he was honest, would feel kindly toward him for this attempt to keep from piling up evidence against Snade. And, when it was over, when Snade had been executed, she would turn to George Calderton.

"Never saw it before?" Noggins questioned.

"I am sure of it, sir," Calderton replied.

"Then how does it happen," Detective Peter Noggins asked suddenly, "that your fingerprints are on it?"

There was a moment of silent tension, and then Calderton sprang to his feet.

"What's that?" he demanded.

"Your fingerprints are on it," Noggins repeated. "Both yours and Mr. Snade's. It is natural that his should be upon it, but how could yours be there if you never saw the cigarette case before?"

"Some mistake —" Calderton said, fear suddenly clutching at him.

"Fingerprints do not lie!" Noggins replied. "The obvious clue: The cigarette case beside the body, where a detective would be sure to find it! But, as I said before, a crook always makes some little mistake. Well, Calderton!"

But Calderton, being made of weak stuff, collapsed now that the crisis had been reached. His brain seemed shocked. He muttered a few phrases that meant nothing, and then Noggins and the others caught some low, coherent sentences.

"I — I must have picked it up — before putting on my gloves," Calderton said. "I remember now — I put on my gloves — after I got outside —"

Noggins nodded to the detective in the doorway. Handcuffs snapped on the wrists of George Calderton. The sound, the feel of them completed his unnerving. A moment later he was babbling his confession.

And fifteen minutes later Noggins was going back to headquarters in the taxicab with the fingerprint man.

"Very simple case," said Detective Peter Noggins. "Very simple — nothing to it, in fact! Too many obvious clues. Always beware obvious clues!"

SLAVE OF MYSTERY

CHAPTER I

THREATS

FROM the large window in his private office, Attorney Richard Z. Peale could look down into the crowded street ten stories below — the street where endless streams of humanity jostled about from sunrise until late at night, diversified humanity, the businessman and the tenement dweller, the social idler and the mentally alert, saints and profligates, good and evil.

Bu raising his head and lifting his eyes, Richard Z. Peale could look out over the city and see the skyscrapers, the patches of green here and there that were public squares, the river in the distance, with its endless fleets of boats passing up and down — the turbulent, restless, busy city that had called to him and had attached him half a dozen years before.

Now, Richard Z. Peale stood before this window and shook his fists at the smoke of industry on the horizon, at the tall buildings, and the passing ships, the hurrying men and women like dots on the pavement below, at the rushing taxicabs and trucks.

"You're unfair — unfair!" he hissed.

For it was a hiss, rather than a spoken phrase coming from between teeth clenched in anger, and ending in a gasp of rage, dying away as if Richard Z. Peale suddenly had realized the utter futility of such an outburst.

He turned away from the window and walked across to the table in the middle of the office. He glanced at the newspapers his stenographer had spread out there, some of them yet damp.

On every front page, the name of Richard Z. Peale was to be found in huge, black type. On almost every front page there was a picture of Richard Z. Peale. Spread on that table was such publicity as any man would have been glad to achieve.

For the name of photograph of Richard Z. Peale was not connected with a scandal, or anything of the sort, but with a work of merit and honor. And yet Peale cursed the city that stretched before and below his office window — not cursed it, exactly, but censured it in no uncertain terms.

"You're unfair — unfair!" he exclaimed again, this time in a mutter that seemed to die in his throat as if the pronouncing of the sentence cost him an effort.

The telephone sounded, and Richard Z. Peale stepped across to the desk and put the receiver to his ear.

"Hello!" he cried.

"That you, Peale?" demanded a raucous voice with a snarl in it. "Well, this is Michael Riley! You think you've done something, don't you? You think that you're a regular little man because you've got your picture in the papers! But I'll get you, Peale! No man in this town ever crossed me yet, and got away with it!"

"*I* did!" Peale snapped.

"Yeh? The game isn't over yet, Peale! There are a few extra innings to be played yet — see? I'll get you, I said — and you can bet that I'll get you good! I'll put you in cold storage before I'm done with you, young man!"

"Is that all you have to say?" Peale asked.

"It is!"

"Then why don't you hang up?" said Peale.

A curse came to him over the wire — and Peale hung up himself before the other man could. He turned away from the desk and walked to the window again.

"Get me, will he?" he whispered. "Maybe he will — but I'll be right here when he does it!"

Richard Peale walked around the office for a time, aimlessly, like a man under a nervous strain, and then he stopped beside the table once more. He did not read the articles in the newspapers — he already had done that.

In the outer office, a stenographer and an office boy were very proud this morning, he knew, because they were working for Richard Z. Peale. In those places where men congregated, nice things were being said about Richard Z. Peale. The city was shouting aloud the name of Peale. And yet Peale was disgusted, discouraged, disappointed!

Richard Z. Peale had reached the city six years before with the determination to make a name for himself. He also had been determined to make money. Peale sought power.

But Richard Z. Peale, being a man who still retained some of his youthful ideals, did not go about it in the proper manner. At the outset of his career, he antagonized Michael Riley, the man who controlled all the power in the city.

For years, it had been acknowledged that Michael Riley was master as far as politics was concerned in that particular municipality. Associated with Riley was a ring of men controlling almost every avenue to position and wealth and all that they meant. Peale had heard of bossism, of course, but never had he dreamed that it could possibly be so absolute.

Having antagonized Michael Riley, Peale was too stubborn — and too honest — to make friends with the boss. Richard Peale had much ability. Michael Riley recognized it, and would have taken Peale into the fold and made a wealthy scoundrel of him. But, finding that Peale was not made of that sort of clay, Michael Riley deliberately raised the bars against him.

Richard Peale's ability as an attorney did not always win out for him. Many obstacles beset his path. Certain judges who took their orders from Michael Riley saw that Peale never won an important case, unless a decision in his favor were absolutely unavoidable. Few clients found their way to Peale's offices; and what money he had saved, and the little that had been left him by his father, began to dwindle. There were months when he did not take in enough to pay his office rent.

The entire city seemed to be against him. He found that he could not fight his way upward. There was no one to offer him a helping hand — on every side he saw nothing but antagonism.

Then came the Walton case.

Walton was a henchman of Michael Riley's who had dared to turn against the boss. As a punishment, Riley ordered that he be rail-roaded to the penitentiary. Walton sent for Peale, told his story, and Richard Peale took the case.

The case happened to develop into a sensational one. Two news-papers that did not cater to Michael Riley disclosed that here was a fight of an honest man against dishonest conditions. Pitted against Peale was a brilliant prosecuting attorney who had two able assis-tants; and there was a host of witnesses in court for the special pur-pose of giving perjured testimony.

Richard Z. Peale entered the fight with anger raging in his heart. The city, through Michael Riley, had held him down. He would make at least one good fight before he acknowledged himself beaten.

Accidents happened from the first that gave Peale a little advan-tage. A judge was ill, and the man who sat in his place made a minor mistake that gave Richard Peale the opening he desired. Before Riley's men realized what was happening, an unbiased judge had been appointed to hear the case.

And Richard Z. Peale, through the efforts of Bob Drake, a private detective who admired him, went into court fully prepared. One by one, he demolished the perjured tales of the lying witnesses. Point by point, he got into the record damaging things that undermined Michael Riley's carefully arranged plans. He had fought continually and carefully during the selection of the jury, and with good effect — for Walton was acquitted.

That meant, of course, that Michael Riley and his cohorts had been defeated, and badly. The foes of the political boss shouted their glee. They started in to make a household word of the name of Richard Peale as a means of reward.

"And there it stops!" Peale told himself upon this morning. "Riley isn't licked! I've won a case — and I didn't get a cent for doing it. I'll get a few more criminal cases on the strength of the victory, where the defendants have no money. Michael Riley will keep remunerative business from reaching me. I've got a lot of publicity, but that'll not pay rent or bring me any corporation business in this town. I'll be like a skyrocket. The public will forget within forty-eight hours, and not even wait to see the stick fall. I'm done!"

Peale snatched his hat from the rack and went to luncheon. As a usual thing, he ate at a soda fountain in the drug store across the street, confining himself to milk and pie, but today he walked on down the avenue and turned into a pretentious restaurant that was patronized by prosperous men. He felt himself called upon to celebrate his victory, though he scarcely could afford it.

Detective Bob Drake hailed him as he entered.

"Well — well!" Bob Drake cried. "I was just fussing around because I had to eat luncheon alone, and here you come along! Can a common private detective sit at the same table with a famous attorney like you?"

"A common private detective cannot, but you may," Peale replied, laughing.

They sought a table in a corner, and gave their orders. Bob Drake possessed a fortune that had been left him by his father, which made him independent of Michael Riley and his ilk. Riley could not touch the fortune even through business channels. And Bob Drake, with an itch for being a detective, maintained an office and kept office hours as if his living depended upon it, and succeeded now and then in tearing aside the veils of mystery that shrouded some important cases.

"How does it feel to be famous?" Drake asked.

"Well, I haven't noticed any particular change," replied Peale. "There is no horde of would-be clients storming the doors of my office."

"Perhaps that will come later," Drake said.

"Not so long as Michael Riley and his precious gang of crooks run the town," Peale answered. "They'll see that no big business comes in my direction. Riley called me up this morning, and informed me that he is out to get me."

"Um! It wouldn't hurt to be a bit careful, Peale, if that gang is on your trail," Drake said.

Peale ate the rest of the meal in silence then, allowing Bob Drake to conduct the conversation, and replying in monosyllables when he felt obliged to reply at all.

Peale was storing up anger against Michael Riley. What right did Riley have to prevent a hard-working man of ability taking his rightful place in the life of the city? What right did Michael Riley have to threaten? If he saw Riley right now —

He did see Riley!

The boss entered the restaurant with two friends, and took a table near that at which Peale and Drake were sitting. It made Peale angry to see how everybody treated Riley. The manager went to the table himself to be sure that his guests were properly served. The head-waiter remained in the vicinity. All that for Michael Riley — grafter, perjurer, enslaver of men — while an honorable attorney was treated as a nobody.

Bob Drake paid the check, and Peale got up and followed him toward the entrance. They were compelled to pass within a dozen feet of Riley. The boss happened to turn his head, and saw them.

"Well, well — if it isn't the boy attorney and his pet detective friend!" Michael Riley exclaimed.

His tone belittled Peale. It was the last straw. The lawyer whirled around as if a rubber band had snapped him back. His two hands shot out and clutched Michael Riley by the shoulders. Riley was lifted out of his chair, bent half back across the table, and well shaken. Richard Z. Peale was an athletic young man.

"You crook!" Peale exclaimed, in a voice that all the diners there could hear. "Don't ever speak to me in public again! Understand that? I want the honest part of the world to know that I'm not on speaking terms with you! A mountain road is a straight line compared to you! You'll threaten to get me, will you? I'm going to hold you with one hand, Michael Riley, and I'll going to slap you with the other. Then you can go and have me arrested for assault and battery, and have me charged with libel, too, if you like. You're a thief and a crook! Hear me? A thief and a crook!"

Michael Riley's two friends were upon their feet by now. The manager, the headwaiter and some other employees came running toward the scene. The diners, businessmen in the majority, rushed forward to witness the trouble. Bob Drake hurried back toward his friend, crying a warning.

Richard Z. Peale held Michael Riley with one hand, as he had said that he would do, and with the other he slapped Michael Riley's face until his head rocked; and then he tossed him to one side.

"This ought to make a dandy story for some of the newspapers you control, Riley," Peale said. "You'd better tell the reporters all about it. And tell them, also, that, after slapping you, I washed my hands in an antiseptic!"

"I'll get you — get you!" Riley screeched.

"Bah!" said Richard Z. Peale.

He whirled around, picked up his hat from the floor, and faced toward the door again.

"One side!" he commanded a couple of waiters who were closing in on him.

He thrust them out of the way, glared around once more at the crowd, and then walked quickly from the restaurant, closely followed by a grinning and delighted Bob Drake.

CHAPTER II

A PECULIAR CONTRACT

"LADY to see you, sir!" said the office boy.

He handed Peale a card upon which was engraved:

MISS GRALIN

It was ten o'clock the following morning. Following the scene at luncheon the day before, Peale had talked for some time with Bob Drake, who had given him some good advice. He had then spent a lonesome evening in his rooms, growing steadily more bitter against the world.

"What sort of a lady?" he asked the boy.

"Um!" the youngster replied, rolling his eyes.

"As good as all that? She certainly must be a dream to get such a compliment from you," Peale said. "Show her in, you imp, and we'll soon see what particular charity she is collecting for or what books she is selling."

Peale turned toward his desk and made a pretense at being busy. Presently, a slight exclamation caused his to look up. Miss Gralin was a woman of about twenty-five. She was dressed elegantly, yet in excellent taste. There was an air of sophistication about her. Peale decided that she was a suffragette of the militant variety, or something like that — a delicious young woman with a will of her own. And she probably was collecting funds for some hospital, he told himself bitterly.

Having placed a chair for her at one end of his desk, Peale at once adopted his professional manner and glanced at her inquiringly. Her eyes had narrowed a trifle, and she seemed to be scrutinizing him carefully.

"Mr. Peale, I hope that you have plenty of time to spare me this morning," she said, "for my business cannot be disposed of in a few minutes."

"I have ample time," Peale replied, with some sarcasm in his voice that was meant for himself and not for her.

"Before stating my business, Mr. Peale, I have a sort of confession to make. I have been looking for you."

"Indeed?"

"I know of what family you came, where you were educated, and all that. I even know that you are playing a losing game here, and that you should not be doing so. Oh, I know all about your ability and honesty!"

"Thank you!"

"You are not displeased?" she asked.

"Certainly not," Richard Peale replied, smiling at her. "Happily, there are no skeletons in my family closet. But why did you go to all that trouble?"

"I wanted to be sure about the man I — I hired."

"Oh, I understand!"

"And now I think we can get down to business," she went on. "I believe that you are not retained by any large corporation — not doing anything that takes all your time and would prevent you accepting a new commission."

"I may safely say that is the truth," Peale admitted.

"For, if we come to terms and make an arrangement, I shall require almost all your time."

Peale sat up straight in his chair. "Your business must be very important, Miss Gralin," he said.

"And peculiar, as well," she added. "I'll state that proposition to you, Mr. Peale, and then you may give me your decision. I want to draw up a contract with you. It is to endure for a year. It is to say that, during the year, beginning at a certain hour today, you are to be absolutely at my command. You are to do exactly as I tell you in all things. You are to be a sort of — well — slave, if you wish to put it in that way. The contract must be binding."

"You spoke truly when you said that it was peculiar," Peale said, smiling at her.

"Please wait until I have finished, Mr. Peale," she went on. "I know that you want to rise in the world. You are eager to make a great success in your profession. You want to go into politics — clean politics — and use your natural ability, make something of yourself. You need money. You want power. Money, of course, is the first essential."

"All that is very true," Peale said.

"Make this contract with me, and I shall bind myself to pay you fifty thousand dollars as your year's salary."

"Fifty thou —" Peale gasped.

"Here are papers and documents from bank officials in this city, which will tell you that I am capable of doing this. My home is in San Francisco, but I have some heavy investments here. I may say that I am rated at almost a million dollars."

"But — what shall you expect me to do?" Peale asked. "What will be the nature of the work?"

"That is something you are not to know at present, Mr. Peale. You are to bind yourself to do exactly as I say — to obey my slightest command. I must be protected in the contract, of course. You may draw it up yourself."

"*You* must be protected!" Richard Z. Peale exclaimed. "But what about me, my dear Miss Gralin? Do you dream that I would enter such a blind arrangement?"

"Oh, I forgot! It shall be in the contract that you can refuse, in case I ask you to do anything criminal — but such a request would render the contract void, of course. We'll put it that you shall not be required to do anything that an honorable man could not do."

"That makes the thing look a bit better," Peale admitted. "But it is a peculiar deal."

"I realize that it is. And the salary is to be fifty thousand dollars a year. You want money, don't you?" Miss Gralin smiled across the desk at him again.

"I do want money — to use in furthering my personal advancement in an honorable manner," Peale told her. "But I want to be sure how I am getting it!"

"I have told you all that I can, Mr. Peale."

"I'll think it over, Miss Gralin."

"But I cannot allow you time to do that," she told him. "I must have your decision immediately. If you make the agreement, you must write out the contract and have it executed before I leave the office. The year is to begin as soon as the contract is signed. I'll give you five thousand dollars down to bind the agreement. My bank references are all right?"

"They are," replied Peale, who had been inspecting them. "You are financially able."

"Then —"

"But it is so unusual!" Peale protested. "I am selling myself for a year."

"Would such a contract be binding?" she asked.

"I can draw it so that it will be binding. And, if I signed it, madam, I'd feel in honor bound to adhere to it."

"I felt sure of that," she said. "My investigations have shown you to be an honorable man."

"Can't you allow me one day to think it over?"

"I am sorry — no!"

"Nor an inkling as to the work —"

"Nothing!"

"Will it take me from the city?" Peale demanded, with sudden suspicion. Perhaps, he thought, this might be some of Michael Riley's work.

"You may include in the contract that you shall not be obliged to leave the city for any length of time unless you desire to do so," Miss Gralin said.

"It seems fair enough!" Peale declared.

He got up and walked across to the window and looked down at the city. He wanted money — power! He wanted to make something out of himself, as Miss Gralin had said, and Michael Riley and his gang stood in the way. Fifty thousand dollars was considerable money, and a year only a short time, everything considered. Fifty thousand dollars would allow him to hand on, to continue the fight.

Peale whirled around and contemplated Miss Gralin again. She did not have the appearance of an adventuress. She had the appearance of a refined, educated, cultured young woman, and the papers she had shown him convinced him that she had ample funds.

He asked himself what the work would be. Was this a trap of some sort? But she had said that he could write the contract himself, that he would not be forced to leave the city, and that the contract would be void if she asked him to do something outside the law. Surely, if he wrote that contract himself —

"May I have a decision now, Mr. Peale?" Miss Gralin asked, smiling up at him.

Peale sat down before his desk once more. Fifty thousand dollars for a year of his life, money with which he could continue the fight against Michael Riley and his gang — and she had said that he could write the contract himself!

"I'll do it!" he said suddenly.

"Thank you. I am very glad," she replied. "Kindly draw up the contract at once."

Peale bent over the desk. Miss Gralin picked up a magazine and began turning the pages, humming a bit of song as she did so. Peale remembered all he ever had studied and read about contracts. He made this one fair to both Miss Gralin and himself, according to the stipulations she had said could be included in it.

"By the way, shall I be able to continue my office here?" Peale asked.

"Certainly," she replied, glancing up from the magazine. "I will demand a great deal of your time, but not all of it. You may even have other clients. I do not mean to cut you off from all chance to extend your business. I merely said that you were to do anything I asked you to do — as long as it was honorable."

Peale bent over the desk again. Half a dozen times he was at the point of tearing up the sheets before him and telling her that he had decided against making the contract. But he failed to see where he possibly could be injured — and the fifty thousand dollars meant everything to him.

Peale read the contract to her when he had finished writing it. She listened gravely, and then took it into her own hands and read it herself.

"One thing more, before we complete it," she said. "I want to be sure that there has been no flaw in my investigation. I understand that you are neither married nor engaged to be married."

"That is true," Peale said.

"And you have no particular feeling — that is, there is at present no woman — no tie —"

"Nothing of the sort, I assure you," Peale declared. "I have not a relative left in the world. And I have devoted my time to my profession. Moreover, my success has not been such as to warrant such thoughts as you imply."

"That is what I understand."

"I stand alone, Miss Gralin. There will be nothing to detract me from the work that you wish me to do."

"That is all," Miss Gralin said.

Peale called in his stenographer and dictated the contract to her, chuckling as he saw the expression of amazement on the girl's face. Then he indulged in small talk with Miss Gralin while the stenographer got the contracts typed. That is, Richard Peale supposed that it was small talk. As a matter of fact, he knew nothing about such things. He always had held himself aloof from society. A visit to the theater or opera now and then had been his only public appearances outside courtrooms.

The contracts were brought in, read, compared, and placed on the desk.

"Satisfactory?" Peale asked.

"Very," said Miss Gralin.

"And the year is to begin —"

"As soon as the contracts are signed," she replied. "Here is the first payment of five thousand."

She took a package of bills from her handbag, and placed the money on the desk before him. Peale hesitated an instant longer. He wished that he could look into the future and see what it would hold for him — wished that he might read the mind of the woman sitting within a few feet of him. But he signed the contracts. The stenographer had called a man from an adjoining office as the second witness; and now she called a notary to take the acknowledgment.

Peale paid the notary and the witness, thanked them, folded the contracts, and handed one to Miss Gralin, who now was smiling at him again. Her first name, he had ascertained for the purposes of the document, was Elizabeth.

The astonished stenographer went into the outer office and closed the door. Peale whirled around his desk chair, clasped his hands, and looked at Elizabeth Gralin.

"And now, sir," she said, still smiling at him, "you are my man for one year, absolutely under my orders as long as those orders are honorable. That is understood?"

"Certainly, my dear Miss Gralin," replied Peale. "And allow me to express the hope that our relationship will be agreeable. Well, I am under your orders, Miss Gralin, as you have expressed it. What is the first?"

"That you call me Elizabeth," she replied instantly. "Miss Gralin sounds entirely too formal."

"But —"

"Are you not to obey my commands? Are you going to refuse to carry out the very first?"

"Er — of course I'll comply — Elizabeth!"

"That is very much better. You are always to call me Elizabeth when we are alone together. And I shall call you Richard — or Dick, when I prefer to do so."

"I haven't been called Dick since my college days," said Richard Z. Peale. "So far, so good! Your first order has been complied with — Elizabeth. And now what?"

Her answer startled him.

"Kiss me!" Miss Gralin commanded.

CHAPTER III

MARRIAGE AND MYSTERY

RICHARD Z. Peale was a serious-minded man. In boyhood he had been one of those unlucky lads who never seemed to fit in with the crowd. He had had no close companions, took part in few sports and pleasures, and kept aloof considerable. Even in college, he had faced the fight to earn a living and win success.

Peale knew little about women. He never had had a sweetheart. He scarcely could remember the time, away back in the years, when he had kissed and been kissed by a couple of tantalizing girls at a party. As an osculatory expert, Peale had every reason to consider that he would be a failure.

And now a radiant woman of about twenty-five was standing before him and insisting that he kiss her.

"But — that is —" he stammered.

"Would it be such a very unpleasant thing to do?" inquired Elizabeth Gralin, smiling at him again, her face flushing a bit.

"I — er — I don't mean anything like that, of course. But — that is — your request is rather unusual, don't you think?"

"It isn't a request — it is a command. And you have contracted to obey, remember. Unless, of course, you can truthfully say that it would not be an honorable thing to do!"

"But your command is — well, rather unusual to say the least."

"I imagine there are lots of men who would be glad to receive a command like that."

"No doubt. But, may I ask why you make such a request?"

"I want to see you carry out orders, Richard. Are you going to kiss me?"

Peale went forward awkwardly, and kissed her. He told himself at the moment that probably it wasn't much of a kiss. Her eyes were twinkling when he stepped back, and the smile was upon her face.

"I doubt whether you have had much experience," said Elizabeth Gralin. "'Tis better that way, of course, than if your experience had been widespread. And now please sit down before your desk, and we'll get down to business."

Peale sat down. He felt that he would collapse if he did not. That kiss had been no small thing with Peale. He couldn't forget it instantly, as Miss Gralin appeared to have done. His lips tingled with it yet. He began wondering what a real kiss would be like.

He was glad that Miss Gralin was going to get down to business now. Perhaps he could compose himself if she presented him with some legal problem. Peale put on his professional manner and bent slightly across the desk, ready to hear his client's confidences.

"It is almost time for luncheon," Elizabeth Gralin said. "You'll take me to luncheon, leaving word with your stenographer that you'll not return today. Before we go, I'll explain what must be done."

Peale touched a button, and the stenographer answered.

"I am not to be disturbed," Peale said. "And I shall not be in the office this afternoon."

The girl made a note of it, and went out again. Once more, Peale bent across the desk.

"And now —" he asked.

"Perhaps what I am going to say may startle you — but that cannot be avoided," Elizabeth Gralin said.

"I am getting used to startling statements," said Peale, remembering the kiss again. "What are your commands?"

"Immediately after luncheon, we'll go to the proper office and obtain a marriage license," she said.

"Very good. And the contracting parties —"

"I am one."

"Ah! I wish you every joy in the world, I am sure," said Peale.

He thought he began to have an inkling as to her purpose, now. She was a woman with a comfortable fortune — undoubtedly she wished her attorney to care for it, probably while she was on her honeymoon for a year.

"And the lucky man?" Peale asked, reaching for a pencil.

"You are the man," she said.

"I beg your pardon?"

"You are to be the bridegroom," said Miss Gralin. "We shall be married by a minister I know — very quietly. And then we shall go to a hotel, where I have engaged an apartment."

"I scarcely contracted for this."

"It is a part of my plan," she said. "It is merely a marriage of convenience — we shall be together a great deal during the year to come. Understand, you are to be a husband in name only."

"But, is it necessary —"

"It is!" she interrupted. "It is a part of my plan. I scarcely see how you can refuse. There are many men, I imagine, who'd be glad to marry me. I have money, I am not bad looking, am educated. Would a man be ashamed to introduce me as his wife?"

"Certainly not!" said Peale. "But — why, I never saw you in my life until a couple of hours ago."

"That doesn't make any difference. I have looked you up and am ready to have told me that you have no relatives, that you are alone in the world. And you are getting fifty thousand dollars for a year, remember. If the bonds of matrimony in name only are so irksome at the end of the year, could you not get a divorce? You are a lawyer."

"I suppose so," said Peale.

"Immediately after the ceremony, we'll go to the hotel of which I spoke. I shall have the remainder of the fifty thousand placed to your credit in your bank — I shall trust you, you see. Then you'll go to your own rooms and pack up and move. We shall have adjoining suites — and I pay the bills, of course — or, rather, give you the money with which to pay them. You'll have to take me around — introduce me as your wife, and so on. People will think merely that there has been a secret romance in your life — that we grew tried of waiting and decided to get married quickly. The public will like it — it'll make you more popular."

"My dear Miss Gralin —"

"Elizabeth, please!"

"Um! My dear Elizabeth, do you realize that you are asking to marry a man you never saw until a short time ago?"

"I've seen you lots of times, Richard. And we are wasting time. Aren't you going to take me to luncheon now?"

Peale reached for his hat. His brain was in a whirl. He blinked his eyes and rubbed the back of one hand over his forehead, not sure that he was not dreaming. A fifty-thousand dollar job and a handsome wife in one day seemed too much.

As they waited for the elevator, and Elizabeth Gralin maintained small talk, doubts began to assail Richard Z. Peale. Into what sort of a trap had he walked? Why had he signed that contract, even to get fifty thousand dollars? Why did Elizabeth Gralin want to bear his name? Peale began to smell a mystery.

They walked up the street three blocks to a restaurant of the better class. Peale began to experience pride of ownership, or something very much like it. He saw that many men glanced at the woman at his side with something akin to admiration. And the women looked at her, too, enviously. But the mystery still bothered Peale.

"Our wedding luncheon," she whispered, as they ate, and smiled at him again.

"You really insist on going through with it?" Peale asked.

"Certainly — as soon as we have finished here. You'd better order a taxicab."

Peale appeared to be in a daze now. He ordered the cab, paid the luncheon check, and went out with her as a man walks in his sleep. Within half an hour, they had obtained the marriage license.

Then they drove to the home of a minister, and were married. Peale still seemed to be in a daze. He made the necessary responses — and finally found himself in the taxi with her again.

Under her orders, Peale took her to the hotel, explained the marriage to the grinning clerk who congratulated him, and left her there while he returned to his own rooms to pack his things. It was almost time for dinner when he finally was installed in his suite adjoining hers.

Married! And to a woman he never had seen until that day! Peale tried to force those facts home in his mind, but found it almost impossible. He dressed for dinner, and waited. He thanked Heaven that he had but few friends to accost him and call him a sly dog and ask embarrassing questions.

She tapped at the door, and entered.

"We shall eat in the hotel, and then go to the theater," she said. "I have the tickets."

They descended to the dining room and took a table in the corner. The headwaiter grinned; so did their individual waiter. Peale glanced around the room, and saw half a dozen other persons looking at them with interest.

"Have you seen the papers?" Elizabeth asked.

"Didn't have time to look at them," Peale replied.

"The story is in the papers. They call it a romance, as I said they would. The minister who married us admitted to the reporters that he had performed the ceremony, and that we appeared to be very much in love with each other." She giggled a bit, like a silly schoolgirl, and then apologized for it. "I must make you proud of me, not disgusted," she added. "I want to be a worthy wife."

Suddenly Bob Drake descended upon them, and stood grinning while Peale accomplished an introduction.

"My — my wife," he said.

Drake made the necessary polite remarks and sat down with them.

"It was, indeed, a surprise," he said. "I thought I was about as close to Dick as anybody, but I never dreamed of this."

Peale almost said that he hadn't dreamed of it, either, but checked himself in time.

"A man named Peale is getting all the good things of life," Bob Drake went on. "He wins a big case, gets famous and captures a splendid wife all in forty-eight hours. Some men have all the luck."

Drake left them after a time, and finally they went to the theatre. They met half a dozen persons Peale knew, and he introduced his wife to them. All had read the newspapers, and knew of the "romance." Peale found that he was quite a personage for a few minutes.

Then they had an after-theater supper, and returned to the hotel.

"You may go to your office tomorrow as usual," Elizabeth told Peale. "Attend to your regular business, but come here for luncheon with me, of course. As I said, I want you to have your other clients."

"But what business are you going to give me?" he asked. "How am I to earn my fifty thousand?"

"By obeying orders, Dick."

"And when there are no orders — Elizabeth?"

"Then go ahead with your own business as if you never had seen me," she said.

She bade him good night, and he went to his own suite. For two hours he tossed about on the bed, wondering what it all meant. Then he slept to dream that half a hundred women surrounded him, each with a package of thousand-dollar bills in her hand, demanding that he marry one of them and take all the money.

He did not see Elizabeth in the morning, but wrote a note saying that he would return for luncheon, and slipped it beneath her door. The morning newspapers had stories of his "romance" too. Everybody he met in his building congratulated him, and men he scarcely knew invaded his office for that purpose.

To escape them, Peale went out on business. He had a client who had given him a minor case, and he set forth to collect certain information and evidence.

It was necessary for him to visit a small, high-class restaurant in the retail section of the city, for he wanted to interview the headwaiter there.

Peale entered the place and sent for the man. It did not take him long to obtain the information he desired. He was about to thank his informant and depart, when he heard Bob Drake's well-known musical laughter.

Peale peered around a bank of ferns and palms. He saw Drake sitting at a table not far away. There was a woman with him. The woman was Mrs. Richard Z. Peale, formerly Elizabeth Gralin.

What on earth could that mean? Peale wondered. When he had introduced his wife to Bob Drake the evening before in the dining room, they had acted as if they never had met before. And here they were, in the middle of the morning, talking and laughing together as if they had known each other for years. Peale, aware that the head-waiter was watching him, turned away.

"Much obliged for the information," he growled, and left the restaurant.

Once more doubts began assailing his mind. Was this a trap? And how was Bob Drake concerned in it? Was it true that Bob Drake was his friend, as he always had believed, or did Bob Drake, too, take orders from Michael Riley, the boss of the city, while pretending to abhor the man and his methods? Those questions gave Peale considerable food for thought.

He did not hurry down the street to his office, as he had intended doing after getting his information from the waiter, and for the time being the case upon which he was working was forgotten. He entered a cigar store on the corner and purchased a cigar, lighted it, and then stood just inside the doorway, from where he could watch the entrance of the restaurant.

CHAPTER IV

FALSEHOODS

IT WAS not a long wait.

Five minutes after he had taken up his position in the doorway, Bob Drake and Elizabeth stepped from the restaurant and went to the curb. Drake signaled for a taxicab, put Mrs. Peale into it, closed the door, gave the chauffeur directions, lifted his hat, and swung up the street as the cab started in the other direction.

Richard Z. Peale hesitated for a moment. He did not want to spy upon his wife of a day, and he did not wish to follow the man he had called friend. There was something peculiar here, he told himself. He began to feel like a man in the clutches of an ulterior force that he could not combat.

He finally decided to follow Bob Drake for a time, for he felt that he owed it to himself. A man was entitled to make every effort at self-preservation, Peale told himself, and was worse that a fool if he did not. He remembered that he was fighting Michael Riley, and that

Riley was a man who did not think it at all necessary to fight fairly if it was necessary to use unfairness to get the proper results. Riley's idea always was to win the battle, not matter by what means.

So Peale followed Bob Drake, the well-to-do private detective, and he promised himself that, if he discovered that Drake was playing a double game, he would thrash him if it was the last thing he ever did in the world.

Drake walked down the avenue for a distance of four or five blocks, and then turned into a side street. Peale finally saw him enter the "family entrance" of a cheap saloon on an unsavory corner. Peale knew about the resort — it belonged to a man who belonged in turn to the Michael Riley gang, and the city police made it a point to disregard anything that happened there.

Peale crossed the street and opened the door cautiously. He neither saw nor heard anyone, and presently he slipped inside, coming into a dark, narrow, evil-smelling hallway. Off this hallway there opened some half-dozen little rooms, each fitted with a cheap table and four or five chairs. Those little rooms had seen many a political plot; if their walls had ears, then they had heard much that might have interested law-abiding folk.

Peale could hear low voices in one of the rooms, and he thought that one of them was the voice of Bob Drake. He went forward through the hall, and managed to get into the room adjoining without having been heard or seen.

There was a thin partition between the two rooms, and halfway to the top of it was a knothole. Peale placed a chair against the partition, stood upon it cautiously, and looked through. There were two men in the other room. One of them was Bob Drake, and the other was Michael Riley!

It was evident to Peale that their conference was about at an end, that he had come too late to ascertain the truth. Drake and Riley were upon their feet, as if preparing to leave. Their talk evidently had been a short one.

"So that settles it?" Drake was asking the boss, standing before him with his hands upon his hips. Peale could not see Drake's face, was unable to read there how he stood with the other man.

"It certainly does settle it, Drake," Michael Riley replied. "I guess there isn't any more to be said about it at all, from any standpoint."

"Well, at least we understand each other," said Drake.

"It's always a good thing to have a perfect understanding," Michael Riley answered. "It's a mighty good thing for a man to know his friends from his enemies."

It certainly was a most excellent thing, thought Peale. He did not pretend to be able to guess what Michael Riley and Bob Drake were talking about. Perhaps they were speaking of him, and perhaps of something else, or of some other man in whom Riley was interested. The big, outstanding fact of all was that Bob Drake was in this den in close conference with the city boss — a man Drake pretended to abhor and fight.

Michael Riley was the first to leave the little room. Drake waited near the door until the boss had been gone for three or four minutes, and then followed. Peale had not been able to get a square look at his face.

The lawyer remained in the little room until he felt sure that Bob Drake was some distance down the street, and then he slipped into the evil-smelling hallway again and started for the door at the end of it. He was halfway there when another door opened, and he found himself confronted by Michael Riley and another man.

The meeting evidently was as unexpected for Riley as it was for Peale. The boss gasped his surprise, took a quick step to one side and blocked Peale's exit.

"What are you doing here?" Riley demanded. "Sneakin' around and tryin' to get an earful, are you?"

"One side — you!" Peale cried.

His voice was charged with anger. The woman he had married, the man he called friend — he felt that they both were against him. He was ready to do battle, if necessary.

Michael Riley merely waved one hand. The man at his back sprang forward, uttering a peculiar cry as he did so. He was a thug, Peale could see, a rough-and-tumble fighter ready to do the bidding of his master. Michael Riley employed many such.

His cry brought two other men from the main room of the resort. Peale found himself confronted by three thugs, with Riley standing in the background. He braced himself against the wall and waited.

"Well, what are you doing here?" Riley demanded again. "I think it'll be better for you to answer the question."

"I was under the impression that this was a public resort," Peale told him, hoping to gain time, to catch the thugs off guard if he argued for a few minutes.

"Maybe it is, but I happen to know that you don't patronize places like this," Riley said.

"I'm glad you give me credit for that, at least."

"Well, are you going to answer my question? How long have you been snoopin' around here?"

"Oh, not very long!"

"You'd better answer, Peale. I've got a score to settle with you, and I don't know a better place or time."

"I'd be a bit careful, if I were you," Peale told him. "You might settle the score, but probably it'd cause you some trouble afterward. It is just possible that other persons know I am here, and that you are here, and there may be an investigation if anything happens to me. And you might not manage to get free this time, especially since a hundred men heard you threaten to get me in that restaurant."

"Bluff!" Riley said.

"Maybe it is, and maybe it isn't. You don't happen to know whether it is or not, so you'll be mighty careful, won't you, Riley? Make your thugs stand aside now, so I can get to the street."

"You'll stay right here until you tell me why you are here at all!" Michael Riley said.

"Want to go ahead with it, do you?" Peale asked. "You'd better call off your dogs, Riley!"

Once more, Michael Riley gave a signal. The three men hurled themselves upon Peale. He was an athletic young man, but he could not fight successfully against such odds, especially in the narrow hall. They bore him backward, utterly disregarding the blows he rained upon them, finally pinioned his arms at his sides, and held him prisoner.

Riley grunted an order, and the three thugs took Peale into one of the little rooms and hurled him into a chair, standing guard over him closely. Riley stood just in front of him.

"I've had about enough of you, Peale!" Riley said. "I promised to get you, and I'm going to do it! You've called me everything from a grafter to a dog — and if I'm a dog, I don't intend to let one poor little flea bother me too much! Understand that?"

"I understand that you and all your gang can't whip me!" Peale retorted. "And you can't bluff me, either! If I've got to fight you alone, I'll do it! But I've a few friends — don't forget that!"

"Bob Drake, eh?" Riley sneered.

"Don't bank too much on Drake, Riley — I'm not! There are a few others, you know."

"My men haven't been able to find them, then," Riley sneered again. "Why, I have every move of yours watched, you poor fool! I can tell you what you ate for breakfast this morning. Now, I want to know what you are doing here!"

"If every move of mine is being watched, you should know that without asking me," Peale told him.

"Think you're smart, don't you? You shyster —"

"Don't you call me a shyster!" Peale cried. "I'm a reputable lawyer. If I was a shyster, I'd have belonged to your gang a long time ago — and you know it. It took more than a shyster to get Walton free and force your gang to lose for once!"

Michael Riley's face went purple with wrath. "I'll get you — and get you good!" he exclaimed.

"If I don't get you first!" Peale replied. "Well, what are you going to do — have these thugs of yours beat me up? That's your usual method, I believe. I suppose I should feel honored that it takes a gang to do it."

Riley stepped closer to him. "Beating up would be a little too good," he said. "I'll attend to you later, and in another way — a better way."

"If I don't get you first!" Peale repeated.

Riley choked with wrath. "Throw him out!" he commanded his thugs. "Take him to the door and throw him out! And if you catch him hanging around here again, give him what's coming to him!"

Peale was grasped and torn from the chair. He was rushed along the hall, the door was opened, and he was hurled into the side street.

He got up and dusted his clothes, and walked rapidly and angrily down the avenue toward his office. His mind was in a turmoil, and he was fighting to control his anger, that he might think properly. Who was this Elizabeth Gralin he had married? Why had she and Bob Drake pretended to be strangers when they were introduced, and then be found on friendly terms the following morning? What was there in common between Bob Drake and Michael Riley?

Peale felt that he was in danger, that the net was closing about him. He knew Riley for an unscrupulous man — and he had angered Riley. After winning the Walton case and making a fool out of the boss, after that scene in the café the day following the trial, after the scene just now, it was to be expected that Michael Riley would not rest until he had conquered Peale. It would be necessary for him to make an example of the lawyer, to show other men that they could not fight Michael Riley with impunity.

Peale reached his office and went to his private room. He made a note of the information he had obtained from the waiter, filed it away, and then forgot the case for the present, while he considered more weighty things.

Luncheon hour approached, and Peale left the office for the hotel. On the street, he came face to face with Bob Drake.

"I'll bet the bridegroom is hurrying to his bride," Drake said. "Fact?"

"Even a newlywed must eat now and then," Peale replied.

"You certainly have a charming wife, old boy."

"I agree with you," said Peale, watching him closely as they went up the street.

"She's the sort of woman to boost you along," Bob Drake declared. "I need one like her myself."

"How can you tell so much after meeting her only once and not exchanging more than two dozen words with her?" asked Peale, trying to laugh.

"Once is enough for that, old boy. I've met her only once, it's true, but I can tell that much."

They separated at the corner. So Bob Drake had lied! Peale had given him a chance, and he had lied!

Elizabeth was waiting for him, and they went to the dining room immediately.

"Been in the hotel all morning?" Peale asked.

"Except for a short time," she replied. "I went out to get some fresh air."

"See anyone you know?"

"And whom should I have met that I know?" she countered.

So his wife had lied! Peale had given her a chance, too, and she had told a falsehood! He did not accuse her. He acted like an innocent; but he determined to keep his eyes and ears open henceforth, to find the reason for these lies.

CHAPTER V

THE BLOW FALLS

LUNCHEON over, Peale returned to his office and spent the greater part of the afternoon trying to find some solution to the puzzle.

He told himself that he had been a fool to marry Elizabeth Gralin, even if it was a marriage of convenience, that he had been a fool to make that contract with her. The marriage changed the status of the contract, of course, yet Peale was not willing to confront his wife and demand that he be released. He wasn't sure — that was the trouble.

"I'll just watch!" he told himself. "I'll watch and see what the game is, and, in the meantime, I'll be mighty careful."

That night he dined with his wife and went to a theater again. He was forced to introduce her to a dozen acquaintances, some men and some women, and she puzzled him all the more.

For this wife of his was all that a man could hope for. She seemed at home in the best society. She gave every evidence of being refined and educated, and she certainly did nothing to disgrace her husband.

But that only made Peale feel more apprehensive. He feared that the blow would fall at any minute. Perhaps the blow would be all the greater because of her perfect conduct now.

He could not help admiring her. He told himself that she was the sort of woman he would have picked for a wife, had he been looking around for one. She was the sort to inspire respect and love. But he remembered the falsehood Bob Drake had told him, and the one she had implied, and wondered.

They had an after-theater supper, and met Bob Drake again. He was with a society girl and her mother, and they all sat at the same table. Peale watched his wife and Drake closely without giving any of them an inkling of the fact; they treated each other as if they had met only once before.

"Perfect acting!" Peale told himself.

Back at the hotel, he asked his wife to talk with him before she retired.

"When do I begin earning my fifty thousand?" he asked.

"You already have begun, Richard. You have married me, you see."

"But business —"

"Are you so eager for work?" she asked. "When I have some business for you to attend to, I'll let you know. By the way, I deposited the remainder of the fifty thousand this afternoon."

"I'd feel better if I was earning it," Peale said, watching her closely.

"Very well. Tomorrow you may transfer some bonds for me, if you are so very anxious to work. And now you may kiss me good night!"

Peale kissed her. He felt that the kiss was more of a success than the first he had given her in the office. He began thinking again that she was the sort of woman he always had wanted for a wife. But the mystery — and the falsehood!

The following day he went to his office as usual. He had some minor matters to attend to in court, and that kept him so busy that he could not go to the hotel for luncheon. After they had been disposed of, in the middle of the afternoon, Peale lighted a cigar and walked the streets, still apprehensive, still wondering when the blow was going to fall, and what its nature would be.

He returned to his office again about four o'clock and went at once to his desk.

"Mrs. Peale called on the telephone about two o'clock," his stenographer informed him.

"Any message?"

"No; she said that possibly she would call again."

But she did not call, and Peale quitted the office at the usual time and walked to the hotel. Peale always walked when he was troubled. He found that he could think better while walking, but in this case he found that he scarcely could think at all. There was nothing to do, he decided, except to wait and watch.

He reached the hotel, went to his suite, and dressed for dinner. He knocked on the door of the adjoining suite, but no voice bade him enter. He waited for a time, until the dinner hour was half over, and knocked once more.

Still there was no answer. He turned the knob and opened the door. His wife, he found, was not in her suite.

He glanced around the rooms. He searched the closets. Her hat and coat were gone, the ones she had been wearing. Perhaps, Peale thought, she was waiting for him below.

Mrs. Peale had no maid as yet, not having found one to her liking. So there was nobody for him to question. He descended in the elevator and walked slowly through the parlors, but he did not find Elizabeth. One of the elevator boys told him that she had gone out in the middle of the afternoon.

Peale sat down where he could watch the entrance, and waited, pretending to read a newspaper. He was hungry, and a bit bewildered. Where had his wife gone, and why, and why had she not left some word? Peale did not want to ask too many questions and make himself conspicuous. He waited until nine-thirty, but she did not come.

At last he went to the dining room and ate a meal, and then went back to the suite. In time, there came a knock at the door, and he hurried to it, expecting to see his wife. He opened the door and stepped back. Before him were the district attorney, an assistant, and a detective connected with the official's office.

"Hoping I'd find you in, Peale," the district attorney said. "We have some business with you."

Peale felt his heart hammering at his ribs. He invited them in, showed them to chairs, sat down himself, wondering what it was all about. Michael Riley owned the district attorney's office, Peale knew. The district attorney and his force jumped when Riley pulled the strings.

"Well, what can I do for you?" Peale asked. "Has some client of mine been getting into serious trouble?"

"I'd like to ask you a few questions, Peale," the district attorney said.

"Fire away! I'll answer them if I can."

"They are of a peculiar nature. You're a lawyer, Peale, and a good one. You need not answer any question that — er — would tend to incriminate you."

"Incriminate *me*? Great Scot!" Peale exclaimed. "What on earth could I do to incriminate myself?"

"You are willing to answer my questions?"

"Certainly."

"Do you know the location of Dugan's saloon?"

"I do, if you mean that dive in the alley off National Avenue."

"That is the one — yes," said the district attorney. "Have you ever visited the place?"

"So that is it!" Peale exclaimed. "The genial Michael Riley is after my skin. Very well. I was there yesterday morning, say about eleven o'clock."

"You admit that freely."

"Of course."

"Peale, you are not in the habit of visiting such places, are you?"

"Certainly not!"

"Can you explain why you happened to go there yesterday morning, Peale?"

"I can, and possibly will do so, if you'll let me know what you are driving at," Peale replied.

"Perhaps you'd just better answer the question," said the district attorney. "Of course, if you feel that you cannot do so —"

"Let's get down to brass tacks!" Peale interrupted. "I suppose that Michael Riley is trying to frame something on me — I wouldn't be the first man. I went to that saloon — yes — about eleven o'clock yesterday morning. I was watching a man. Is it anything unusual for a lawyer to watch a man if he is gathering evidence in favor of one of his clients?"

"It is usual, I believe, under certain conditions. Will you tell me the name of the man?"

"Not at present," said Peale.

"You were married a short time ago, I believe."

"Yes," Peale replied, "but that has nothing to do with Dugan's saloon, has it?"

"Where is your wife now, Mr. Peale?"

"I expect her at any moment," Peale said.

"You do not know where she is?"

"Not exactly — at this moment."

"Peale, as a matter of fact — I know it well, and so do you, so there's not use beating about the bush — as a matter of fact you are not blessed with the world's goods to a great extent, are you?"

"Well, I'm no millionaire," Peale said.

"Isn't it a fact that you have had trouble making both ends meet?"

"Not exactly that bad," said Peale. "But I haven't been enjoying many luxuries."

"Yet three days ago you moved to this hotel, to an expensive suite, did you not?"

"After my marriage — yes."

"And it is the truth, isn't it, that your bank balance is somewhere near fifty thousand dollars now?"

"How the deuce did you know that?"

"I am the district attorney, and sometimes it is my duty to know certain things."

"Well, you're right," Peale said, remembering that Elizabeth had told him she had placed the remainder of the fifty thousand to his credit the day before.

"Do you mind saying how you got that much money so quickly?" the attorney general asked.

"That is scarcely your business."

"Perhaps it is," the district attorney said. "I am afraid that your answers are far from being satisfactory. I regret it, of course, though we are not exactly friends. I hate to see a member of the bar in trouble."

"Trouble?"

"You were in Dugan's saloon yesterday morning about eleven o'clock, so you admit. At that hour, Mr. Peale, the sum of forty-five thousand dollars was stolen from a desk in the rear room. It had been put there by a certain contractor who was about to settle a bill for materials, and pay off his men. You were seen following that contractor into the saloon. You were seen, before that, watching him as he drew the money at the bank."

"What utter rot!" Peale cried.

"Careful, Mr. Peale. I am merely stating the case to you. You followed the man into Dugan's saloon. You were seen coming from the rear room. Mr. Riley and three other men saw you."

"They saw me, all right!" Peale said. "But they saw me in the hall, and I had a bit of a row with them."

"All four are ready to swear —"

"I don't doubt they'd swear to anything to get me."

"They are ready to swear that you were the only man in that room after the money was left there. You came from the room, and fled when they tried to stop you and ask you questions. A few hours later, your bride deposited forty-five thousand dollars to your account. It was her own check, of course, but she had made a similar deposit in her own bank before making the deposit for you. I am afraid that my man must serve a warrant on you, Peale."

The accused man sprang to his feet. "And do you think you can get away with a raw deal like that?" he cried. "I can explain about that money — my wife can."

"Just where is your wife, Mr. Peale?" the district attorney asked. "Perhaps I can enlighten you. She is in a place where she'll be kept until you are sent to prison for theft, Mr. Peale. Without her testimony, which would carry little weight with a jury at best, you are helpless! You can't fight Michael Riley and get away with it!"

"You can't frame me like this!" Peale screeched. "Don't think you can!"

But the district attorney's detective, grinning, snapped the handcuffs on the wrists of Richard Z. Peale.

CHAPTER VI
AN UNEXPECTED VISITOR

FOR a moment Peale fought against the indignity of the handcuffs, scarcely realizing what he was doing, but it availed him nothing. He knew, of course, that he could expect no mercy from the henchmen of the vindictive boss. Riley had planned his downfall, and was trying to put it into effect.

"No sense — in these!" Peale gasped, shaking his manacled wrists toward the district attorney. "I'm no — murderer, am I? Take the things off — !"

"That is entirely up to the officer — but I imagine that he will not care to take a chance in a case of your kind," the district attorney replied. "You would not be an easy man to handle if you attempted an escape, and you are accused of the theft of forty-five thousand dollars, remember. That is no small sum. However, we'll call a taxicab — you won't have to go to the jail in a common patrol wagon."

The word "jail" seemed to beat into Peale's brain, and force him to realize his predicament. It was all a trap, he guessed now — Elizabeth Gralin, Bob Drake, everything! And Peale knew enough of Riley's work to feel sure that there would be an abundance of evidence forthcoming that would point to his guilt.

The district attorney ordered the detective to let him put on a business coat in place of the evening-dress affair. Then they went out, and Peale locked the door of the suite and handed the key to the hall-boy.

Down the elevator they went, and through the crowded lobby. Peale tried to hide his manacled hands, but could not. Two or three who knew him started forward, as if to offer help, but the glares of the detective and the district attorney warned them away. Men and women of the better sort glanced at those telltale handcuffs and turned away as if from a pestilence.

Peale raged at first, and then, as they got into the taxicab, he almost sobbed. He had come to this — just because he dared to be honest and try to get along in his profession. He had come to this because he had opposed a crooked political boss.

He wondered where his wife had gone. He was almost convinced now that it was all a trap. Of course, the district attorney had intimated that his wife was being detained forcibly until Peale could be dealt with — but Peale did not believe that. She had planted the trap — that was all. There was the money in the bank, that he could not explain. Perhaps, after his conviction, she would get a divorce on the grounds that he was a felon, and then Michael Riley probably would pay her handsomely for having aided in sending an innocent man to prison.

Now a reaction set in, and Peale told himself that he would fight! He would tell his story straight, and force men and women, and above all a jury, to believe it. There was his copy of the contract in his office — the contract between himself and Elizabeth Gralin. That would show that he had expected to get forty-five thousand dollars beside the five thousand received when the contract was signed.

The next instant, he told himself that he was doomed if he depended too much upon that contract. Michael Riley's witnesses would kill that, and the district attorney would make every effort to show that the contract was made purposely to cover up some theft. With Elizabeth missing, the evidence for the defense would be slight. Peale could not hope to gain much through the testimony of his stenographer.

The taxicab reached the jail, and Peale was conducted inside. He said nothing as his name was entered on the blotter. He merely glared at the deputy sheriff in charge for the night, and when he faced the district attorney, who had accompanied them to the jail, he sneered openly.

"You and all your crooked gang can't get away with it!" he told that official. "You've overlooked a few things in your eagerness to get me. Go back to Michael Riley, your master, the man who has bought you and owns you, and tell him for me that he has made the big mistake of his career."

"I don't want any more of that kind of talk out of you!" the district attorney snarled.

"You'll get a lot worse before we are done!" Peale promised. Then he faced the turnkey. "Put me in a cell, if you're going to; I don't like my present company," he said.

"Got a right to use the telephone, if you want to call counsel," said the turnkey, from force of habit.

Peale walked across to the telephone on the wall. The handcuffs had been removed, and he had been searched as if he had been an ordinary criminal. He hesitated a moment, and then called Bob Drake.

Before very long, Bob Drake's valet answered the telephone. Mr. Drake was not home, he reported. He had not seen him since morning, he said. Yes, he would give him Mr. Peale's message when he came in.

Peale turned away from the instrument to see the district attorney grinning at him. He told himself, then, that Drake was in the plot, of course, and probably would manage to keep away. With a heavy heart, Peale went into the cell assigned to him.

He did not sleep at all that night. He walked back and forth in the narrow confines of the cell, and sat on the edge of the bunk for an hour at a time, and tried to think it out. He tried to arouse himself, to tell himself that he had to fight — yet he seemed unable to do so. Peale was numbed by the blow that had struck him.

Morning came, and he sent out for his breakfast. The papers were taken in to him, and he saw that Michael Riley had done his work well. The name of Richard Z. Peale was held up to scorn. He had descended to theft, the articles said, because he needed money to support his bride in a lavish fashion. He was stealing for a woman!

It revealed that Peale had very little money of his own, very little business. His wife had disappeared, it was said, and there was some possibility of her being arrested as an accomplice when she was located. The newspapers made it appear that Richard Peale and his bride were criminals and confidence workers not worthy of a kind thought on the part of any honest man or woman.

Peale raged when he read the articles.

"They're unfair — unfair!" he cried.

He cursed the name of Michael Riley beneath his breath. He wanted to fight — fight! And it seemed that he didn't have a friend in the world.

They arraigned him that day, of course. Peale pleaded "not guilty" and asked to be admitted to bail. The judge, owned by Michael Riley, fixed the bail at forty-five thousand dollars, the amount of the alleged theft.

Then Peale tried to raise the bail. They allowed him to use the telephone in the office of the jail, and grinned as he did so. In the first place, he could not use the money Elizabeth had deposited to his account. That had been tied up by the court on the supposition that it was stolen money. And Peale had only six thousand of his own, and that included the five thousand Elizabeth had given him when they signed their contract.

He did not know where to turn. He telephoned Bob Drake again, and was informed that the detective had not yet returned. Peale knew of no other man who would arrange that large amount of bail for him. He went back to his cell.

His stenographer braved the jail that morning, and took him news that the office had been robbed the night before. The safe had been opened, and papers stolen, she reported. His contract with Elizabeth Gralin was among them.

So even that small bit of evidence for the defense was gone, Peale told himself. Michael Riley's trap was complete. They were going to railroad him to prison. He could not get out on bail to gather his own evidence. He could not get it gathered by anybody else. He could only engage some attorney to aid him — and run the risk that the attorney was a man of Riley's. If he allowed the court to name an attorney, he knew it would be a Riley man.

"They can't do it — can't do it!" Peale told himself.

But he knew that they could do it, unless something akin to a miracle happened. It is comparatively an easy thing to railroad a man to jail. Two or three unscrupulous men can band together and tell a story, and have an innocent man confined for months awaiting trial — and then, their purpose perhaps served, they can let the case fall to bits and escape trouble themselves. It is being done everyday, and Peale knew it. The courts make it a point to deal in the law, but not always in justice!

There seemed to be nothing that he could do. The long day passed, and he ate his evening meal. It was an hour or so afterward that the turnkey and another man came along the corridor.

The other man was Michael Riley. The turnkey went away and left the boss standing just outside the cell door.

"So the famous attorney is in trouble, is he?" Riley asked, chuckling. "I thought I'd drop in and see how you were getting along, and whether I could do anything. Always willing to oblige a friend, of course."

"I'm no friend of yours, you crook!" Peale exclaimed.

"Now, isn't that too bad. If you were a friend of mine, this little matter might be arranged. It is just possible that I have enough influence to get you out of jail."

"I don't doubt it — you had enough to get me in here!" Peale said bitterly.

"That was because you have been a naughty boy," Riley declared. "Will you be good if I let you out?"

"What are the terms?" Peale wanted to know.

"I'll have you released on your own recognizance, and the case continued indefinitely," Riley said. "You'll leave the town, and stay away. If you return, the case will be called."

"You mean that you want me to pretend to run away, so everybody will believe me guilty!" said Peale. "You'll hold this thing over my head all my life, try to force me to do your bidding if occasion ever requires it! Not much, Mr. Riley! I'll go free, with my name cleared, or I'll go to the pen an innocent man! Get that? I don't make any compromise agreement with a snake like you!"

"Better think again!" Riley snarled. "I seldom make an offer more than once."

"Don't waste your breath making this one again," Peale told him. "And don't think the game is over yet!"

"It isn't!" said Riley. "It'll not be over until you've had your head shaved and have been given a number!" He whirled around and stamped his way up the corridor. Peale heard the door at the far end open and clang shut again. He knew that he had thrown away his last chance, but he did not care very much. Riley would hold no whip over him for the remainder of his life! He'd be free entirely, or he'd go to the big prison up the river, and trust to luck that he'd be cleared some day. He remembered that Walton had been framed — and he had saved Walton. Perhaps Riley would make some mistake this time, and he could save himself. That was the only chance he seemed to have remaining.

Peale prepared to get some sleep. He was getting a bit used to the cell now. He stretched himself on the bunk, wrapped in the blanket that had been furnished him, and closed his eyes. The lights had been extinguished, save those in the corridor. The jail was quiet. They had put Peale in a corridor where there was no other prisoner near him, and for that much he was grateful.

Two hours later, something awakened him suddenly. He sat up on the bunk. He saw that the turnkey was at the door, beckoning him.

Peale slipped from the blankets and stepped softly to the door.

"I'm takin' a big chance, Mr. Peale, and I hope that you appreciate it," the night turnkey said. "I ain't a Riley man, and never was, but I don't aim to cut my own throat by gettin' careless where the boss is concerned."

"What's all this about?" Peale demanded.

"There's a friend of yours called to see you, Mr. Peale. I'm going to slip him in here for a little time. He wants to talk to you, but you'll please be careful?"

"Certainly," Peale said.

The turnkey slipped away, and an instant later a second man came quietly along the corridor and stopped before the door of the cell. Peale looked at him in surprise. It was Walton, the man Peale had saved from prison.

CHAPTER VII

TO DOWN THE BOSS

THE arrival of Walton was a complete surprise to Peale. He had not thought that his recently acquitted client would be likely to come to his aid. He had hoped that the mysterious visitor was Bob Drake, for he still wanted to think that Drake was his friend, though appearances were to the contrary.

Walton's face was very pale, and he glanced around the jail nervously and wet his lips like a man filled with dread and apprehension. He grasped the bars of the cell door and put his face close to them.

"I — I've got to be careful, Mr. Peale," he said. "I got here just as soon as I could after hearin' about it. That turnkey is a friend of mine. He let me in — and we've got to protect him, of course."

"Certainly," Peale said. "What is it, Walton?"

"What is it? Why, I want to help you, Mr. Peale. I hope you don't think I'm the kind of man that forgets. You're in trouble right now because you saved me from bein' railroaded to the pen, and I ain't forgettin' that, you can bet. I guessed what you're up against. That Riley is a devil, Mr. Peale. But I'm goin' to help you."

"How can you, Walton?"

"Ain't it the truth that you can't find out things because you can't get out on bail?"

"Yes."

"Well — I'm out, thanks to you! And I don't see why I can't do things for you. I can arrange to get in here every other night or so, and make my reports and get my orders from you."

"That's fine, Walton!" Peale said, and he meant it, too. "I'm glad that I've got one friend in the world."

"You've got a few scattered here and there, but most of them are afraid to let it be known," Walton told him. "You let me help you, Mr. Peale!"

"Can I trust you, Walton?"

"You bet you can! Didn't you save me from the pen? Or maybe the electric chair? Riley was after me, and you sidetracked him, didn't you? And do you think I'd do his dirty work now? You think I'm doin' this for Riley — that I've made up with the boss after what he tried to do to me?"

Peale looked him straight in the eyes, and then put his hand through the bars, "I trust you, Walton!" he said. "But, what can you do to help me now?"

"Why, didn't I do some of Michael Riley's dirty work for about ten years or so?" Walton demanded. "Don't you reckon I know his ways? I know his gang, too, and about everything connected, of course, since I don't belong to the crowd any longer, but I can be careful in this case, all right. I'll stay under cover, but I'll work."

"And how do you intend to begin?" Peale asked.

"All I know, Mr. Peale, is what I've read in the papers, and a few extra things I picked up yesterday. Your office has been robbed, ain't it? That means, I suppose, that Riley got some papers that might help clear you."

"Exactly."

"Well, I'll try to get 'em back, if they ain't been destroyed. And your wife can't be found, can she?"

"So they say, Walton."

"There's somethin' funny about that. 'Course I don't know the lady, Mr. Peale, and I suppose you do, she bein' your wife. Do you reckon she's been taken some place and is bein' held?"

"I was given to understand as much, Walton, but I'm not sure about it," Peale replied. "There are some things I can't tell you, Walton. You'll just have to work as well as you can."

"Well, I'll scout around and find out," Walton said. "If they're keepin' her some place, I'll know it before long. Anything else you can think of, Mr. Peale?"

"Yes. See if you can find Bob Drake and get him to me. And find out for sure — for sure, Walton — whether he belongs to Riley's gang."

"You can bet he don't. Didn't Mr. Drake get evidence that helped you get me off?"

"He did that — yes. But there have been some things that appear peculiar —"

"Why, you ought to be ashamed of yourself, Mr. Peale. Mr. Drake is a square man, all right. You want me to look him up?"

"I haven't been able to get in touch with him since I was arrested," Peale replied. "Find him, if you can — and if he is a true friend of mine, he'll come to me."

"I'll do my best, Mr. Peale. Anything else now?"

"Isn't that a pretty big order for one night?" Peale asked.

Walton grinned. "Well, you see, I want to help you all I can," he said. "And I won't be alone, either."

"What do you mean by that, Walton?"

"I ain't the only one that's got an idea he wants to hand it to Riley," Walton replied. "There are men right in his gang —"

"Be careful, Walton! They may double cross you!"

"Not these men. They want to hand it to Riley, I tell you — and I know. That little game he tried to put up on me scared them some. They want to get out from under. I've been busy ever since that case against me was dismissed, Mr. Peale — before you was arrested, I mean. We've got it all planned to get Michael Riley, and get him good, and this trouble of yours just gives us a big chance. Don't you worry any, Mr. Peale. We're strong for you! We're strong for anybody that has the nerve to fight that big crook!"

"Thanks," Peale said. There didn't seem to be anything else to say just then.

"Well, I'll blow out of here now," Walton went on. "I don't want to get our friend the turnkey in trouble. I'll make a report just as soon as I can, and you just keep a stiff upper lip, Mr. Peale! You ain't licked yet, and don't you believe you are!"

Without another word, Walton slipped down the corridor like a shadow. Peale heard him whispering to the turnkey in the distance, heard the door of the corridor opened and closed as softly as possible.

Peale sat down on the side of his bunk and held his head in his hands. He did not know whether to be optimistic. He wanted to trust Walton fully, but he was getting to the point where he did not dare trust any human being.

Even if Walton was true and sincere, there was little possibility that he could do anything, Peale told himself. Even if Walton did have with him three of four disgruntled members of Riley's gang, that did not mean that the boss would be undone easily. Walton was not noted for his mentality.

But Peale did not know Walton entirely. He might have been lacking in education as the world accepts it, but he had education along certain other lines. He knew every square foot of the city. He knew every dive, every resort — knew where thieves congregated, and where a man could get the latest gossip of the underworld. He could have told where politicians of the poorer class met to have their little private talks. Walton knew many things.

He had not told a falsehood about the others, either. There were six of them, six men who had sworn to get square with Michael Riley, because they felt that the boss had not treated them fairly in a certain matter. They had been nursing their wrath for some time, and now the spark of anger was kindled into a flame. They were unscrupulous, as might be expected of Riley's men — and they could be just as unscrupulous against the boss as they had been in his behalf.

Walton managed to slip out into the street without being seen, much to the relief of the turnkey. He kept to the shadows until he was some distance from the jail, and then pulled his hat down over his eyes and made his way rapidly toward the poorer section of the city, alert for officers of the law. He did not want to be questioned; he wanted to be forgotten for the time being, while he did his work.

It took him some time to reach the section of the city toward which he was heading, and it was almost daylight when he did reach it. He made his way down a dark, evil-smelling alley and came to a little door that opened into a tumbledown shed behind a cheap lodging house. Walton knocked on the door in a peculiar manner.

A bolt was shot, the door was opened, and Walton slipped inside. The bolt was shot back again, and Walton put one hand against the wall and followed another man through the darkness.

They came to a second door, passed through it, and were in the building proper. They went through a dark hall, ascended a short flight of stairs, and entered a small room at the back of the building.

A single candle was burning on the table there. Five men were sitting around a table, playing cards silently. The man who had led Walton in stepped up beside them, and the card game ceased.

"Well?" one of them whispered to Walton.

"I saw him," Walton whispered in reply.

"Will he let us work for him?"

"Yes."

"That's the stuff. And what did he have to say?"

"It's like this," Walton said. "We've got an idea that Mrs. Peale is bein' held somewhere against her will. There's somethin' funny about that woman, but Peale wouldn't open up to me. And he wants to find Bob Drake worst of all. He had half a notion that Drake was tryin' to double cross him, but I told him different. We've got to find his wife, and find Bob Drake, and get back, if we can, them papers that was taken from his safe when his office was robbed. That's the first thing to be done."

"Well, that hadn't ought to be a very hard job," said one of the others.

"We'd better scatter now, and meet here tomorrow at midnight," said Walton. "And for Heaven's sake, don't make any break and give the thing away. You know what it'd mean to make a break, don't you? Riley would get his fingers around your throat mighty quick!"

"There won't be any mistakes made," one of the others growled.

"And we've got to be careful gettin' in and out of here. Go one at a time, and about five minutes apart — and don't everybody turn south toward the avenue, either. We'd ought to gather some information today, I reckon; don't you?"

"Sure!"

"And we want to make it as quick as we can," Walton added. "Gee, it almost make me sick to see a gent like Mr. Peale in a cell! And him a white man with nerve enough to fight Mike Riley! We've just got to save him — that's all!"

"We'll do it, all right," another promised.

"Start goin', then," Walton ordered.

The first man slipped away like a shadow, darted through the door and was gone. One by one they went, five minutes apart, until only Walton was left in the little room.

CHAPTER VIII

TWO BURGLARIES

THE following day was spent by Richard Peale in reading the newspapers, eating his meals, and exercising by walking up and down the corridor. He shaved and brushed his clothes, and tried to make himself as presentable as possible. He applied to the court for a reduction in bail, more to show that he still was in the fight than anything else, and had the judge refuse him promptly.

Peale had expected the refusal, of course, but he argued his point well. Yet it did him little good — for the evening papers gave him no credit. All but one were controlled by Riley, and that one did not happen to have a courthouse reporter brainy enough to realize the points that Peale had made.

Then came the night, and though Peale retired, he could not sleep. He wondered whether Walton would make another visit, and whether he would have anything to report. One o'clock came and passed, and two and three o'clock, and Peale finally fell asleep because he could remain awake no longer.

Morning broke, and another long day began. Peale had nothing to do. He was innocent, but his hands were tied. He paced the corridor, and ate his meals — and just before evening Michael Riley visited him once more.

"I'm giving you a last chance, Peale," the boss said. "Want to make a deal with me?"

"I don't make deals with the devil!" Peale told him.

Michael Riley laughed. "Oh, I don't blame you for being sore, Peale," he said, "but I do blame you for not knowing when you are licked. I just want you out of this town — that's all. Promise to get out, and I'll see that you are released the first thing in the morning — have you released tonight, if you say so. You can even take with you that money in the bank."

"Very kind of you to let me have my own money!" Peale sneered. "I'll make no deal with you, Riley. You might as well save your breath instead of talking to me. Maybe I've got a few cards up my sleeve."

"If you have, they're probably deuces," Riley told him. "I'm holding all the big cards myself."

"You think you are!"

"I am!" Riley declared. "You're a stubborn fool, Peale. If you had seen the light, you could be rich and famous today. But you came into this town and started in by treading on my corns — and that always makes a man mad."

"I never had an ambition to be a crook!"

"You might as well have been as to have that reputation now. For nothing on earth can save you, Peale. If you don't make this deal with me, you're going to the pen."

"Get out!" Peale said.

Michael Riley growled his rage, and departed. Peale paced the corridor again, and finally sat down on the bunk in his cell. He was waiting for the night.

When it came, he still waited — waited for the turnkey to bring Walton to him. But the turnkey did not. That official entered the corridor about three o'clock in the morning, and shook his head at Peale.

"Haven't heard a thing from him," he whispered through the

bars. "Don't know what's become of him, or what he's doing. I wouldn't put too much confidence in anything, or build up hopes too strong, if I was you."

Peale was nervous, and he almost sobbed. He slept fitfully during the remainder of that night, and faced the new day with his courage considerably lessened. Why, it wasn't to be believed, he told himself! How could an innocent man be subjected to such a thing? Was there no justice in the world at all? Was Michael Riley greater than law and the courts?

He trusted Walton; and he supposed that Walton had made some blunder and had been caught, and that Riley had taken care of him in his own way.

But Walton had made no blunder. He was working night and day with the six others, and they were beginning to accomplish something. On that second night, as the turnkey was talking to Peale, they were at work.

It was a few minutes before three o'clock in the morning when two men slipped along a little used lane on the outskirts of the city, and approached a ramshackle house far back from the road.

It was a night of pitch blackness. They crept forward slowly, stopping now and then to listen and to make sure of their position. They came to the house, and stretched themselves on the ground for a time, to listen again. Finally they crept forward once more, always alert. One of the men was Walton.

Now they were at the side of the house, near a window. The man with Walton lifted himself and felt at the bottom of the casement. He drew an instrument from beneath his coat, and worked swiftly. The catch snapped, the window was raised.

"Have to be careful," Walton whispered. "It ain't just gettin' to the prisoner, you know. We don't want anybody to know we've been there, see? That'd put Riley wise and spoil everything."

They slipped into the house like thieves. It was not the first time any one of them had entered a house in such a manner. They closed the window again, went through a room, and came to a hall.

Two men were on guard there. One was asleep, and the other was sitting beside a table, reading, his head nodding. Walton and the other man slipped down the wall without being seen, and started up the flight of stairs.

"The room at the back?" Walton whispered.

"Yes," his companion replied.

"Got the key?"

"Sure. Riley had me guardin' here last night. I just made an impression of the key in a cake of soap — and the rest was easy. We can get in, all right."

"Why didn't you talk to the prisoner last night, and put him wise to what was comin' off?" Walton demanded.

"Didn't have a chance, that's why. The other guard was with me all the time. After he's locked up for the night, they don't look at him again until mornin'."

They had reached a door on the upper floor now. Walton took the key and unlocked it, and they stepped inside. The other man flashed an electric torch as Walton locked the door again.

It was a prison room. There were heavy steel bars at the one window, and the door was a strong one. There were a bed, a table, and two chairs. On the bed, a man was sleeping. He was Bob Drake.

As the light from the torch was flashed in the sleeper's face, he awoke.

"Steady, Mr. Drake! We're friends!" Walton whispered.

Drake sat up in the bed. He looked the two men over, but did not speak a word.

"Friends, eh?" he said presently, being careful to whisper. "Well, what's the idea?"

"I'm Walton. Don't you know me?"

"By George — yes! Good boy, Walton!"

"I got in to see Mr. Peale, and I'm workin' for him. I've got half a dozen other men helpin' me, Mr. Drake."

"Tell me about Peale. What's happened?"

Walton and his companion stepped nearer and the torch went out.

"Got to be careful," Walton explained. "This is ticklish business. We was goin' to get you out at first, then we thought that would put Riley wise and we couldn't get the goods on him."

"Very good! But what about Peale?" Drake persisted.

"They pinched him — accused him of stealin' forty-five thousand dollars from Dugan's saloon. It's a frame, of course. And his wife can't be found. Seems she deposited that much to his credit the day they say the money was swiped and —"

"I understand — regular frame-up," Drake said. "Don't waste time telling me that. What else?"

"I guess Riley's got Mrs. Peale, and is holdin' her so she can't help her husband with her testimony. He ain't got anybody to help him but us. They tied up the coin in the bank — said it was stolen — and he can't get bail, which is forty-five thousand bucks. That's some coin, of course. And then you disappeared —"

"I did!" said Bob Drake. "I was decoyed, nabbed, and put in here. I walked right into a trap when I wasn't looking for it."

"And Mr. Peale was afraid you had turned against him."

"What? Dick thought a thing like that?"

"He had some reason for doin' it, but I ain't sure what it was — more of Riley's work, I reckon. I promised I'd find you — and I have.

You goin' to help him?"

"Let me think," said Drake.

He was silent for a minute or so, and then he grasped Walton by the arm.

"You're a wise lad, Walton," he said. "Maybe this is a chance to get Mike Riley for good! We don't want him to know we are wise, of course. I'll just stay here as a prisoner for a little longer, and try to give the impression that I know there's no possibility of escape. You can work for me on the outside."

"Yes, sir."

"We'll even keep Peale in the dark. I'll see that he gets out on bail, and that he has legal help. He can work for himself after he gets out, and we'll work for him on the side. Get the idea, Walton? Riley will be so busy watching Peale that he won't watch anybody else. How about Mrs. Peale?"

"Oh, Riley's keepin' her prisoner somewhere," Walton declared. "I guess maybe we'll find out where before tomorrow night."

"Get word to her if you can, Walton. Tell her that everything is all right — that Bob Drake says so — and that she is to remain a prisoner for the time being, if she is being treated all right. If she is not, you must rescue her, of course. That woman has nerve — she isn't a delicate doll! We want to make Riley watch Peale, and Peale only. Flash the torch again!"

Walton flashed the torch. Bob Drake took a fountain pen and a notebook from his pocket, and filled a sheet with fine writing. Then he folded the note and handed it to Walton.

"Take this to Mr. Belknot, my attorney, the first thing in the morning," he instructed. "Tell him to follow the instructions I have written, but do not tell him where I am. If there is anything I must know, get the knowledge to me as soon as you can — but be careful about it. We don't want to endanger Peale's case, and we don't want to lose our chance to square matters with Riley."

"You bet we don't!" Walton exclaimed.

"Tell Mr. Belknot that he is to obey every instruction I have written. Be careful when you go to his office, Walton — some of Riley's men might be watching him."

"I'll get it to him without goin' to his office," Walton said.

"Good boy!"

"Well, we'll blow out of here now."

The torch was extinguished. The door was unlocked again, Walton and the other man passed through, and the door was locked. They went down the stairs, found that both guards were sleeping, got from the hall into the side room, went through the window, and closed it. Unless somebody noticed that the window catch has been broken, nobody would guess that Walton and his companion had visited the prisoner.

Walton did not intend to go to Belknot's office the following morning and be seen by one of Riley's henchmen. He had a better plan than that. He left the other man at a certain dark corner, and hurried toward the better residential section of the city.

Walton knew where Belknot lived. To tell the truth, he knew a great deal about the Belknot residence. Years before, he had played burglar there, under the direction of Michael Riley, and had obtained some papers from the attorney's desk.

Block after block he hurried, for he knew it would be daylight within the hour. He reached the residence, looked around it, and finally made his way to a side veranda.

It did not take Walton long to get inside, but once there he was forced to move with care. He made his way to the upper floor, where the sleeping rooms were located. He entered three before he located the one in which the distinguished attorney was slumbering.

Belknot came from a deep sleep to find a bright light shining in his face and to hear a harsh voice whispering:

"Not a cheep, or you'll be plugged!"

Then, sure the attorney would remain quiet for a moment, Walton went on:

"I ain't any burglar. I'm from Mr. Drake — got a letter for you. I slipped in this way because Mr. Drake don't want any of the Riley gang to guess you're communicatin' with him."

Belknot's courage had returned. "There is a light switch at the head of the bed," he said, "and the shades are drawn."

Walton found the light switch and turned it on, and the two men regarded each other.

"I'm Walton, the man Mr. Peale defended," the intruder explained. "I've been workin' to help Mr. Peale."

"But, how about Drake?"

"He's bein' kept a prisoner by Riley."

"Why, the infernal scoundrel. I'll —"

"You'll sit tight, that's what you'll do!" Walton told him. "Mr. Drake wants to go on bein' a prisoner for a time yet. He wouldn't even let me tell you where he is. We're after Riley, and if Riley gets wise we won't be able to land him. Here's the note Mr. Drake wrote and told me to give you."

He handed it over, and Belknot read it quickly.

"No doubt about it!" he said. "This came from Mr. Drake, all right."

"Think I'm workin' some sort of game?"

"Certainly not, my boy! I think that you are a true friend to Mr. Peale and to Mr. Drake — and hope you'll be one to me. A man needs friends of your sort."

"Aw! Mr. Peale did a lot for me — and Mr. Drake, too. I didn't have a cent, and Riley was on my trail, and if it hadn't been for them two men I'd be in the pen right now. I'm not forgettin' that, Mr. Belknot."

"Will you get the chance to communicate with Mr. Drake again?" the lawyer asked.

"I might, if it's necessary."

"Come to me here tomorrow night — say at about one o'clock in the morning," Belknot instructed. "Come to the side door, and I'll let you in, and not even a servant will see you."

"You want to be careful!"

"I'll be careful," replied the attorney, smiling.

"You goin' to get Mr. Peale out on bail? Mr. Drake said you would."

"I'll do it if I can, my boy. Those are Drake's instructions. I'll get him out myself — understand? Mr. Drake's name is not to be connected with the case yet."

"I got that! We don't want any slips," Walton declared. "Guess I'd better blow out of here now. It's almost daylight, and I've had a pretty busy night. I'll be here tomorrow night, all right."

Belknot let him out the side door. Walton slipped through the shadows and made his way to the poorer part of the city, to the little room where the others probably would be waiting.

CHAPTER IX

ANOTHER BLOW

AT ten o'clock the following morning, the turnkey stopped before the door of Peale's cell.

"Into court!" he said.

"What's the idea?" Peale wanted to know. The date of his trial had been set, and it was a month away.

"Don't ask me what the court wants, Mr. Peale," the turnkey protested. "I got troubles enough of my own without tryin' to run the court."

Peale followed him through the corridor, up the winding stairs, and to the judge's chambers. Belknot was there.

"Peale, I have come to bail you out," he said. "I've arranged case bail, and must put you on your honor, of course —"

"I consider myself so," Peale said.

The arrangements were made almost instantly, and Peale went from the courthouse with Belknot, a free man for the time being, at least. He took a deep breath and glanced around.

"Hereafter, I always shall get a client out of jail as soon as possible," he said. "Heavens, what a relief."

They got into Belknot's automobile and started for his office.

"Understand, I am doing this on my own behalf," Belknot explained.

"I beg your pardon?"

"I am putting up the bail myself. I do not think that you are guilty, Peale."

"Thanks for that!"

"And I hate to see a man like you in jail to satisfy the spite of Michael Riley. The boss cannot hurt me, for I am an old man, and established. So I dared to affront him by bailing you out. That isn't all, of course. You've got a fight before you yet. But now you have the chance to prepare for it."

"Where's Drake?" Peale asked suddenly, looking closely at the older man.

"Peale, I don't know. I haven't seen Bob Drake for several days. But that is nothing. He often is away on that confounded detective business on his. I attend to his property and all that, but I don't need him often. I tell you the truth — I do not know where he is."

And that was the truth, of course. Peale looked ahead at the busy street, and wondered.

"Funny!" he commented. "I didn't think that Bob would desert me at such a time. Surely he doesn't think that I am guilty."

"I feel sure that he doesn't," Belknot replied.

Peale remembered again the mystery of Drake's meeting with Riley, and the mystery of Drake's meeting with his wife. He wondered what had become of the woman he had married under such peculiar circumstances. She must have been a tool of Riley's, he thought. Riley would be willing to risk five thousand, or even fifty thousand, to remove an enemy.

They reached Belknot's offices, and remained there for a time. Peale telephoned to his own and found the faithful stenographer on duty. He announced that he had been released on bail and would be at the office later in the day. Then he engaged a taxicab and hurried to the hotel.

A wide-eyed clerk handed him the key to his suite, and he went up immediately. He had a bath, and changed his suit, and then walked around the rooms, and also through the suite his wife had used. Nothing seemed changed.

He was about to leave for the office when there came a knock at the door. The manager was there.

"I'm sorry, Mr. Peale," he said, "but I'll have to ask you to vacate, I'm afraid."

"Worrying about your money?"

"It isn't that, of course. But you are — er — under a cloud, and of course other guests might not wish to mingle with you. Your wife has disappeared, it appears, and that is bad, too. If you'll kindly have all the things packed — I'll send in a maid to pack your wife's trunks."

"Very well! Send her in!" Peale said. "And tell the porter to come for the trunks in half an hour. I suppose I may use the telephone without contaminating anybody? You can have it fumigated afterward, you know."

"Certainly you may use it, Mr. Peale. I'm sorry about this, really, but what else can I do?"

"Nothing, when you are under the thumb of a man like Riley," Peale said.

"What do you mean, sir?"

"I mean that you've had a message from Mike Riley — that's what I mean. He has ordered you to make me get out — wants to humiliate me all he can!"

The look on the manager's face told Peale that he had guessed correctly. He sneered at the man, and turned to his packing. A few minutes later her used the telephone to engage rooms in a less pretentious hotel. Half an hour later, he moved, sending his wife's trunks to a storage warehouse.

Then Peale went to his office, heard the office boy and stenographer declare that they believed him innocent, paid them their wages, and told them that business would go on as usual.

For Peale was not whipped. His fighting blood was thoroughly aroused now. The hotel manager's words had put the finishing touch to his anger. Peale was out to fight Michael Riley to the last ditch.

He called in a young attorney in whom he could put some trust, and engaged him to help gather evidence. He wished that Bob Drake could be there to help him. Drake had a way of gathering in elusive evidence that was charming. He didn't know what to think of Drake; the old doubts began assailing his mind again.

He began thinking of his wife, too. Surely, he thought, she must have been merely a tool. Else, where had she gone? Why had she not come forward and helped him?

Once more he told himself what a fool he had been to sign that contract with her, and to marry her at her request. Yet she had seemed such a refined, cultured woman — the sort any man would be proud to have as a wife.

Peale tried to think of other things, but it seemed that he could think of nothing except Elizabeth. Despite appearances to the contrary, he could not force himself to believe wholly that she had been engaged in a plot against him. But her absence seemed to indicate it.

During the afternoon, he received a telephone call.

"This is Walton," came the voice over the wire. "Glad to see you're out, Mr. Peale. Hope you never get in again, but you'd better watch for the big boss and his gang."

"What do you mean, Walton?"

"I've got it straight that he's mighty sore because somebody put up the bail, and he's busy plannin' his little tricks right now. But don't you worry! You just keep your eyes peeled. You've got a few friends watchin' over you, you know."

"Thanks, Walton."

"And you don't want to worry about Bob Drake, either."

"Have you found out anything about him?" Peale asked.

"Nothin' that I'm ready to report yet, Mr. Peale."

"And how about my wife?" Peale wanted to know.

"I ain't ready to report on that, yet, either, Mr. Peale, but maybe I'll have some news for you tomorrow. I'll let you know just as soon as I can."

Walton stopped the conversation, then, though Peale wanted to pour questions at him, give him instructions and advice. Where was Bob Drake? Where was Elizabeth? Why had everybody deserted him? Why had Belknot bailed him out with cash? It wasn't at all like Belknot, who was a conservative attorney of the old school.

The Belknot business worried him a bit. He felt sure that Belknot had been acting for a client. But the old attorney had declared that he did not know where Bob Drake was, and so Peale got the idea that he had not been acting for Drake.

Peale left the office at five o'clock, went to a small restaurant for a meal, and then walked toward the little hotel where he had engaged rooms.

It was growing dusk as he made his way down the street. At a corner of the avenue, he was jostled by two men.

"Look where you're goin'!" one of them cried.

Peale stepped back to apologize. The two men launched themselves at him.

"Double up your fists at us, will you?" one of them shrieked.

Peale found that he had a fight on his hands. It flashed through his mind that these men were not intoxicated, that they were deliberately forcing him to fight.

Then he guessed the truth. This was another trick of Michael Riley. The police would come, and he would be arrested with these two men. He would be charged with fighting and disorderly conduct, and the newspapers would play up the story. He would have to put up more bail — perhaps even the court would cancel the other bail and order him back to jail, saying that he could not be trusted at large with such a charge pending against him.

Peale fought back as well as he could. Suddenly more men ran from the gloom and got between him and his two adversaries, and he heard the voice of Walton in his ear:

"Beat it, Mr. Peale! This is a trick! Beat it, before the cops get here!"

Peale ran. Walton and his companions had knocked the two men out before they could be recognized, for they had been busy watching Peale, and supposed the men plunging out of the gloom were officers come to make the arrest. When the police did arrive, they found two men unconscious and groaning on the ground — and that was all.

Peale got to his room and bathed his bruised knuckles. He sat down before a window, breathing heavily. The fight was beginning to get on his nerves. He wanted to whip Michael Riley, put him out of the way politically forever, but he didn't know whether he could make the fight longer alone.

He didn't want to run away; he couldn't run away with that charge hanging over him. He was not the sort of man to skip his bail.

"There are too many mysteries!" Peale told himself. "My wife — Bob Drake — the bail! I'm a regular slave to mystery, that is what I am!"

But he still could fight, he told himself. Walton, at least, was working for him — Walton and his friends. He was at liberty, he had a chance to prepare his case for trial. Surely, he could break through the perjuries of Riley's people and tear their case to shreds. If he only could find Elizabeth — and she proved to be loyal to him! But he did not dare think of such a thing.

"She was one of Riley's people," Peale told himself. "The whole thing indicates that! And I walked right into the trap — signed that contract, married her, let her put that money into the bank for me. If I hadn't gone into Dugan's that day — ! That must have been a part of the trap, too. Drake must be in it! He knew I had seen him, would follow him —"

Peale stopped. He simply could not bring himself to believe fully that Bob Drake was with Riley and against him. Had not Drake fought Riley in the Walton case? Did not Drake have a fortune that made him independent of Riley?

The telephone rang, and Peale hurried across the room to answer the call. It was from the young attorney he had engaged to aid him.

"Well, they're playing another card, Mr. Peale," the young lawyer said.

"What now?"

"Riley isn't going to give us time to plan our case. The judge, last thing before court adjourned, fixed up the calendar again. Your case has been put ahead."

"When?" Peale asked.

"Called for tomorrow morning, Mr. Peale. Shall I come up there?"

"Yes!" Peale cried.

Called for the morning! And Peale knew very well that Riley's judge would not grant a continuance. Riley and the district attorney were going to get him before he could arrange his defense. Riley's men would pack the jury panel. Peale saw but little hope!

CHAPTER X

A BOLD PLAN

WALTON appeared at the residence of Belknot at the appointed hour, and the aged attorney let him in.

"My boy, you must get word to Mr. Drake as soon as you can," he said. "He must help us now. They have put the Peale case forward on the calendar, and the trail is to begin in the morning."

"Gee!" Walton said. "Mike Riley don't lose any time, does he?"

"This is a serious affair, my boy! Mr. Peale can delay the case the greater part of one day, perhaps, through the selection of the jury, but that will amount to little. He has not had time to prepare his case, if you know what that means. They'll have him in prison, if we don't save him. Go to Mr. Drake and tell him this. He'd better get away, if he can, and try to help."

Walton left the Belknot house like a shadow. He crossed the city as swiftly as possible with safety, for he didn't want to be seen by some officer. He did not have time to send the alarm to the others. He would help Drake get free, and then they would work together — that was Walton's idea.

He was almost frantic now. For he realized what it was that Riley was trying to do. A Riley judge would rush the case, a Riley district attorney and assistants would talk to a Riley jury, and Riley witnesses would perjure themselves for Riley. Unless help reached him, Peale was doomed.

Walton came to the house and crept through the yard until he was beside the building. He stopped there to watch and listen. Finally he slipped the window up, an inch at a time. Next he took a revolver from his pocket, thankful that he had it with him, which he seldom did. He expected to find the two guards there, and he did not intend to let them stand in the way.

He opened the door that led to the hallway, and peered through. One of the guards was asleep, but the other was awake and playing solitaire. Walton did not hope to be able to get through this time without being seen. He knew the guard — a burly thug who would hesitate at nothing.

It was two o'clock now. Walton's task was to free Bob Drake, and if he made a wrong step, that would not come to pass. He slipped into the hall and stepped forward, keeping his eyes on the back of the man who was dealing out the cards.

Walton watched his chance and sprang forward. The butt of the heavy revolver crashed against the man's head, and he toppled from his chair with a groan. The sound awakened the second man.

Walton whirled around in time to dodge the other's blow. Once more he struck, and it was his good fortune to have the blow go home. The second man toppled to the floor.

They would not be out of the fighting long, of course, and Walton had no time to bind them, and nothing with which to do so. He searched them and took a revolver from each. Then he sprang up the stairs.

Bob Drake, sound asleep, heard Walton's call and jumped up from the bed. The door crashed in, and Walton flashed his torch.

"Take these guns!" he cried. "Two guards, below! We've got to make a getaway! Belknot said for you to come —"

There was time to explain more fully, and Drake did not need anything more. He was on his way down the stairs already, dressed only in his underclothing. One of the guards was getting up from the floor; the other was sitting there, feeling his head, trying to collect his scattered wits.

Bob Drake went into action immediately. His blows found vulnerable spots, and the guards were unconscious.

"Watch 'em!" Drake cried. "Don't let 'em make a move if they come back to earth! I'll dress!"

He darted up the stairs again, and Walton remained on guard. Bob Drake dressed in record time; the guards were still unconscious when he hurried down the stairs again.

"Which way out?" he cried.

Walton led the way. They got through the window and ran down the dark lane, and so reached the first street. Walton was gasping out his information.

"We've got to get Riley after this!" he said. "One of them thugs recognized me, and it'll be all day with me if we don't beat Riley. What you think we'd better do, Mr. Drake?"

"Get away from this neighborhood first — get some place where we can talk. You didn't tell me very much the other night, you know."

"You come with me and meet the rest of the gang," Walton told him. "They might have some news, too, especially about Mrs. Peale."

Walton led the way across the city, and Bob Drake found himself admiring the manner in which it was done. Walton seemed to know just how to avoid police officers.

"We don't dare take a taxi," he explained. "It'd be quicker, but not so safe this time in the mornin'. We'll be there in half an hour, Mr.

Drake."

It was less than half an hour later when they crept into the dark alley and Walton gave the signal at the door. He led Drake through the narrow hall and to the little room where the single candle burned. The six were there.

Walton explained again, and they looked at Drake.

"Well, boys, we've got to work fast!" Drake said. "We have about two hours and a half until daylight."

"We're ready!" one of them said.

"What about Mrs. Peale?"

"I spotted her," replied another.

"Well — out with it!"

"She's bein' kept in a house on the other side of town. She's been treated all right, except that she's a prisoner. Riley ain't been around there, of course, and the men who have will get a wad of coin and be sent out of town when they let her go."

"We can rescue her later, then," Drake said. "If she is in no danger, there are more important things to think about. Did any of you recover those papers taken from Peale's safe?"

"I guess Riley's got them," said Walton. "We found no trace of them."

"Well, we can get along without them, if we have to," said Drake. "You fellows got your nerve with you?"

"Try us!" Walton exclaimed.

"I'm going to. We understand, of course, that Michael Riley is behind all this — that everybody is taking orders from him. He ordered that trial advance, of course. He probably didn't have time to order anything else. Riley still lives in the same place?"

"Sure!" said the chorus.

"Now, if Mike Riley was missing, as I have been missing, he couldn't give orders, could he? And if he couldn't give orders, his gang wouldn't be quite sure what to do, would they?"

"Sure not!" said the chorus.

"Well, boys, we're going to take a leaf out of Mike Riley's own little book," Bob Drake declared. "We're going to take the law into our own hands for a bit — just as Riley has done so often. I'm a registered detective, and I'm working on this case — understand? And right here and now I name you as my assistants."

"What's the scheme?" Walton asked.

"We're going to Riley's place, boys, and we're going to make a prisoner of Riley. I'll arrest him technically. And we'll keep him hidden until we can get the upper hand. Are you with me?"

They gasped at that. It meant something to tackle the big boss like that. But Bob Drake's enthusiasm was contagious, and they hated Riley.

"We're with you!" the chorus said.

"We'll scatter, then, and meet at the corner by the Riley place as soon as possible. Remember, every minute counts! We haven't all the time in the world!"

Walton was the first to whirl toward the door.

CHAPTER XI

IN THE ENEMY'S HANDS

MICHAEL Riley was a product of the city. As a boy, he was reared in a certain district thereof, and attaining manhood's state, he did not move, even when prosperity came.

That certain district was not the best in the world, but Michael Riley often declared that it was good enough for him. There had been a time when he had torn down his house and had a finer one erected it its place, but that was all the concession he would make. He would not move to a better part of town; probably he knew that he would not be welcomed there, despite his power.

Riley was a widower, and his only child, a daughter, was away at school. He had an aged cook, and a manservant who attended to everything except preparing the meals.

On this night, Riley had retired about the hour of eleven, after having made sure that the trial of Richard Z. Peale had been called for the morning. He wanted to be up early and attend the trial. He was eager to see Peale get the worst of it at every stage of the game. He wanted the city to know that, in some peculiar manner, the man who had triumphed once over Michael Riley, finally had been conquered.

It was about two o'clock in the morning when the manservant shook the boss of the city and caused him to awake.

"What's the trouble?" Riley growled.

"Private telephone message, sir."

Riley got out of bed and went to the telephone. The voice that came to his ears was that of one of the guards who had been watching Bob Drake. He told his news in a few sentences.

"There were more than half a dozen of them, sir," the man lied. "They caught us before we knew they were at hand, and rescued Drake and took him away. We did the best we could, sir."

Riley cursed and hung up the receiver; took it down again and called certain of his henchmen. Bob Drake had been rescued, he said. Riley wanted the man found and watched as soon as possible. With Drake at liberty, many things were possible. Drake simply had to be found and cared for again.

Then Riley went back to his bedroom and sat before his desk

there for a time, chewing at a cigar and vowing that he should have better men working for him. Finally, he tumbled back into bed.

Bob Drake, at that moment, was making his way across the city, carefully and cautiously, alert for signs of anybody who might be working for Michael Riley. Drake guessed that the boss would be informed of his escape — and that was the one thing that was worrying him.

He reached the district where Riley lived, and went down a dark side street until he was on the corner nearest the Riley house. There were some trees along the edge of the walk here, and they cast deep shadows.

Drake crouched in the shadows and waited. One by one, the others came to him, Walton being among the first. Drake issued his instructions in whispers, and they got over the fence and moved toward the house.

They saw no light, heard nothing to indicate that those inside were awake. They gained the side of the house and waited for a time in the darkness there, listening, watching.

"Careful, boys!" Drake warned. "A little slip will ruin all of us now, you know. Who's going to open a window?"

Walton announced that such would be his pleasure. He selected the window and worked at it, finally raised it inch by inch, reaching in and drawing down the shade to prevent a draft that might give an alarm. Walton was the first to enter the house, too. He found himself in an empty room, and turned to signal the rest.

Drake followed him in, and the others followed Drake. Finally, all were grouped in the room.

"Scout, Walton!" Drake ordered.

Not a light flashed. Walton opened the hall door, went out, closed the door after him. The others waited, not speaking, scarcely daring to breathe. The most of them had entered houses in this manner before, but never the house of Michael Riley. Determined as they were to outdo him, yet the very name of the boss carried fear to their hearts. They knew what it would mean, if anything went amiss.

Walton returned; he had located Riley's sleeping room, and he said that the boss was asleep.

Now Bob Drake led the way, and the others followed at his heels. Walton pointed out the room, and Drake entered it boldly. The others remained in the hall.

Drake switched on his electric torch, located the light button and turned it on. The lights blazed up, and Michael Riley sprang from his bed to find himself looking down the muzzle of an automatic pistol.

"Easy!" Bob Drake warned.

"You, eh?" Riley snarled, instantly awake. "Playing burglar, are you? You'll suffer for this!"

"Don't make me laugh!" Drake said. "My manner of entrance may be a trifle unceremonious, but that should not bother an individual who has a man kidnapped."

"Are you crazy?" Riley shrieked.

"Easy!" Drake warned again. "I have a dozen of my men in the hall. You are under arrest, Riley."

The boss sneered again. "Under arrest for what?" he asked. "Got a warrant?"

"I haven't — and I don't need one at the present moment. I am arresting you as a suspect, Riley, and I think there'll be at least a dozen charges to back up your arrest. You've gone a bit too far, you see!"

"You fool! What does this nonsense mean?"

"It means, Riley, that you are at the end of your rope," Bob Drake told him. "You are about to kick off, to speak with more truth than elegance. Every dog has his day, and yours is done."

Drake gave a call, and Walton and the others came in from the hall. Some of them looked at the boss defiantly, some fearfully.

"Nice bunch you've got with you," Riley sneered.

"I thought you'd appreciate them, Riley, since they've been in your gang so long," Drake said. "They are all my men — taken in emergency to help me bring a lawbreaker to justice."

"Justice, eh? You poor fool! And you men! You know what you'll get for this, don't you? Grab this fool of a Drake for me, and maybe I'll forget it!"

"Grab you if we grab anybody!" Walton exclaimed. "Try to railroad me to the pen, will you? I'm the man that put the skids under you, Mike Riley! I found Drake, and I rescued him — and I've done a few other things, too. Now you're goin' to get yours!"

Michael Riley was glaring like a beast at bay. He got upon his feet and took a step forward, Bob Drake menaced him with the automatic.

"I said that you are under arrest, Riley!" Drake announced. "Make a wrong move, and you'll get yours! A lot of persons would thank me if I sent a couple of bullets through you."

"Well, goin' to take me to jail?" Riley sneered.

"Not just at present, Riley. And don't raise your voice again, please. If that old manservant of yours comes in here, we'll simply have to wreck his nerves."

"What are you goin' to do, then?" Riley demanded.

"I'm going to hold you for investigation, Riley," Drake told him. "You'll probably take a lot of investigating. You've been concerned in a lot of crooked work."

Still watching Riley, Bob Drake felt in a pocket of his coat and brought out a small bottle. He motioned toward the others, and they seized Michael Riley and stifled his cries, held him on the edge of the bed and kept him from struggling.

Drake lowered the automatic, took a handkerchief from his pocket, and removed the cork from the bottle.

"A little dose of chloroform won't hurt you, Riley," he said. "I had to stop and get this bottle on my way here, and had to show my badge before I could get it. It was a lot of trouble, but it's worth it, you crook!"

Riley started to gurgle something, but Walton choked the gurgle back into his throat. Drake saturated the handkerchief and approached the bed.

Michael Riley fought, but he could not fight with success against the determined men who held him. Soon, he was unconscious, and Bob Drake stepped back from the bed and put the handkerchief and bottle into his pocket. Even in such a case, Drake did not intend to leave evidence behind.

One of the men had been watching in the hall, and he brought in the news that the manservant evidently had not been aroused, and neither had the cook. Riley was carried through the hall, and out of the front door. He was borne across the narrow lawn, to the shadows cast by the trees.

"Walton, you'll find a taxicab at the corner, waiting for Mr. Drake," Bob said. "Have it drive up here — and be sure nobody sees you. Don't worry about the chauffeur — he is a friend of mine and knows all about this business."

Walton darted away through the darkness, and within a few minutes the taxi was at the curb. They lifted the unconscious Michael Riley in.

"I want Walton and one other man. The rest of you can scatter," Drake said. "If I need you later, I'll communicate with you."

Walton selected the other man, and they got into the cab. The others slipped away through the shadows. The chauffeur had his instructions, and it was not necessary for Drake to speak a word. The cab started, left the curb, turned into the first cross street and sped toward another part of the city.

Once more, Drake applied the saturated handkerchief to the nostrils of Michael Riley.

"This is a great pleasure," he told Walton and the other man. "I have not told you, but I am taking our prisoner to my own rooms, and there you two are to guard him. I arranged everything by telephone while I was on my way to the Riley house."

It was a journey of more than half an hour to the bachelor apartment house that Bob Drake called home. When it was reached, the chauffeur stopped the cab on the side street, and Drake got out and went to a tradesman's entrance.

He was back again almost immediately. Walton and the other

man carried the unconscious Michael Riley across the walk and into the building, and up the stairs to the third floor. Drake went ahead and unlocked the door.

"Put him on the bed," Drake instructed. "We didn't have any too much time — it'll be daylight in half an hour or so."

"What's the orders, boss?" Walton inquired.

"Simply to keep him prisoner on that bed, Walton. I shall expect you two men to do that. You know what might happen to you if you fail me, don't you? Very well!"

"We'll keep him, all right!" Walton declared. "But he's goin' to come back to earth in a few minutes, and then —"

"We cannot keep him under the influence of chloroform indefinitely," Drake explained.

"Then we'd better gag him. He'll howl his head off when he gets conscious," Walton declared.

"He must not howl!" Drake declared. "And he must not be injured. In an hour or so, I'll have breakfast sent up here for you men. I have done a similar thing before for some of the detectives in my office — when I used to have assistants — so the restaurant will think nothing of it. Then I'll go to court, and you'll have to guard the prisoner. I expect to use him before the day is done."

Detective Bob Drake walked over to the bed and looked down at the unconscious Michael Riley once more — and grinned.

"I have a faint suspicion that there are going to be some persons badly shocked today," he said.

CHAPTER XII

DRAKE GIVES HOPE

THERE was no sleep for Peale that night. With the young attorney he had engaged to appear for him and help him fight the charge of robbery, he sat up throughout the night in his office, trying to prepare what looked to be a hopeless case, searching out points to defeat the purpose of Riley and his henchmen.

"What do you think, sir?" the young attorney asked, as dawn was breaking.

"I think that it looks hopeless," Peale said. "That is my honest opinion. Unless something happens — something upon which we are not banking — I am doomed."

"They can't convict an innocent man!"

"No?"

"Certainly not, sir."

"That," said Richard Peale, "is an old statement that is accepted in certain quarters. It no longer is true. Honest men are convicted every year, some through damnable circumstantial evidence and others through the work of their enemies. Don't entertain the idea for an instant that an innocent man is always safe."

"What can we do, sir?"

"Fight like the blazes!" said Richard Peale. "In a criminal case, a man never knows when something will come up that will change the complexion of things. We're not whipped until there is a verdict against us — and we're not necessarily whipped then, not if we can command a certain amount of money."

Then Richard Peale threw himself on the couch in one corner of his office and tried to get some sleep.

But he could not sleep. The case was bothering him; and he was thinking of Bob Drake and Elizabeth. He thought of Walton, too, and wondered whether Walton was doing anything. Walton was a willing instrument, but a weak one, Peale thought.

The courtroom was jammed when the Peale case was called, for all the morning papers had carried articles about it, saying that it had been advanced on the calendar because Peale himself had insisted that he be given an immediate trial. Peale made a face when he read that, and then forgot it. It was one of the least of the things that Riley's henchmen were doing to him.

The grinning district attorney was there, and his grinning assistants. The judge did not grin, for that would have been going too far, but he did almost everything else.

Peale's attorney asked for a continuance which was not granted. This move was made just to show that the trial had not been advanced by his request. The plea for a continuance was eloquent, but he knew that only one reporter was making a note of it — the others worked for papers controlled by Michael Riley.

During the morning, while the jury was being selected, Peale's attorney kept up the fight. Every ruling of the court was against him, except minor ones that made little difference. The young lawyer scarcely saved himself from being committed for contempt.

After the noon recess, Peale went into court feeling like a beaten man. Half the jury had been selected already, and Peale had hoped to drag the process through two or three days, so that he could have time nights to arrange his case — and time for the unexpected to happen.

It was an hour before adjournment in the afternoon when the last juror was selected. The district attorney's address outlined the case he proposed making against Richard Z. Peale. He said some bitter things, and the objections of Peale's lawyer went over the head of the judge.

And then Peale, happening to face about as the first witness for the prosecution was called, received a shock. He saw Bob Drake entering the courtroom.

The sight disconcerted Peale. He looked at Drake anxiously, and the detective made some sort of a sign; Peale could not guess what it meant. He got up and walked to the railing, and Drake stepped down the aisle to him.

The district attorney saw Drake, too. So did the assistants, and the judge, and several witnesses Michael Riley had obtained for this particular case. Some of them knew that Bob Drake was supposed to be kept a prisoner until this trial was over. The district attorney at once suggested to the court that the taking of evidence be left until the morning, since it was almost time now for adjournment, and the court agreed.

"Bob! Where have you been?" Peale asked.

"Answer that later!" Drake said. "Come along to your office — or mine. I've got a lot of things to tell you!"

"But —"

"And don't try to talk now where the enemy can hear you!" Bob Drake added. "Have you lost your wits, man? Cheer up! That's enough to tell you at present."

He went down the stairs with Peale, and got into a taxicab with him. But they did not go to Drake's office — they went to Peale's and while they talked, the young attorney stood guard outside the door, ready to give a signal if anybody made an attempt to overhear the conversation.

"Now — tell me!" Peale begged.

"Well, our genial friend, Michael Riley, has been keeping me a prisoner," Drake said.

"I feared that!"

"Did you? I understood that you doubted my loyalty and friendship a bit."

"Who told you that?" Peale asked.

"Walton! And Walton is the man who rescued me, too, and helped me do several little things. You did suspect me, didn't you?"

"I'm ashamed to say that I did, Bob — for a time," Peale confessed. "Things looked so black. You were missing just at the time I needed you most — and Mrs. Peale —"

"Is missing also?"

"Yes."

"And you thought, I suppose, that your wife and myself had been working for Riley?"

"I — I scarcely knew what to think, Bob."

"Well, I suppose that things did look bad. But they aren't bad, Peale! Don't think it for a minute. We're going to dinner together, and then I'm going to give you a big surprise. I don't think that you could endure it on an empty stomach."

"You mean — my wife?" Peale asked.

"I didn't mean anything about her — but I'd not worry about her, if I were you!"

"But," said Peale, "it is all so mysterious. When I went to the hotel that evening, she was gone. And she has not communicated with me since. Bob, I want to tell you something about my marriage — if you care to hear."

There Richard Peale stopped for a moment. He had remembered that his wife and Drake had acted like strangers when he introduced them, and that the following morning they were acting like old friends.

"Worried about your wife?" Bob Drake asked.

"Naturally. Wouldn't any man be worried if his wife was strangely missing — and he had other troubles —"

"I suppose so. I've never had a wife," said Drake. "I'd worry if anything I owned was missing. Think a lot of her, don't you?"

Peale glanced through the window for a moment, got up and walked across to it and looked down at the city, then turned back and sat down before his chair again.

"Bob, I want the truth!" he exclaimed. "You knew my wife before I married her, didn't you?"

"What on earth makes you think that?"

"Well, when I introduced her to you, you acted as if you never had met before. And the next morning I saw you at a certain little restaurant, talking and acting as if you had known each other all your lives!"

"Great Scot!" Drake gasped.

"I watched up after you left her — and you went to Dugan's. I am ashamed to confess it — but I followed you into Dugan's, Drake. I know that you had a conference there with Michael Riley. When I started to leave, Riley saw me —"

"What happened?"

"He had some of this thugs throw me out. And then he framed this thing on me. I gave him the chance, of course, by going into the Dugan place. Do you wonder that I suspected you — and my wife?"

"Good Lord! It did look bad, didn't it?"

"It certainly did, Drake," Peale said.

"Well, I'll confess to you, Peale, that I did know your wife before you married her. I had met her in San Francisco once or twice while I was out there. When you introduced us, we acted as strangers just for a joke."

"And the meeting the following morning —" Peale asked.

"I suppose it looked bad, but it was innocent. I know a little about your marriage, Peale. Didn't Elizabeth Gralin say that she had been looking you up? I was the detective who looked you up for her."

"Oh, I see!"

"I know about the contract you signed with her, know that she asked you to marry her for convenience."

"But, what does it all mean?" Peale cried. "Where is she now? Why did she insist upon the marriage?"

"One question at a time, old boy. And before I answer any of them, let me tell you this — your wife is a good woman, a reputable woman, and she has nothing to do with Michael Riley!"

"Thank Heaven!"

"You seem to have a lot of interest in a wife in name only," Drake said.

"I was just beginning to admire her deeply," Peale confessed. "If — if this thing had not come up, I think I should have tried to win her for my wife in fact."

"Bully!" Drake cried. "There isn't a better woman in the world than she!"

"But everything is different now. I don't know where she is. I suppose she ran away when she learned about this trouble — probably believes that I am guilty —"

"Didn't you ever suspect what might have become of her?" Drake asked. "Don't you realize, you ass, that with her at hand Michael Riley couldn't put this over on you? She'd explain about the bank deposit, wouldn't she? She'd go into court and tell about that contract. She'd knock the bottom out of Riley's case!"

"But she isn't here and hasn't done any of those things — and so I am doomed!" Peale declared. "Even my office safe was robbed, and my copy of the contract stolen. I suppose she has her copy, but I haven't the slightest idea where she put it — some safe-deposit box, I presume. And what good is it doing me?"

"How about the case?" Drake asked.

"I'm as good as sentenced now! They have a bunch of witnesses ready to commit perjury. The judge is Riley's, body and soul! The district attorney is a Riley man! They didn't even give me time to plan a defense after I was admitted to bail."

"By the way, I had Belknot furnish the bail."

"And where were you?"

"A prisoner, I said. But I sent instructions by Walton. I didn't want to let Walton help me escape at first, you see — afraid that Riley would get busy too quick. But I had to escape, understand, when I learned that the trial had been rushed."

"You can't help me now, Bob — it is too late!"

"Yes? There are several things you do not know!"

"What, for instance?" asked Peale.

Bob Drake lighted a cigarette, puffed it, and smiled across at Peale.

"In the first place," he said, "your wife has been forcibly detained by some of Riley's men. Walton and those precious thugs who are helping him have ascertained where, and they will rescue her tonight."

"She's in danger?" Peale cried.

"Been treated with every consideration, I have been given to understand. The intention was, I believe, to keep her a prisoner until you were safe in prison. Then she was to be released, and if she had anything much to say, Riley was going to have her arrested as an accomplice. Nice plot, eh?"

"Drake! Don't you understand, man? You've escaped, and Riley knows it! He'll guess that we have found out about her! He'll have those thugs of his move her to some other prison, and we won't be able to find her in time. She won't be able to give testimony and help me —"

"I fancy nobody would move her unless he had orders to that effect from Michael Riley," Drake said.

"And how long will it take Riley to give the orders? About two minutes! He's probably given them before this. She probably has been moved by now."

"Not a bit of it!" Bob Drake declared. "Riley has not given the orders, and he will not give them."

"Why, the man wouldn't hesitate now!"

"You see, Peale, he is forced to hesitate. I neglected to tell you that, with the help of Walton and the others, I kidnapped Riley last night — and he is a prisoner in my own rooms this minute!"

"What?" Peale almost yelled.

"Fact, I assure you! So you go into court tomorrow, Peale, and hammer at that case. We'll spring a few surprises, and I think that the district attorney will be asking for a recess. He will want to locate Michael Riley and get a few orders. And he will not be able to find Riley! Understand? The bottom is going to fall out of this case harder than it did out of the Walton case."

"But, Drake —"

"And even that is not all!" the detective interrupted. "I am going to handle Michael Riley tomorrow!"

"What do you mean?"

"Never you mind what I mean! I'm doing this, and what you don't know you can't swear to afterward. You let the prosecution get through, and then there'll be a surprise or two. I have a faint suspicion that they are looking for Riley now, since they have seen me show up."

"But they'll suspect the truth, Drake! They'll get a search warrant and go through your rooms —"

"Yes?" said Bob Drake. "Why, if I may be so bold enough to ask?

Has Michael Riley anything to do with your case — on the surface? Has Riley anything to do with me — on the surface? Why should they search my rooms for Riley any more than the rooms of some other man? If they try it, it will not be with the sanction of the court. They wouldn't dare go into court and get a search warrant — it'd give them away. See? And, if they try it without the sanction of the court — well, Walton and another man are there in my rooms now, and you can bet that I'll be there during the night — and Heaven help the gent who comes prowling around my castle!"

Bob Drake glared at Peale and smote his hands together.

"Is this all you are going to tell me? Am I to work in the dark?" Peale demanded.

"You attend to your little case in court, and leave the rest to me!" Bob Drake told him. "You for the highbrow stuff — leave the rough stuff to me!"

CHAPTER XIII

ANOTHER RESCUE

BEING a political boss, Michael Riley was a man of many secret conferences in out-of-the-way places. He often was missing for days at a time, but generally there were two or three trusted lieutenants who knew where to get a message to him.

On this occasion, however, it appeared that Michael Riley had not taken anybody into his confidence. The district attorney tried to get a message to him, and failed. A lieutenant returned with the intelligence that nobody seemed to know where Riley had gone. His aged manservant declared that the boss retired to his own room the last that he knew, and that in the morning he was missing, and his clothes were gone, hence he supposed Mr. Riley had dressed and set out about his business without leaving word.

The district attorney had a message left to the effect that he desired to get into communication with the boss at the earliest possible moment, and let it go at that. The presence of Drake in the courtroom had disconcerted the district attorney. He knew that Drake was to have been kept out of the way. If Riley had changed his plans, the district attorney wanted to know it. He was a Riley man, but he didn't want to be caught in the corner and suffer for it.

As for Riley, he was learning what it was like to eat crow.

Bob Drake had returned to his rooms from Peale's office and had seen that Riley was given a meal. It was a delicate undertaking, since it was to be expected that the boss would attempt to create a disturbance and attract attention, but it was carried out successfully. Riley was stretched on the bed, well gagged, and Walton and the other man bent over him while the waiter from the café below put the meal on the table in the other room. And then the boss was conducted to the table, his gag removed, and informed that he would be throttled if he as much as raised his voice.

"This is goin' to cost you a lot, Drake!" Riley said. "I've always let you alone —"

"Because you couldn't get your hooks into me, you crook!" Drake told him. "My fortune is invested in such a manner that you can't touch it — that's why."

"And I'll get you for this piece of work!" Riley said. "We'll see if a citizen can be kidnapped from his own house and —"

"Why, you ignorant prune! You are under arrest and being held for investigation," Drake told him, grinning. "I am a regular licensed detective, and have every right in the world to do what I am doing. It is a little peculiar, keeping you here instead of putting you in a jail, of course, but I am doing that out of consideration for your standing in the community!"

Bob Drake grinned again, and Walton and the other man chuckled freely.

"Well, what are you goin' to do?" Riley snarled, when he had finished eating. "You can't keep me here forever, can you?"

"Let us hope not, Riley. These rooms constitute my home, and I'd hate to think that you'd be here forever."

"You would, eh?"

"I certainly would! You rest easy, Riley. Have a nice, little sleep tonight, with the boys watching you, and in the morning we'll have a talk."

"About the Peale case, I suppose?"

"You've said it! They are going to begin taking testimony in the morning, Riley. All your little witnesses are ready to say just what they have been told to say, and your district attorney and judge will do their share."

"Since you seem to know that much, then you must know that Peale is going to prison for a long term," Riley said.

"Don't think it!" Drake told him. "Just forget it until morning, Riley."

The boss was conducted back to the other room and put into bed, and Walton and the other man, having received their instructions, began their guard. Drake did not fear that Michael Riley would be able to get away from them.

Drake remained in the rooms until after midnight, reading a magazine as if he had experienced no excitement whatever during the past three or four days. Shortly after midnight, he put on coat and hat and descended in the elevator.

"If anybody calls for me," he told the night clerk, "I am in my rooms, but have left word that I am not to be disturbed for any reason whatever unless the house is burning down."

"I understand, sir," the grinning clerk replied. This man admired Bob Drake immensely; he had visions of being a wealthy detective one day himself.

Drake walked slowly down the street, as if taking the air before retiring. He was much alert, however; he half feared that he would be under surveillance of some of the Riley gang.

Finally he went through the lobby of one of the city's big hotels, emerged on another street, engaged a taxicab, paid the chauffeur in advance, and ordered that he be driven to a certain railroad station. Halfway to the station, on a dark street, Bob Drake opened a door of the cab, slipped out — and let the cab roll merrily on its way.

He felt sure that he had shaken off any shadow who might have been following. He stood in a dark doorway for a time, and then began walking rapidly toward the poorer section of the city, watching all pedestrians he met, cautious not to be recognized by anybody who might report to Michael Riley's lieutenants.

In time, he reached the dark alley and knocked at the door, which was opened to him. Three of the men were in the little room in the rear of the building. Bob Drake gave them their instructions in a few words, and then left the place again.

Half an hour later, he was at a deserted spot near the river, far below the town, and the other three had joined him. A taxicab was waiting, the lights out, the chauffeur a man Drake could trust.

Drake led the three along the bank of the river, one of them indicating the way.

"There'll be only two men watchin', boss," the man said. "They've got the lady in a room like the one you was in, only it's on the river side, where she couldn't get out without jumpin' three stories into the water."

They came to the building, presently, an old fish cannery that had been fitted up by Riley's men for such purposes as this. They got in through a broken window, and made their way carefully to the third floor.

Half a dozen rooms had been fitted up there, and a hall connected them. The two guards were playing cards and expecting no trouble. But suddenly there was a rush, and they found themselves engaged with four men.

There was no attempt at concealment now. Drake and the three went into the fight with the intention of making short work of it. The battle was over almost before it began, and the two guards were powerless on the floor.

Bob Drake ran to the door of one of the rooms and pounded on it with his fists.

"Well?" asked a woman's voice.

"That you, Mrs. Peale?"

"Yes."

"This is Bob. Get ready quickly, please, and we'll take you out of here."

He heard a gasp of pleasure and surprise on the other side of the door, and then silence. He went back and looked down at the two captives.

"You'll get yours for this!" one of the men growled.

"Don't make me laugh," Drake told him.

"You wait until the boss —"

"What boss?" Drake demanded.

The man on the floor suddenly was dumb.

"You see, you have been detaining a lady against her will," Drake went on. "We'll have to take you to jail for that, of course."

"Yeh? And how long do you suppose we'll be there?"

"For longer than you think, my man. The boss — as you just called him — will be in no position to help you this time. You may help yourself by giving evidence against him, but that'll be the only way."

"If you think that I —"

"Oh, wait until you know all about the situation," Drake told him. "You won't be so sure, then."

He went back to the door.

"Ready?" he asked.

"Yes, but the door is locked on that side, Bob."

Drake took the key from one of the prisoners and unlocked the door. Mrs. Richard Peale stepped out, smiling, and Bob Drake clasped her in his arms for a moment.

"This way," he said. "I have a taxicab waiting a short distance down the road. We'll have you in a nice hotel room within an hour — and then you can get a good sleep."

"What does it all mean, Bob? Why has this been done?" she asked.

"Too long a story to tell you now — tell you in the taxicab," Drake said. "You men stay here and guard the prisoners — do as I told you — understand? If any of Riley's men come around, get these fellows away and keep them safe. I'll communicate with you before night — and don't forget that I'll reward you, too."

And then Bob Drake went from the old cannery with Mrs. Richard Peale, and led her down the dusty road toward the taxicab.

CHAPTER XIV

TWO STRONG MEN

MICHAEL Riley slept but little that night, while Walton and the other man took turns guarding him, watching his every movement, ready to use violence if the boss attempted a trick and make an effort to escape. Walton and his companion were very determined.

Bob Drake returned just before dawn, but did not retire. He read the early editions of the papers, and smoked considerably. From the expression of his face he was a bit determined himself.

Breakfast was served at the usual hour, and Riley was watched as he ate. After a while he found Drake sitting across the table from him, looking at him narrowly.

"Well, what's the idea?" Riley wanted to know.

"The time has come for me to attend to you, Riley."

"When the time comes for me to attend to you, you'll realize what a fool you've been!"

"You growl like a bear, Riley, but you're harmless. Haven't you realized that yet? Don't you know that you're done?"

"Done, am I?"

"I said it — done! Your little day is over, Boss Riley. I am going to explain a few things to you — and then I'm going to issue a few orders, and you'll carry them out."

Riley sneered at him and sat back in his chair. Walton and the other man were just behind him, ready to throttle him if he started an uproar.

"We won't say anything about the many tricks you have played," Bob Drake said. "We'll skip all that and come down to the Peale case. You've been after Dick Peale ever since he struck the city — because he was the one attorney of ability you could not buy or get into your clutches. He beat you when the Walton case came up — and that set you against him more than before. You threatened to get him — and you have tried it.

"Now, I'll show you where you stand, Michael Riley. Some of your own men have turned against you, as you know. With their help, I was rescued, and a short time ago, I took Mrs. Peale from the place where you were having her kept prisoner."

"You can't prove I had anything to do with it!"

"Oh, yes, I can, Riley! The two men guarding her have a bit of fear in their hearts — and they are ready to tell the truth. You decoyed Mrs. Peale from her hotel by means of a telephone message purporting to come from her husband, so she tells me. You decoyed me by another telephone message. In other words, men acting under your orders committed two abductions — and those men are ready to tell it and ask the court for mercy."

"The court, eh?"

"Oh, not one of your judges, Riley. We'll have an honest judge this time — and we'll have an honest jury. Then you framed this case against Peale. It looked pretty bad for him until yesterday. But it doesn't look bad for him now. I know just how the thing was framed, Riley. And do you know what we are going to do? We are going to keep you here and let your witnesses give their perjured testimony. Then we are going to spring the truth — and have every one of them indicted for perjury. They'll have somethin' to say about you and your instructions, of course."

"Think so?" Riley sneered.

"I know it, Riley. We are going to catch you in one of your own traps. Your district attorney and your lieutenants are trying in every way to locate you now. They are beginning to get afraid — understand? They are beginning to feel that they are over a powder magazine and that somebody is about to touch it off. They know that I was to be kept prisoner until after the trial — and they are afraid because I am at liberty."

"Why tell me all this?" Riley asked.

"I just want you to know where you stand, Riley. I want you to realize that you're done! You've played your last trick!"

"You're talkin' big!"

"We are ready to knock out every bit of perjured testimony, Riley, and you know what that will mean to you."

"Well, I suppose you want me to let Peale alone so he can make a senator out of himself, or something like that!"

Drake laughed. "He'll do that without any help from you," he answered. "I'll tell you what you're going to do, Michael Riley. You're going to get that crooked contractor on the telephone, when I give the word, and give him certain instructions. Then the court will be told that it was all a mistake about that theft — that the package of money has been found in the desk, or something like that."

"Then we'd better get busy. Those witnesses —"

"Exactly!" Drake interrupted. "You'll not do this until after those witnesses perjured themselves."

"But, man —"

"Again, exactly! Everybody will know, then, that it was a frame-up, and that the perjured testimony was given by your orders. You are going to be caught in your own trap, I said — and I meant it! Your kidnappers are going to jail, and your perjurers, and your crooked officials, and you are going, too."

"Got it all arranged, ain't you?" Riley sneered. "Well, Mr. Bob Drake, you're a fool! I'll just sit tight, and we'll see. There may be a few funny things pop up, but I guess they can be handled, all right! I've been in bigger fights than this."

"Don't you believe you have! You don't realize just how big this is! You're going to do just exactly as I say, Riley. You're a big brute! And so you can only be conquered in a brutal way."

Bob Drake got out of his chair suddenly, his eyes never leaving those of Michael Riley, and began pulling off his coat. He tossed the garment to one corner of the room, and began rolling up the sleeves of his shirt.

"What's the idea?" Riley snarled.

"I'm going to handle you, Mike Riley! I'm going to give you a taste of violence. You've got it coming to you, for what you did to Peale and Walton and scores of others — and for subjecting Mrs. Peale to indignity. I'm going to break you with my bare hands, Mike Riley! I'm thirty, and you're forty-five, but you're a bigger man, and you're in the prime of life! Get on your feet, you crook! I'm going to break you, I said! And then I'll drag you into court and make you tell the truth!"

CHAPTER XV

SOME EXPLANATIONS

RICHARD Peale had not heard from Bob Drake again, and he did not know that his wife had been rescued and was at a certain hotel. He went into court trying to appear cheerful and hopeful, but found it hard to do so. He seemed to need more than the fact that Riley was held in Drake's rooms to make him hopeful and cheerful.

The taking of testimony began, and one by one the witnesses, acting under orders from Riley, committed perjury. Peale's young lawyer hammered at them in cross-examination, but could not shake their stories, and every decision of the court was against him. Some of the jurors were smiling — Riley's jurors.

The noon recess arrived, and the district attorney made frantic efforts to get into communication with Michael Riley. It appeared that the boss could not be found. The district attorney began to fear that there was something wrong. His detectives had informed him that Bob Drake had been acting mysteriously the evening before, and had seemed well satisfied with himself and the world — and for Drake to appear that way meant possible trouble.

The district attorney held a conference with the judge. They had to get Riley before they could go on, they decided. They didn't want to make a mistake and jeopardize themselves.

Court convened again, and the district attorney presented the last witness for the prosecution. The young lawyer, under Peale's prompting, hammered at him in cross-examination but to no avail. Peale was beginning to experience a little fear himself now. This was the last witness for the prosecution, and he had none to offer for the defense. Bob Drake had not put in an appearance — and neither had Mrs. Peale.

But the district attorney saved him. The district attorney announced that he had another important witness, that deputies were searching for him, and asked that court be adjourned until the following morning.

Peale sprang to his feet. He objected. "I demand that this trial go on!" he said. His heart was hammering at his ribs as he said it, for he was afraid that the trial would go on — but he wanted the district attorney to think that he was ready, that he had a surprise in store. "I have a right to expect this trial to go on," he declared. "The prosecution has had as much time to prepare this case as I have had."

The judge appeared to weigh the problem. He began to give his decision. He was inclined to adjourn until the following morning, to give the district attorney a chance to find his important witness. There had been some criticism about setting the case forward, the court explained; some persons had intimated that the defendant had not been given time enough to prepare. The court wished to be fair and just — and an adjournment would give the defendant a chance to perfect his own case.

There was a commotion at the door, and half those in the courtroom sprang to their feet. A bailiff pounded for order.

Down the aisle came Michael Riley, his left arm clutched by Bob Drake. Riley had on no coat, and the sleeves of his shirt were torn and bloody. His face had the appearance of a piece of raw beef. He was whimpering like a whipped cur.

Bob Drake was in little better condition, but he was smiling — and he glanced at Richard Peale.

"What is the meaning of this?" the judge roared. "Mr. Drake, I shall adjudge you in contempt! This is a court of law —"

"This man has something to say regarding the present case," Drake interrupted. "He is my prisoner — I have him under arrest. Tell the court, Riley!"

The boss whimpered again.

"Tell the court!" Drake commanded, in a stern voice.

Michael Riley's whimpers now turned to words.

"I — Mr. Peale is innocent!" he said. "I — I framed him! He never stole that money — there wasn't any to steal. The witnesses — have lied — my orders!"

"What's that?" the judge cried. The judge realized that Riley was a broken man, and his first thought was to protect his own interests.

"It's — the truth!" Riley declared. "I — framed it up — hated Peale!"

The district attorney waxed indignant. He, too, wanted to save himself. He called for the instant arrest of Michael Riley and the witnesses who had given perjured testimony. The Riley ship was sinking — it was a case of every man for himself.

"It took a tough scrap to do it, but it has been done!" Bob Drake whispered to Peale.

Peale heard the judge dismissing the case against him, instructing the jury to acquit, and saying how he regretted that a reputable member of the bar had been subjected to such an ordeal. Peale knew how much he regretted it!

And then Peale turned toward the door again, and saw his wife coming down the aisle toward him — Elizabeth, smiling and dimpling and blushing a bit.

Ten minutes later, Peale and his wife and Drake were in an anteroom where Drake was washing the blood from his hands and trying to make himself presentable.

"Take it easy, Dick, and I'll explain," Drake said, as he bathed his knuckles. "You see, your wife happens to be my half-sister. My mother went to California and married again after my own father died, and I always remained in the East, was educated here, and all that. I used to go out and visit them once in a while. Elizabeth is a child of the second marriage, five years younger than I am. My own father left me a fortune, and her father left her one. Plenty of proof if you want it, old man. That's why we were so friendly in that little restaurant."

"Why didn't you tell me?"

"Would have spoiled everything," Drake explained. "Elizabeth was playing a little game, and didn't want to be bothered."

"I don't understand."

"You see, Peale, the silly young woman had fallen in love with you. She always said she'd never marry the first man who came along and asked her — wanted a real man who could make something out of himself. She came along here to buy clothes and things, and I happened to tell her about the fight you were making against Riley. She watched you during the Walton trial, and — well, she got interested. You never would look at a woman, you know — thought you had to be rich and famous first.

"So she planned that silly contract, and then made you marry her. She had an idea that even by being wife in name only, you'd be thrown together a lot, and she could study you. If you turned out to be the man she expected, she was willing to let the marriage stand — providing you were wise enough to fall in love with her during the year. Otherwise — Reno and a divorce. She wanted to be sure, you see — didn't want to take a chance on her happiness. Look at the silly thing blush!"

Peale looked at his wife — and felt his own face flaming.

"You two get together and fix it up," Drake said. "If I were you, Peale, I'd fall in love with her before the end of the year."

"That — er — may not be so difficult," said Peale.

"Great!" Drake exclaimed. "Hope you do. She's a fine girl, Peale — make a senator or something out of you before she is done."

"Please clear up a couple of more things," Peale begged. "What were you doing at Dugan's talking to Riley?"

"Had an appointment with him. Told him he'd have to step aside and give you your chance or that I'd go after him strong — that's all. He decided to fight, of course."

"And the forty-five thousand dollars. Er — Elizabeth, you deposited it to my account — your own check. But they were ready to show — did show, in fact, that you also deposited the same amount in cash in your own bank the same day. They meant to prove that I stole the money, gave it to you, you deposited it in your own bank, and then transferred it to me in another check."

"Oh, Bob sold a piece of property for me," she explained. "And it just happened to bring that amount."

Peale sat down weakly.

"Well, I'm looking pretty decent again," Bob Drake said. "Let's go to the best hotel in town and have a real dinner. Hope everything will be all right after this. See what a lot of trouble a woman can cause by picking a husband in her own original manner? Elizabeth, never do it again."

"I should say not," Elizabeth said, looking at Richard Peale.

www.ingramcontent.com/pod-product-compliance
Lightning Source LLC
Chambersburg PA
CBHW030519020726
47494CB00004B/1161